By Leslie Glass

OVER HIS DEAD BODY
TO DO NO HARM
MODERN LOVE
GETTING AWAY WITH IT

FOR LOVE AND MONEY

A Novel of Stocks and Robbers

LESLIE GLASS

BALLANTINE BOOKS •NEW YORK

For Love and Money is a work of fiction. Names, characters, places, and incidents are the products of the author's imagination or are used fictitiously. Any resemblance to actual events, locales, or persons, living or dead, is entirely coincidental.

2006 Ballantine Books Mass Market Edition

Copyright © 2004 by Leslie Glass

Published in the United States by Ballantine Books, an imprint of The Random House Publishing Group, a division of Random House, Inc., New York.

BALLANTINE and colophon are registered trademarks of Random House, Inc.

Originally published in hardcover in the United States by Ballantine Books, an imprint of The Random House Publishing Group, a division of Random House, Inc., in 2005.

ISBN 0-345-44795-6

Cover design: Tony Greco

Printed in the United States of America

www.ballantinebooks.com

OPM   9   8   7   6   5   4   3   2   1

FOR DAN & BOBBY AND
ROBIN & ANNE & GEORGE &
MARY ANN & BARBARA

acknowledgments

Thanks to the three special people who keep me
going—Jim, Alex, and Lindsey.

one

ANNIE CUSTER WORKED FOR A FORCE SO POWER-
ful that nothing on earth could control it. Sometimes it
acted like a perfect summer of endless sunny days with
showers that came and went only before dawn. And
sometimes it brought season after season of hurricanes
with tornadoes and tidal waves that wreaked destruction everywhere. When times were good, the whole
world wanted to get into the stock market and ride its
highs to the top. When it turned bad, everyone wanted
to run away and hide from its devastation. The funny
thing about the stock market, though, was that anyone
could take a vacation and miss the highs; but no one
could escape the tsunami waves, the avalanches, the free-
fall crashes. They affected everyone. Everywhere.

God or the devil or nature itself, the stock market was
the true dictator that ruled the earth. No one could con-
quer it forever, not its former chairman, who took too
much pay, or anyone else. For better or worse, when it
started to move in any direction it changed lives. On
Monday, September 18, it was Annie Custer's turn to
get caught in the deadly currents.

That day there was mixed feeling on Wall Street. The
good news was that after the deluge of 9/11 and several
years of market free fall, recovery of the Dow and
NASDAQ finally seemed firmly on track. The bad news

was that parts of the economy hadn't followed suit. Turned out there couldn't be such a thing as a jobless recovery, or a recovery of jobs in only one sector. From sea to shining sea, millions of people in many fields were still out of work and suffering.

In the brokerage business, customers were still licking their wounds and regarding their brokers with suspicion for bad investment advice from years past as well as the financial irregularities that had surfaced in the fall of giant companies and the toppling of dot-coms. Billions of dollars in paper gains had disappeared forever, and not without repercussions. Above all, the United States is a free and *litigious* country. Clients were suing their brokers left and right, placing the blame for all their woes squarely on them.

Annie Custer's old-line firm, Hall Stale, was taking a big hit. The firm had so many complaints to defend that there was a logjam of arbitrations looming years into the future. It was costing a lot of money to settle the legitimate cases, and costing even more to fight the clearly ridiculous ones. For Hall Stale—and the brokerage business in general—it was a lose–lose situation.

In addition to the lawsuits, something else was making business difficult for brokers. New standards for consumer protection had cut commissions to pennies. Former million-dollar-a-year brokers were struggling to make six figures, and six-figure brokers were out of the game altogether. Offices were emptying, and people were without work of any kind. The climate was as uncomfortable for brokers as it had been decades ago in the early 1970s when all the small investment houses went out of business and thousands of people lost their jobs.

That Monday morning, Annie was worrying about the usual subjects: money, her husband, her daughters.

Money, her husband, her daughters. Money . . . husband . . . daughters. Every day it was the same thing. She had a greatly reduced income and the same old bills—and *she* was one of the lucky ones. Her husband had not died in the World Trade Center attack, her clients were still solvent, and she hadn't been sued. All in all, she was an unusual person—and she'd worked hard. She'd never been just a stock jockey who pushed the stocks of whatever companies, bonds, or funds Hall Stale happened to be promoting at the moment. She was more than the money managers who specialized in different areas but never did the actual transactions. She logged in most of the trades for her clients herself—hundreds of thousands of them a year—and she didn't rely solely on her assistant to do the scut work, either. She wasn't above doing paperwork. She opened accounts, closed them, transferred money when people bought houses, and explained everything along the way.

She'd been a broker for a long time and had helped her clients understand all the sectors that so many investors had trouble keeping straight: the Blue Chips, the Steady Value companies, the up-and-coming Growth stocks, the Cyclicals that performed well in different economies, and the Tech and Fixed-Income sectors. Every stock and bond in every sector traded every day. The prices varied minute by minute. When you were placing orders in the tens of thousands, every penny-a-share counted. There was a lot to know, and a lot to watch out for. People went crazy under the pressure. She had close personal experience with some of the victims of the business. Her own husband, Ben, was one of them.

She didn't want to end up like him, so she was up at dawn every weekday with a clear head, and in her office on the fourteenth floor of the Lipstick Building before the opening bell sounded at the New York Stock Exchange. Today had been no exception. She'd pulled herself out of her recurring nightmare of New York under attack. She'd drunk a cup of coffee all alone in her kitchen. She'd dressed in a pleasant enough early-autumn suit that was far from new. Then she'd bused twenty blocks down Lexington Avenue to her office on Fifty-third Street and Third Avenue. As usual, Petra, her pretty blond assistant, was already at her desk fielding calls. A second line was ringing as Annie waved and walked into her large and airy office. Petra answered the phone, then called through the open door.

"It's Carol."

Annie picked up the phone before sitting down. "Hey, cutie, what's up?" she said, sipping from the Starbucks she'd bought across the street.

"Annie, I need your help." Carol's plea was the cry of a wild animal, which was not unusual for Carol.

Instantly Annie was a faithful dog on point. "No problem, whatever you need." Carol Mack was her best friend, after all. Furthermore, her mother was dying of cancer. Annie had lost her own mother to the same sad fate years ago, and the catastrophe still felt brand-new to her. "What can I do?" she asked quickly.

"You have to help me with the stash."

Uh-oh, here we go again, was Annie's first thought. *The stash* was the hoard of securities Carol's eccentric father claimed he had hidden in the house. No one knew the value of it or where it was hidden. For years he'd tormented both Carol and Annie with hints of it, but nothing either of them said to him could persuade him to hand it over to a brokerage house to be invested properly. Annie sank into her leather desk chair and turned away from her computer, its screen already full of numbers and the tape running. "How's your mother doing?" she asked softly.

"Not well, but one thing is a blessing. She doesn't know what's going on, and Dad is in complete denial. You told me what would happen if she died before I took care of her estate issues." Carol sounded even more frantic than usual.

Annie shivered. The air-conditioning in the building was still on full force, and her hands were frozen, but the cold air wasn't what chilled them. Carol's situation was truly upsetting. "How do you want to handle it?"

"Look, I really think that Dad is ready to do things properly this time. I have a strong feeling he'll do it today if we handle it right," Carol said craftily.

"Well, that's good news," Annie replied slowly. She'd heard this before, and for her own sake she didn't want to hope for a new account, only to be disappointed again.

"He says it's big. Really big. The trouble is, he'll hand over the stash only if you go out there and take care of it yourself. You'll go, okay." Carol wasn't asking the question. She'd made up her mind.

Annie was silent. This was the last thing she ever would have expected from the most secretive person she knew. Carol had asked for her help a hundred times, but had never invited her over to meet the parents. How could she go there out of the blue and collect their money? It made no sense.

"Please, Annie. Please. I wouldn't ask you to do this if it wasn't an emergency." Carol had that tone in her voice. She was used to getting her own way and didn't mind begging when she had to. "You know what it means to me."

Annie kept thinking, *Poor Carol, her mother is dying.* It was the worst thing in the world. Obviously she couldn't handle it. She was freaking out.

Then Carol said, "I've been loyal to you, kiddo!"

And that hit Annie right in the gut because it was true. Three years ago Carol's husband had sued Annie's husband. The bitter fight contributed to the trauma Ben had experienced on 9/11. Carol's husband, Matthew, a litigation lawyer, had won his case. Ben sank into a quagmire of disillusionment about pretty much everything. He'd stopped working, and Annie's life had become a juggling act of painful allegiances. Now she was torn again. If she did what Carol asked and took someone's assets out of their house, her branch manager would have a cow. If she didn't do it, Carol's assets—whatever they were—would be in jeopardy, and she might have a meltdown. There was also the prospect of a new account to consider: Annie wanted, and needed, new accounts. Besides that, she was curious as hell. Carol's meltdown began anyway.

"I waited until you got into the office to call, didn't I? I didn't bother you at home, did I?" Carol said as she launched into her tirade.

"Honey, I've been telling you all this for years—"

"I know, I know. I should have taken care of it, but they're soooo difficult," Carol said sullenly.

Well, yes, parents could be very difficult, but that wasn't Annie's fault. She'd already done her best with Carol's parents. She'd talked and advised and been there for dozens of hours of phone debate with Carol's father, Dr. Dean Teath. Just his name alone put Annie's teeth on edge. And he probably didn't have that much money anyway.

"Please, I promise you won't be sorry," Carol wheedled.

Annie exhaled and realized she'd been holding her breath. She knew she shouldn't succumb to the plea to go that extra twenty miles. She was a stockbroker, not a courier, not a bodyguard, not a cop! She had no armored vehicle. And there was no insurance for what Carol was asking her to do: to intervene in her private life, to take possession (of whatever) from a notoriously skittish old man who'd been resisting custodial care of his assets (as well as himself) for the whole fifteen years that Annie had been a broker.

She shivered with swelling anxiety. Okay, okay. She reminded herself that her husband wasn't working, so she couldn't afford to do something wrong and lose her job. As if she needed any reminders about that! But those things aside, she didn't *want* to do anything wrong. So many terrible things had happened to people because of their brokers, or lawyers, or big corporations. She couldn't forget that. There were lawsuits left and right because of the bad things people had done. The firm would punish her if she generated one. She was an honest person and never did anything wrong.

. . . But she was curious, and not so far in the back of her mind she wondered if she could pull it off. She debated with herself. Certainly Carol could be harmed by her father's negligence. On the other hand, she knew that if she took any assets out of Dr. Teath's possession, the water could get very muddy very quickly. There were rules about this kind of thing. And even if she had been dead-of-winter-wolf hungry—which she was—it was not in her job description to travel to someone's home to dig assets out from under their mattresses. No, no, and again no! She decided she could not do it.

"Carol, you know I love you. I really do, but you have to go out there and get the certificates yourself. Bring them to the office where we can officially document them in your and your father's presence."

"But you *know* he doesn't trust me," Carol wailed.

"He *will* trust you if bring him into the office with

you. I'll be here waiting for you. I'll explain everything to you," Annie promised.

"Please, please, please. You're my best friend, my only hope here. If he hides all this stuff again and forgets where he put it, or God forbid he dies without telling me, I might never find it. Remember when Mom forgot that she'd put all her jewelry in the Goodwill box and told me to take it in. It was just an accident that I checked it first."

Something clicked. Something cracked in an honest person's mind. Annie didn't know what it was. Maybe the dirty tricks of politics. Maybe war. Maybe all the events of the past few years together just caught up with her. She didn't know. All she knew was that the little voice inside her head, whose job it was to separate right from wrong, was strangely absent right at that moment. She caved.

"Okay, Carol, I'll do it. But you'd better pray for both of us that this isn't one giant mistake." With those fateful words, she put her whole life on the line.

two

NERVOUS AS SHE WAS ABOUT WHAT SHE PLANNED to do, Annie acted normally at work for two hours. She made and received calls, placed some orders, and watched the tape on her computer and the news on Bloomberg TV. She didn't leave her office to talk to her manager about Carol's request. She didn't consult the compliance people. She had a lot of second thoughts and knew she was guilty as hell. But quite frankly, the more she mulled it over, the more eager she was to uncover the truth about Carol's life before Matthew. She felt almost elated at the prospect of finally learning her friend's deep family secrets.

At ten, Annie stuffed a stack of blank powers of attorney in her briefcase just in case Dr. Teath had the securities that he claimed he had. Then she hurried downstairs and got into the waiting black Lincoln Town Car that she'd ordered for the trip. As soon as she was in the car, she started thinking about her husband. She had two opinions of him that she went back and forth on several times a day: He was a good guy who'd been disappointed by his work and his friend and had been badly damaged by circumstances beyond his control. And, he was a wimp who'd put her, the children, and their entire way of life at risk by collapsing instead of being resourceful in the face of adversity and finding something new to do. In fact, she knew both were true, and ambivalence was her downfall. Right then she was using the wimp opinion to justify her action that day. For an hour or more she actually told herself that if Ben hadn't stopped working, they wouldn't need money, and she wouldn't have to go out on a limb like this to get a new account. Normally she didn't do this kind of thing. She didn't take shortcuts. The farther they went, the easier it got to rationalize; she happened to be taking a very long way to Staten Island.

She'd had no idea how far it was. Staten Island was located practically in the Atlantic Ocean off the coast of New Jersey, five watery miles from Wall Street and the Statue of Liberty. To reach it, she could have gone in a taxi downtown to the tip of Manhattan, then taken a ferry.

But after the ferry crash that killed ten people the previous fall, the ferry idea was unappealing. Her solution had been to take a limo the long way around through Brooklyn and across bridges she had never traveled before. Unfortunately, there was no alternative. Staten Island was where Carol Mack had grown up, where Dr. Dean Teath had lived all his life, and where the much-heralded but unknown assets were.

It was a longer trip than Annie had anticipated, and when she finally arrived at the address Carol had given her, she was shocked. Staten Island had a wonderful charm about it, but the Teath house was far, far from what she'd expected. Annie was so surprised, in fact, that she had to check the address twice. She couldn't believe that the family she'd always believed to be extremely affluent lived in a tiny brick Cape-style bungalow with a garage that was neither fully enclosed nor attached. In addition, the paint on the bricks was peeling, and so ancient that it was impossible to tell what its original color had been. The roof was curling asphalt, and, horror of horrors, perched on top of it was an ancient Christmas sled pulled by two nearly fossilized reindeer. Equally prehistoric icicle lights hung from sagging gutters across the front. Uneasy, and certain that she'd come to the wrong place, Annie slid over to the car door.

"Wait for me, please," she told the driver. He didn't get out to open the door for her, or even bother to answer.

Outside the car, Annie was further disoriented by suddenly balmy Indian summer air and the delightfully briny smell of ocean. There was no water view from here, but on the distant horizon the tall buildings of Manhattan were etched into the sky. She felt as if she had traveled to another world, far away from her safe office in Midtown and the large apartment on Central

Park West where Carol Mack lived with her evil husband, Matthew. So this was Carol's secret.

The little suburban block was quiet. Nobody was walking around, and hardly any cars cruised the street. In Manhattan there was always noise and traffic. Huge trucks rumbled on the avenues at night, and sirens from police and emergency vehicles pushed cars and people out of the way at all hours. Brakes squealed, and from time to time there was the crunch of metal on metal, one vehicle connecting with another. There was always the hum of many blended sounds. In Manhattan it was never, ever quiet. Here the silence was deep and a little scary.

Uncertain, Annie walked to the front door and rang the bell. No one came. She tried again, and then again. Nothing except birds twittering in the trees. The quiet was so unnerving that she had the chilling thought that the old people were dead inside, and she was the one destined to find them.

Nervously, she walked around to the kitchen side of the house, where a battered old Toyota was parked in the carport. The screen door was streaked with dirt and dead bugs, and the paint on the kitchen door was cracked and peeling. There was no bell here, either, so Annie tapped on the glass. Minutes passed and nothing happened. Then she wondered if something had happened since she and Carol had spoken, and her mother had been taken to the hospital. Again she considered aborting the mission. She didn't want to go inside.

Just as she was about to turn away, she heard the sound of shuffling footsteps. An old man opened the door, and Annie was further stunned by his appearance. Dr. Teath was tall and thin. His face was covered with stubble. His clothes were old, faded, and wrinkled. He was wearing slippers. His white hair was long enough to curl at the ends. His blue eyes were watery behind his glasses. But his voice was strong, and he boomed at her through the dirty screen.

"You didn't have to go to all this trouble for us, Annie Custer," he said, frowning in the direction of the Town Car with the driver parked by the curb.

"It was no trouble at all. What a charming sled you have up there." Annie couldn't help referring to the appendage on the roof. It didn't go with the Carol she knew. Thank God no one was dead.

A happy smile transformed Teath's face. "Isn't it a treasure? I found it in the garbage years ago . . . Carol loves it," he added, about the sled.

Annie found that hard to believe.

"Please, come in." He opened the creaky door and stepped back to let her enter a kitchen where the appliances were antiquated, and the worn-out linoleum on the floor and counters could easily have been much older than she was.

In her banker's blue business suit, silk blouse, and high heels, Annie panicked. In that split second, she knew she'd made a giant mistake. She was in the wrong place at the wrong time, overdressed and doing something she shouldn't be doing. The ancient kitchen was filled with piles of garbage, and now she *really* wanted to flee. But then something else happened. With a dawning horror, she realized that the thick folders stacked on the counters and on the kitchen table were actually filled with stock certificates, dozens and dozens of them. *Oh my God, the old man really does have a fortune!* And Carol really had sent her out here to retrieve it. It was a dream come true and a nightmare at the same time . . . and the very last thing in the world she should do was touch a single piece of paper.

three

DESPERATELY, ANNIE LOOKED AROUND FOR HELP. "IS Brad here?" she asked tremulously. A witness would help a lot. No one at the office would believe this.

"Brad?" Dr. Teath tilted his head to one side and scratched his head as if he'd never heard of his own accountant. White flakes from his dry old scalp showered onto the shoulders of his worn green sweater. He looked like a desiccating bird, long dead and falling apart in front of her.

"Your accountant," she prompted. Now she was horrified by what appeared to be Carol's frightening neglect of her own father and mother. She was having trouble processing this man as the father of the competent and compassionate friend she thought she knew so well.

"Oh, him." Dr. Teath remembered his accountant. "He's not so great. We can start without him. How about some coffee?"

Annie's eyes slid over to the ancient stove. On one of the burners sat the kind of coffeepot that had pretty much gone out of style with electricity. Like everything else on the premises, it was discolored from age and use. "Not right now, thanks," she said.

After the hours of travel, she needed to use the bathroom. On the other hand, she didn't want to see any more of the pitiful condition of the tiny house. She searched her mind for some reference to anchor this upsetting situation with all the other clients she'd known over the years, and after a moment she found one. Old Sal, a florist with a corner shop near her apartment, had been like this. Sal's place was such a dump it didn't even have a name, but the plants were really cheap for the upscale neighborhood, and despite its sad appearance the shop had been a booming, all-cash business.

Every month or so Sal used to summon Annie to the store, load her up with free plants, then give her a shopping bag stuffed with ten thousand dollars in small bills with the order to go invest it for him. She'd carried the cash back to her office and done just that. Back in the innocent good old days when people had trusted each other to do the right thing, Sal had relied on her, and investing ten grand in cash hadn't been against the rules. Now his son ran the place. It was drop-dead designer gorgeous with computers and a refrigerated van for deliveries. The shop had a fancy name, and the flowers cost the earth. It was all run on the up-and-up, and no one who frequented the place remembered what money was. Times had changed, but it was clear that the Teath family hadn't changed with them.

Annie was more than uncomfortable. She was terrified. The rules were *really* different now. Brokers couldn't walk around with cash in a bag, and for good reason. Advantage had been taken left and right of people like this. If Sal tried to give her cash now, she wouldn't be able to deposit it for him even if he got on his knees and begged. Packing up the Teath stash was an even bigger no-no. Carol had promised her that the accountant would be there. If Brad didn't show up, she would have to leave without touching anything. She knew she should call her friend anyway. *Phone home,* she told herself. *Now!*

Dr. Teath cleared his throat. "Have a seat. Mamie will be up in a few minutes." The old man's eyes seemed to harden at the mention of his dying wife.

"Good, that's great, Dr., um . . . Teath." Annie couldn't help stumbling on the name. *How do people live with such oddities?* she asked herself. Dr. Teath, the dentist, didn't actually have very attractive teeth himself. She curbed her wandering mind. *Phone home.*

"Do you know the reason for my visit today?" she asked.

"Yes, yes, of course," the old man said impatiently.

"Can you spell it out for me? I want to be sure we're all on the same page." Now she was a social worker—not an entirely new role for her.

"You're that stockbroker friend of Carol's." Teath eyed her with a bit of a sparkle.

"Yes, that's right." Annie nodded.

"Well, you're a pretty girl, but you're probably a thief. I'll bet you're here to steal my money," he told her contentiously.

Annie's breath caught. "What?"

"Brokers, pah," he muttered.

"Ah, Dr. Teath, let's sit down and talk about this for a minute."

"Okeydokey," he said, suddenly genial. "Whatever you say."

Annie felt the heaviness of big trouble settling on her as she pulled out a chair and sat. The stale air in the old house, the pervasive atmosphere of neglect, and the deep fear of doing something very wrong all seemed to be conspiring to stifle her.

The old man fumbled with his chair. "Don't get me

wrong. I appreciate your coming. Would you like a hot dog? I have a few left over in the freezer. Nathan's. You like Nathan's, don't you?"

"Oh yes, but I just had breakfast." Several hours ago, anyway. In her distress, Annie's hand brushed a folder. The edge of the cover peeled back to reveal five thousand shares of an oil company that had merged with another oil company thirty years ago. Beneath it was a certificate for five hundred shares of a defunct railroad. *Oh boy. Oh boy.* Southwestern Bell Telephone. One hundred shares. *Oh boy.*

"Maybe some cake . . ." Teath scratched his ear as he went down his menu. "A bagel. I could go out for some—"

"No, no. We need to talk business." Her eyes slid around the room. *Carol, what did you get me into?*

"Ah, business." Teath waved a shaky hand at the air, as if business was of no interest to him.

"Are all these folders full of stock certificates?" Annie indicated the stacks of files that covered all the visible surfaces.

"Yes, I put a little aside for a rainy day. And now you're here to take it from me." He wagged a finger at her. "This is Carol's idea."

Annie shook her head as she thumbed through the certificates in the closest folder. They were all colors— orange, yellow, green, blue, rose. Some were dated back in the 1930s, some in the 1950s. Others were many decades later, right up to the late 1990s. The number of shares was different on each certificate, and they didn't seem to be arranged in any particular order.

"I'm only here because Carol is my closest friend. She's like an aunt to my daughters," Annie murmured. She wanted to flee. Something was not right about this, something beyond the obvious. But she didn't know what.

"Oh yeah, what about the stock market crash?" Teath demanded.

"What?" Annie frowned.

"I'll bet you're going to pilfer the account." He grinned in a most disconcerting way.

Annie could see that he was not following the conversation. Or else he was following some conversation of his own that had nothing to do with her, but she'd dealt with people like this before. "Let's not talk about me for the moment—" she murmured.

"I like getting my checks," he interrupted.

"You mean your dividend checks? I understand, but you'll still get a check at the end of every month," she assured him. For anyone else she would have explained in detail how the computerized system would greatly simplify his life.

"But why can't I collect them myself the way I always do?" he replied in a bellicose tone. "I've heard about those computer robbers. They can steal you blind."

Annie wasn't sure what he was talking about now. "We're protected and insured. That won't happen to you," she said. She could be very patient, and didn't want to get technical. She was also worried. It looked as if there was a *lot* of money here.

"I feel protected right now." Teath waved his hand at his bulging folders, enjoying his importance. "I keep meticulous notes. Are you sure you wouldn't like a hot dog?" There was no question that he looked kind of crazy.

Annie's cell phone rang in her purse. He jumped.

"What's that?" he cried.

"My cell phone." She grabbed the phone and glanced

at the caller ID. When she saw it was her home number, she picked up.

"Mom?" It was Mag.

"Hi, what's up?" Annie asked, pleasantly surprised that her daughter was up by noon.

"Dina's daughter is getting married. She's leaving us to make the wedding dress and take care of her." Mag sounded distraught.

"No." Annie was shocked. On top of everything else, Dina was leaving. She stared at the table in dismay. How could they live without Dina? "Honey, I'll have to call you back."

Then she saw something that distracted her from the catastrophe. Sticking out of one of Dr. Teath's bulging folders was an old-fashioned bearer bond with a bunch of uncashed coupons that anyone, including herself, could redeem for instant money. On the street those coupons were called hangers, and the rule was that no one was allowed to touch them. No one.

For decades this kind of bond had been the hedge that helped rich people and gangsters avoid paying taxes, transfer funds to spies and bad guys of all kinds, and launder money. The bonds had no owner names on them and read simply "Pay to Bearer." Bearer bonds had been so fraught with tracking, theft, and tax problems for the government that none had been issued since the late 1980s. They were the ultimate no-no, and Annie was pretty sure Carol didn't know a thing about them. The hair rose on the back of her neck, and her jaw felt numb. What was going on here?

She checked the date on a coupon and saw that it, and several others, had come due months ago—and were worth $150 a pop. A tap on the glass of the kitchen door stopped her investigation short. Brad, the accountant, had arrived.

four

"WHAT'S GOING ON?" MAMIE TEATH SAID, WANdering into the kitchen vague as a fine mist. Wearing a long nightgown and robe, she resembled the other Mamie, Mamie Eisenhower, only this Mamie had a lot more hair and no sweet and wistful smile.

Annie jumped up to greet her. "I'm Annie Custer."

"Who's he?" Mamie pointed a bony finger at the accountant, a tall, pudgy, red-faced thirty-something-year-old who badly needed a haircut and was so nervous he couldn't keep his sweaty hands from shaking. "I'm Brad Rosen, your accountant," he said.

"Brad Meltzer is my accountant," she corrected him.

"Brad retired five years ago, and lives in Florida," the young man told her.

"No one told me." She eyed him suspiciously.

"Well, I'm the other Brad," he replied.

"Sounds fishy to me." She sniffed.

Brad looked around miserably. "I don't know about any fishing," he said after a pause.

She turned to Annie with a shake of the head that said, *Men aren't so smart.*

"I'm Annie Custer, Carol's friend," Annie told her in case she didn't know.

"Shhh. Follow me, you'll need a shopping bag." She shuffled across the small room to a walk-in pantry by the door and rummaged through the mess inside until she found a huge, tattered Lord & Taylor shopping bag and pulled it out. Then a large collection of used tinfoil and clear plastic wrap distracted her. "You never know when you're going to need something," she murmured.

The old woman looked so thin, so profoundly sad and neglected, that she actually seemed to be starving to death. "Do you have everything you need?" Annie asked suddenly. *Food, medicine, care?* Nothing seemed right here.

Mamie Teath glanced quickly at her husband, then lifted a shoulder. "I'll be happy when it's out of here. It's all mine, and I know he wouldn't give it to her."

"Carol?"

She put a finger to her lips as if she was afraid to say her daughter's name. That was the defining moment, the moment Annie knew she had no choice. She had to take the stock certificates and the perilous bearer bonds because Carol's mother wanted her to. She took a deep breath. "I'm going to need your signature on all these powers of attorney so we can open an account for you," she told her.

They were whispering in the pantry. Once again Mamie glanced at her husband, who was talking to Brad the younger. "I want it in my name alone and that's that."

"Are you sure?"

She nodded, looking very sharp for a moment. "And you and Mr. Brad there are my witnesses." She shuffled out of the closet just as her husband raised his voice to a thundering roar.

"I know what she has. I keep meticulous notes."

Annie had a lot of questions, but she didn't take the time to ask them. In the next three hours, in an atmosphere of complete unreality, she and Brad made a careful list of everything she was taking with her. There was a lot, but in the end she was not fully confident that Teath had shown her everything he had; nor did he tell her what he had done with all the dividends he had most certainly collected over the years. Clearly he hadn't spent it here. But that was Carol's problem.

Mamie pressed her hand as she said goodbye. "Got him," she said with a straight face. "I finally got him."

Annie pondered this remark and the sad, sad situation all the way home with Teath's stash nestled tightly between her feet. At three thirty, more than five hours after she'd left her office, Annie emerged from the Town Car on Third Avenue and Fifty-third Street, clutching the huge Lord & Taylor shopping bag that was now full of stock certificates and more than three hundred thousand dollars in bearer bonds of five-, ten-, twenty-five-, and fifty-thousand-dollar lots.

Where did it come from? Why hadn't they used it to take care of themselves? And why wasn't Carol doing something about it? That was what Annie wanted to know. As she crossed the sidewalk to her office building, she was both very upset about Mamie's condition and conscious of having done a great service. All of this could have disappeared in a fire, or a burglary. She was no longer thinking of her own gain, but rather of Carol's salvation.

She reached the doors of the Lipstick Building, named for its oval shape, and breathed a sigh of relief. *Made it.* Then, as on every other occasion when she entered the building, the surly security guard on her bank of elevators demanded to see her employee card as if he'd never laid eyes on her before. And just like every other time, it was not easily obtainable. Annie had to dig around in her purse to find her card. This was one of those changes in the world that made life so difficult. As Annie struggled to find her ID—which she knew for certain was there (so did he) because she'd already used it once that day—she was overwhelmed by a sense of loss for all that used to be so safe and good in her life.

Annie knew that she did not resemble the Teaths in any way. Quite the opposite; she wasn't an indiscriminate hoarder who'd pushed her children far away. Annie Custer was a spender, a replacer, an upgrader in every way. She'd spoiled her loved ones by thinking of them and trying to help them at every step. She was present for them in every meaning of the word. Still, there was a nagging message of severe dysfunction in her visit to the Teaths that troubled her even back here in familiar territory. The message that she'd received from them was that family was tricky and treacherous, and it wasn't always clear what was going on. She thought of herself as the very opposite of them, yet in some ways her own family was just as dysfunctional.

Ah, there it is. She found the photo ID and produced it for the guard.

"Thank you." She got into the elevator and exhaled with relief.

Okay, one thing done. She'd completed her mission. She'd made it back to base with the precious package intact, and she could breathe again. On the fourteenth floor she exited the elevator and slid the all-important ID card into the slot that opened the door. Inside Hall Stale, she picked up her pace on the path around the outer bank of offices. Her large office was in the narrowest curve, a sweep of windows facing northeast. Her apartment happened to be exactly one mile north, on the twelfth floor facing south. Over the years the juxtaposition of the two buildings had always made her feel that she was almost within view of her two beloved children, actually quite close to home and in control of her world.

Petra was on the phone when she came into view. "Mr. Vole from Stockholm," she mouthed.

Annie's eyebrows shot up.

"Yessir, I'll tell her. Yes, yes, I have it all. You're sending the two hundred million by courier. And you'll be talking with Greenspan tomorrow. I'll definitely tell her. No, no, and I won't forget that you need the twenty-five million in your account by Monday." Petra hung up and swung around in her chair grinning. "Market's up twenty-three," she said. "And Mr. Vole has a new associate in Stockholm. He's bringing in two hundred million next week." It was clear she thought this was a great thing. Anybody would.

No stranger to big deals in the old days, but unused to them now, Annie shivered with excitement. "No kidding."

"He's in his Mercedes," Petra added with a little smile, tapping her chin with the pen she'd used to take the message.

"Oh?" Annie frowned at the odd note. "He said that?" What kind of person said he was in his Mercedes? Rich people didn't have to say it.

"Oh yes, he said it. And he's meeting with Greenspan tomorrow in Washington."

"Yes, I heard that." Uneasiness shot through Annie.

"Did you get what you went for?" Petra asked, changing the subject.

Annie glanced down at the frayed handles of her shopping bag. "Yes, it's right here."

"Well, that's good. It took long enough." She glanced at her watch.

Annie exhaled. "It did indeed." But it was okay. She was safe now.

"Brian came by three times. He wants to see you ASAP. He said to be absolutely sure not to let you go home without talking to him. It's very important."

"All right. No problem." Annie smoothed her skirt and jacket around her hips, ran her fingers through her hair, and hurried to the other side of the building, still lugging the precious stash.

five

MAG CUSTER LAY ON HER BED AND STARED UP AT HER awful ceiling as she waited for her mother to come home. A heavy weight held her down, and she couldn't have gotten up if she'd wanted to. It was like being chained to the floor of a flooding basement with only a few hours to go before the water rose above her neck and filled her mouth. Her heart beat so fast with terror for her own death that sometimes she thought it would burst. She knew she was sick and dying of cancer, but no cancer was visible yet on the scans she'd had. It was one of those mysterious things that happened in her family that couldn't be explained. Things went wrong, but the causes could not be logically ascertained, so steps could not be taken to fix them.

The temperature in the apartment, for example, was uncontrollable. It went from hot to cold in seconds, and at least one of the lights went on and off at odd times for no apparent reason. She'd shut it off, and it'd come on again. It was very woo-woo, and the dog went nuts whenever it happened. Sudden cold flashes made the apartment smell like an old attic, and a strange damp-ness seemed to concentrate in the center of her ceiling where the chandelier was hung. Ugly patches of peeling paint pocked the ceiling. Whenever the superintendent of the building came to check things out, the tempera-ture was normal, no knocking on the radiator pipes was in progress, and the light fixtures all checked out. As for her ceiling, that was clearly damp and cracking, yet the moisture meter brought up by the super always deemed it dry. Furthermore, nobody could find a leak upstairs or a single thing wrong with the building. Not only that, her mother talked regularly to a cigarette-smoking ghost no one else could see. This was not just some TV show stunt; it was happening to them.

To Mag, these little unexplainable, but irritating, things were warnings of some terrible, and all too real, event to come. The country was at war on many fronts. There were no jobs for the graduates, so she personally might as well be dead. There was probably lead poisoning in her building—her father was as sick as she was—and her sister wasn't doing much better. And everybody just denied everything. Only she knew the end was com-ing. And that end she feared didn't have to be just her own. It could be another attack on New York. Another war. Another market crash. Another parent out of work. Or more likely, her mother would finally get it together to leave her father—leave them all, just like Dina was leaving them. Then she and Bebe would have nobody to take care of them. Her dad was completely out of it.

Mag brooded a lot about her mother. She understood why her mother wanted to bolt. Unlike herself, who had no interest in escaping her moldering room even for an hour, her mother wanted to fly away and be free. She said it often enough. It was pretty much the same as hearing that your mother hated you and wished you were dead.

Sometimes Mag's ceiling even seemed to undulate a little. It actually appeared to shimmer for a while as if to remind Mag that the family was indeed falling on its ass and breaking up. Their future couldn't be anchored on shifting sands anymore. That was what her mother said, and it was scary. It reminded her of the fire that had almost killed her. For years she'd forgotten the fire. She'd almost stopped being afraid of lights and light switches, but now that the lamps and sconces, as well as the temperature in the apartment, seemed to have minds of their own, she thought about that fire often.

One night the chandelier in her bedroom had burst into flame and might have burned the apartment down if her mother hadn't been there to save her. If she had been alone in that room, she'd have burned up for sure. The chandelier had been her grandmother's, an elegant wrought-iron five-light with painted wooden spools around it—five candles as in five years, her age at the time. She'd gone to bed, then called her mother to bring her a glass of water and read her another story, just one more. A short one. At that time she used to do it often, and it always worked. Her mother came quickly and didn't mind lingering.

That night, in the faint glow of her night-light, she saw her mother open the door. She saw a pale hand reach for the light switch, and when the switch went up, the five candles on the Italian chandelier instantly ignited into shooting spits of flame that shot up to the ceiling. The fire made a windy kind of sound.

"Fire! Fire! Stay there!" her mother screamed.

Margaret's bed was by the window. She and her mother were separated by the torch in the middle of the room. Her mother moved toward her, within reach of the flames. She was terrified that her mother would catch on fire trying to save her.

"No, no, Mommy, don't!" she shrieked.

But instead of walking into the fire and burning up, her mother switched off the electricity, ending the conflagration even before her father arrived with the fire extinguisher. It fizzled out almost instantly without having harmed anything but the ceiling, which turned black and cracked like an egg. That was the first magical thing that happened. Her mother saved her by switching off the light. No one but a goddess could do that, she'd thought.

Later, after the wires had all been checked, the ceiling was repainted. Mag insisted that the chandelier be replaced, too. She didn't want the old one rewired and rehung. She wanted it out. Her mother had let her choose a French one with lovely colored glass fruits dangling from it. She repeatedly reassured Margaret that the fire had been caused by a short in old wiring, and no such thing would ever happen again.

"But how can you be sure?" Mag had demanded of the all-powerful.

"I just am," her mother had replied, smiling. "Trust me."

Back then, it had been easier to trust. Mag loved that new ceiling and chandelier all through elementary school and junior high. Then three years ago on September 11, when she was a sophomore in high school, a pipe burst three floors above them, and water poured down through the opening in the ceiling. The chandelier held, but the plaster on the ceiling fell. In fact, her whole sky fell that day when the plumber couldn't get through to stop the flood and save her room. Her father went missing for five hours, she and her sister couldn't get home from school, and so many other tragedies occurred at the same time.

Since then, she'd marched like a soldier, as her mother told her to do. Her room was redecorated, but the ceiling never recovered. No amount of fresh plaster would dry it out. Every new coat of paint cracked and flaked. Mag was afraid something was very wrong up there in the ceiling, or up there in the sky. If she left home, worse things would happen to her family. Right now, for example, she was pretty sure her baby sister had cut school to go shopping and was now home way too early, smoking a joint behind the closed door of her room. The smell of marijuana was strong, but she didn't think she would tell. Anyway, not unless Bebe really annoyed her.

six

"WELL, WHAT SHOULD I DO?" BRIAN REDFIELD FIN-ished telling Annie about his girlfriend's snub and waited for her response.

He sat on the green plaid sofa in his large office, ignoring both the TV playing endless Bloomberg as well as the ticker rolling on his computer screen. Annie stood in his doorway and stared at him in disbelief. Sometimes she had trouble believing this was her manager—the man who had to deal with every employee and customer issue that hit the fan. Here she had some real problems on her mind, a fortune hanging on her wrist, and the urgent reason for Brian's summons was to get some dating advice. She swallowed and rose to the occasion.

What was this again? Oh yeah, the ever-difficult Mary Beth had canceled a long-standing date for an important game at Yankee Stadium in favor of dinner with her posse, which consisted of two other unmarried women in their thirties and her mother. In Annie's day such bad behavior would have been dating suicide.

"Dump her," she said flatly. "Now can we get down to business?" She wanted to unload the minefield, pronto.

Unfortunately, Brian wasn't ready. His handsome, clean-cut features performed acrobatics as he considered the consequences of breaking up with Mary Beth. She could feel his brain working on it. He'd been married for a number of years and had learned that women had different priorities these days. His needs didn't happen to be at the top of the list anymore. His unguarded expression showed his hurt about the broken date, and his indecision about such severe retaliation. "Are you sure? Isn't that a little harsh?"

"She doesn't hold you in high enough regard, Bry. How long are you going to put up with that? Now, we've got to discuss the Teaths. It's nearly four."

Brian sighed and licked his lips. "You're *really* sure about this?" He tended to trust her judgment in this area.

"Yes! There are lots of much better girls who'd be thrilled to have you."

Annie's eyes rolled up at the ceiling. She'd accommodated the opposite sex her whole life, so she didn't have much patience for the Mary Beths of the world. As on all other occasions, she was on Brian's side. She wanted him to have a happy life. End of story. Sometimes people in the office thought she and he were a tad too close, but she never paid any attention to gossip involving herself.

Needing the comfort of the ladies' room after her long ride back, she wanted to dump the securities and pee. She stood in the doorway clutching the bag and feeling like a complete fool because she'd rushed in there for another round of the dating game.

Brian shook his head, still unsure. "But you know how personable she is . . ."

"That's not a good reason," Annie said scornfully.

"But I can take her anywhere. She's got the right look, and she knows how to talk to people. Not like Sally," he went on.

Sally was Brian's ex-wife, his college sweetheart who'd turned out to be a poor dresser and a cokehead. Annie evaluated him, as she did several times every day. At thirty-eight, he was still thin and preppy. He wore nice suits that fit him well, and had pleasant blue eyes and an engaging smile. Emotionally he was a little worse for wear, but he worked out, made a good living, and still had hopes to love and be loved. Unfortunately, while he wanted a relationship, all the women he met seemed to want their independence. What was that about? Annie figured he was between an eight and a nine, and frankly—between her and herself—she wouldn't mind having a man just like him. But that was another story.

"Would you please ask Darian and Frisk to come in?" she asked.

Brian nodded absently, still elsewhere in his mind, bobbing up and down on the seesaw of revenge. Annie knew she'd have to stay on hold until he returned. She sighed. He was the youngest of three divorced men in the office. The other two were fifty and sixty, but they were pretty much all the same. Before their wives had left them, they used to talk about politics and war, terrorism and world markets. The pace of their stride had been quick and their heads held high. But now they'd lost their starch and, more important, their conversation. They'd lost their ability to talk about anything beyond the women they were dating, the women they used to date, and the one perfect woman they were seeking. In other words, sex, sex, sex. None of them had any responsibilities or real worries beyond work. They had their independence—whatever that was. Since Annie didn't have hers, it was hard to sympathize.

"I have to go home," she announced.

With that, Brian finally focused his deep blue eyes on her as if he'd suddenly gotten a brand-new idea. "Why don't *you* come with me?" he said.

She was puzzled. "Where?"

"To the game." His eyes came to life with the possibility of Annie at his side. "Wouldn't it be fun? Carl and Bill are going. You could be our fourth."

"Well, that's tempting, but I really can't. I have to go home." She actually looked longingly at the hallway behind her. Three divorced men covered with peanut shells, swilling beer, and looking for girls? No thanks.

"Why not?" Now he was giving her a long, speculative look. A first. *Annie; why haven't I thought of her before?*

What? She raised an eyebrow. Nobody had looked at her like that in a long time. *What?* A little shiver took her by surprise.

"It's just business. How about it?" he wheedled.

She hid a pleased smile and shook her head. "Call Mary what's-her-name and tell her she's history if she doesn't pull up her socks and cheer for the home team."

"I already did that. She laughed in my face," he admitted sheepishly.

"She laughed?" Annie was incredulous. This reaction was shocking.

Only five years ago, when Annie had been thirty-five, she'd had a husband, two children, a full-time job, and a household to run. She'd thought those things were what women wanted. Now all these thirty-five-year-olds who'd never been married didn't seem to care a hoot for any of it. Mary Beth—who was by no means perfect, let that be very clear—was actually laughing in his face for wanting her. Brian might be a little self-involved at times, but he didn't deserve that kind of contempt.

He squirmed uncomfortably at his admission and finally turned his attention to the shopping bag. "What do you have there?"

"Ah." Annie finally entered the room and collapsed in one of his green plaid wing chairs. "You know, I went out to Staten Island to visit Carol Mack's parents." She said it slowly because *Mack* was not a welcome name in the office.

"And?" Brian frowned and tapped his fingers on the desk, eyeing the bundle that she'd wedged between her feet. "What makes me think this isn't going to be a short story?"

"It was unbelievable. Those poor old people are living in a dump with a fortune in securities sitting around on the kitchen counters."

"Really?" He leaned forward, suddenly interested.

"They were both kind of confused, and I don't think they had any idea what was there."

"Oh no." Suddenly Brian put a hand to his forehead. "Please God, don't tell me you took their fortune, after everything that's gone on with the Macks."

"Well, yes, it's right here. Carol is my best friend. She asked me to. I had to. Her mother is dying. Her father is out of it . . ." Annie shrugged. She was their hero.

Brian groaned. "Oh, Annie, you shouldn't have *done* that."

"It's all right. I made a list." She pulled the handwritten tally out of her handbag and waved it at him.

"It was wrong. Why didn't you call me?"

"Ah . . ." She didn't have a quick answer for that. She'd thought about him, certainly. She'd thought about him often. But she hadn't considered actually *consulting* him.

"Okay." He waved his hand, resigned. "What's in there? Let's see it."

Annie exhaled and reached down between her feet to hand over the heavy bag. She couldn't wait to let it go.

"I don't know what you were thinking. This was a really stupid move," he muttered. "Why couldn't *he* just bring it in?"

"He's not regular. You had to be there. You had to see them."

Brian didn't reply as he opened the bag wide enough to see in. The usual thing was for people to bring in a few certificates they'd found in a drawer or in a safe-deposit box. A few thousand dollars' worth—sometimes as much as ten or twenty thousand. Nothing to cheer about. Then one of the assistants would scurry to get the proper papers to re-register the issues so the shares could be added to the person's account. It was all pretty routine. Generally speaking, if someone was stupid enough to bring a shopping bag, there wouldn't be much in it.

"Let's see what we have here." Brian pulled out a fistful of IBM and GE certificates and quickly thumbed through them. Then he moved on to the chunky utilities wad. The bag was really stuffed. "Wow." Brian was impressed.

His fingers stopped moving at their furious pace, however, when he reached a five-thousand-dollar bearer bond with a bunch of hangers still attached. He stared at the dangerous bond for a second or two. Then, as if it and the uncashed coupons were tainted by rat poison, he pushed them quickly away and exploded.

"Jesus, Annie, are you crazy?"

She hunched down in her chair guiltily.

"You shouldn't have touched this," he said angrily. "What were you thinking?"

"I don't know," she replied in a small voice, biting her lip because there was a whole lot more where that one came from.

"Oh shit! You should have alerted me!" He got up, went to the door, then spun around and hurried back to grab the phone on his desk.

Annie knew he didn't want to leave her alone in the room with the bonds, which was silly because she'd already been alone with them for hours. She shivered at his rage.

"Bev, I need Darian and Frisk in my office now," Brian barked. Then he returned to the sofa and sat down heavily. "Do you have an idea how big an account this is?"

"Over three million, maybe as much as three and a half," Annie said softly.

Brian whistled. *Way to go, Annie.* "You should not have done this," he said sternly. "But congratulations."

seven

A FEW MINUTES LATER DARIAN STRODE INTO THE room. She was a petite woman with short dark hair that was stiffly gelled to stick straight up, as if to remind everyone that as the branch's regulatory compliance manager, she was as tough to get around as a razor fence. About Annie's age, she had an excellent figure that showed even in her conservative gray suit and pink silk blouse. She was the kind of woman whose lipstick was never on crooked, never smeared on her teeth or faded inside the lines like everybody else's. Her nail polish was always perfect, and she'd never been known to have a run in her panty hose or a food stain on her blouse. Annie, who was often a mess, envied her.

"What's going on?" Darian demanded.

Annie sucked in her stomach to prepare for an attack.

Before she could answer, Sean Frisk swaggered in. "Hey, Annie, what's up?"

"New account," she murmured.

"Great."

Like Brian, Frisk was a wholesome-looking guy in a Brooks Brothers suit. He had a straight-up kind of face, a brush haircut that had gone white in a single day, and a Brooklyn-boy sense of black humor. Frisk had been at the Hall Stale office in the Trade Center before it went down, and he was the first one to go back into the vault in the threatened building next door, where several billion dollars' worth of street name securities had to be recovered and locked down before that building, too, succumbed to its terrible fate. He'd done his job without blinking and was in a recovery site at the mouth of the Holland Tunnel before noon. After that, nobody called him Sean anymore.

"Well, we have a mess." Brian indicated the piles of certificates he'd begun stacking on his desk. "Annie picked this up from a client this afternoon. We have bearer bonds, too."

Oh boy. Darian and Frisk both looked at the ceiling.

"That was wrong," Brian said.

The rule was that no one was ever left alone with a bearer bond. They all knew that, so no one commented.

"Now we have to get this locked down for the night." Brian glanced at his watch.

"What do we have?" Darian made a face that said she wasn't leaving the office for a second, not to mention the whole night, with a potential problem on their hands. They'd have to deal now.

"Just about everything, all jumbled together. This is a real rat's nest going in."

"I have signed powers for every block of stock," Annie said defensively. "I have a list of everything I took. It's completely manageable."

"Why don't you let me decide that?" Darian's dander was up.

"Okay, calm down. Let's just not screw this up," Frisk said.

Brian shuffled some papers, ignoring them both. "What we have here are certificates in all amounts. There have been stock splits several times over on some of these. Some companies are defunct, and others have merged a couple of times with other companies. We've got stuff that goes back sixty years." He threw up his hands. "Let's lock it in the vault for the night. We can't begin to untangle it now."

"Uh-uh," Darian protested. "We've got to check it and accurately record what we're putting into our vault. We can't just dump it in there."

"Yeah, and if you've got bearer bonds, security is a problem," Frisk added. "Let's do it now."

"Well. We have to gear up for a huge project. And I don't want anyone with this alone," Brian said, casting a dirty look at Annie. "This could take all night, even with several of us working on it."

"Doesn't matter. Whatever it takes. I don't want problems down the road." Darian was gearing up to be a bulldog.

Frisk nodded. The operations manager and the compliance officer were one on this.

"Okay." Brian capitulated for the moment. "Fine. Let's just see what we've got. We can check it against Annie's list, then lock it in the vault for the night."

"Compliance is going to be a nightmare on this," Darian muttered to herself.

"Annie, go copy the list," Brian ordered.

Annie thought of calling Petra to do it, but quickly changed her mind. Since Petra came in promptly at seven thirty, she liked to leave at four. She didn't want to make her stay. Anyway, she had to pee. She grabbed the list and left the room.

Only a few minutes later, when she had returned feeling better and armed with several copies of her list, the three of them were deep in it, stacking papers everywhere. Annie's heart spiked with dismay. It seemed to her that the pile of bearer bonds looked a little thinner than it had when she'd put them in the bag. She frowned. How could that be?

Her three colleagues looked completely innocent as she handed out her list and they began making little checks on their copies. She frowned. They wouldn't . . . not even to prank her . . . would they?

No one looked up. They were busy checking. IBM, all present. GE, all present. Southern Bell . . . and so forth. About half an hour later Brian locked eyes with Annie. Then, after a few seconds' scrutiny, he threw up his hands and ordered Frisk to bring in his staff from the cage to lock down what they had.

"This is a massive project. We'll have to finish in the morning," he said, checking his watch again.

Annie stared at him. *What?*

He didn't respond.

"You know better than this," Darian scolded. "We should finish it now." But she knew she couldn't argue with Brian. He was the boss. The buck stopped with him.

When the stacks of certificates were taken away, and Annie and Brian were alone in the office, he gave her a hard look.

"Are you sure your count was right?"

She gulped and nodded. "There was an accountant with me. We did it together—more than once because some of the stock splits didn't come out right. What's the problem?"

"Does he have a list?"

"The accountant?" She shook her head. "He was a young guy. He didn't know about anything. He just asked for a copy when we were done."

"Did you leave a receipt of any kind with the customer?"

The customer? Her heart pounded. "No, I said I'd send it when it was properly recorded and the account was open. Tomorrow afternoon at the latest."

"We have a problem," he said quietly.

"You're teasing, right?" Annie wasn't certain she'd heard him correctly.

Brian blinked. "I do not tease. Does anyone else—other than the four of us—have this list you made?"

She shook her head. If Dean Teath had made a list of his certificates, he hadn't shared it with them. Suddenly she knew where Brian was going with this. He was thinking they could cover it up if they had to.

Her heart throbbed in her throat. She couldn't cover up a loss if she wanted to, certainly not a loss to her best friend. "What are you saying?"

"I'm not accusing you." He looked out the window.

"Please, Brian."

"I said I'm not accusing you. We'll figure something out. I'll see you in my office first thing tomorrow," he said, speaking to her sharply for the first time ever.

"Brian, I didn't take anything," she said wildly.

"I trust you. So if you don't want to go to the game, just go home," he said angrily.

What was going on? Annie left the office in a daze. She was so upset by Brian's implication that she was a thief and a liar, and by his hostile tone, that she forgot to ask him what was missing.

eight

LATE IN THE AFTERNOON CAROL MACK CALLED HER
father from work. She was in no hurry to go home, even
though her office was no grand affair like her husband
Matthew's. In fact, her office was kind of a dump. She
had a medium-sized room without a great view that
would have been more than adequate if it hadn't been
loaded with sample items that she'd collected from all
over the world and never discarded. She'd had different
specialties over the years, moving down from large furniture to smaller and smaller accessories. Her office was
filled with knickknacks and accessories of all types. Carol
had turned out to be the very opposite of her mother
and father. Every cell of her body pulsed with the command to *buy*. Buy now, buy more, buy better, and put
those products out where the public could buy them, too.

She loved being a buyer. She had the perfect job, and
one that had swelled in importance over the last decade
as consumers at nearly every economic level acquired
more money and clamored for nonessential items. The
myriad selling sites that blanketed North America had
gone crazy with candles and candle accessories and
plates and pillows and tableware and glassware and just
more and more terribly attractive large and small items
for big-eyed customers to scatter about, or simply put

away for infrequent use. Things that nobody used to
care about had become vital must-haves. Lamp shades
had been a nothing business. Now they were made of
ostrich skin and hung with crystal. Suddenly they were
valuable, absolutely necessary finishing touches.

Potpourris to make rooms smell better used to be only
for people who had everything else. Now anybody and
everybody had to have them. Potpourri had become
such a big seller that more attractive holders had to be
created to infuse with indispensable elemental aromas.
The new potpourris had names like Sea Spray or Beach
or Cozy North Woods: places where urban consumers
longed to reside. Piles of dried flowers and candles were
not good enough anymore. New carriers for the smells
had to be dreamed up. Shells and braided twigs and
beaded fruits and glitter-covered candles in every shape
imaginable had to be invented. Interesting containers in
which to put the attractive items had to be manufac-
tured. And Carol orchestrated her trends for a name-
brand distributor with catalogs and stores nationwide.
It was a stressful job, and every inch of her office bulged
with quality-of-life-enhancing possibilities.

She had an eye for beauty in unexpected places the
way a perfumer had a nose for blending scents or a chef
had a palate for new taste sensations. In different seasons, she developed different ideas and traveled to exotic places to find the items that expressed the mood she
wanted to create—Alaska or the Caribbean, the North
or the Deep South, the faraway or just around the corner.

Carol spoke to her parents regularly, almost every
other day, but she did not travel to Staten Island to visit
them any more frequently than she went to Thailand.
Staten Island had changed around her parents, but they
lived exactly as they had when the difference between

dessert and no dessert had been ten cents, and more often than not they had gone without. Money had remained a complicated issue for them, and so it was for her. So also it was for Matthew. Maybe it was for everybody, she thought.

In any case, both her husband and her parents were incomprehensible to her. Her parents seemed to her just like the uneducated people who couldn't believe bacteria in their drinking water was responsible for the dysentery that killed their babies. Her parents could not accept the fact that the world had moved on, and they could move on, too. At any time in their lives, they could have relocated to an attractive garden apartment or town house in a warm place and never have seen their unrenovated cottage again. She hadn't known it when she was growing up, but she knew it now. Her parents refused a better life. She had no idea how anybody could be so stubborn.

"Dad, how did it go?"

"Carol?" came the wheezy voice.

"Yes, Dad, it's me."

"Well, that pretty young woman stole my money." He sounded very upset.

"What, Dad?"

"You're a bad daughter, Carol. You robbed me blind. You and that girl. Both of you. Did you give her a commission? Did you pay her off? You know those brokers are thieves. How could you do this to me?"

Carol's blood pressure soared. Her whole body tensed with intolerable conflict. "Dad, we've talked about this. We agreed we had to do this. Everything is going to be fine."

"Nothing doing. You all railroaded me. I want it back," he yelled.

Whenever he yelled at her, she wanted to tear her hair out. "Dad. You can't have it back. It belongs to Mom. She wants it safe. This is her call."

"What are you talking about? It's safe right here."

"You know you have no security, no alarms. What if you had a fire, or someone robbed you?"

"It hasn't happened. Get it back here. I won't sleep at all unless you do."

Carol went into her own special downward spiral whenever her mind was ripped from the rational (her thinking) to the supremely irrational (her father's thinking). His point of view always led her to the bottomless pit of old recriminations and pain. Her young life with her father had been a nightmare. His view had never coincided with hers on any point whatsoever. They were diametrically opposed, and she'd never been able to improve the situation. A long time ago a therapist had told her that some people were toxic. If they happened to be your parents, the only way to survive was to flee. She'd struggled with flight all her life.

"Dad, you can't have it back. It's not yours," she said again.

"Yes, some of it is mine. A lot of it is mine. How will I live? Who will take care of me?"

"I will take care of you," Carol said.

"You? Who are you? A stranger. Let me tell you, your mother changed her mind. She wants it back. I want it back. I'll go to the authorities, Carol. I don't care what you say. I'll sue my own daughter, mark my words." Then he hung up before she could reply.

nine

WHEN ANNIE GOT HOME, DINA, HER HOUSEKEEPER
of six years, was leaning against the counter by the stove
languidly stirring vegetables and chorizos in the paella
pan for *arroz con pollo*. The TV was on and she was totally engrossed in a rerun of her favorite Mexican soap
opera. Annie stood there for a moment, trying to dis-
perse a new feeling of intense uneasiness that was distinct from all the others in her life. Something was new.
Something felt different even though a familiar episode
was playing. Annie loved Spanish TV.

In this scene a bunch of weeping women crowded
around a hospital bed where a gorgeous blind girl had
either just been raped, just given birth to a deformed
baby, or just lost a baby. In Spanish it was hard to tell.
The scene changed to a prison cell where the victim's
father/brother/boyfriend was in prison awaiting imminent execution for a murder that he either had, or had
not, committed. The high drama always reminded Annie
that life could be worse.

"Hola, Dina, que tal?" she said.

Dina turned around. She was about Annie's age. She
had very short hair that had been pitch black but now
was red. She'd tied a white apron that read KISS ME I'M
ITALIAN over tight black pants and a red and black

sweater. She was wearing gold earrings, lipstick like the movie stars she avidly followed, and street shoes that looked a lot like Pradas.

"Hello, Mrs. Custer. Not much happening. It was a quiet day," she reported in perfect English.

Annie tried again. *"Quien esta en la casa?"*

"Everybody's home. Nothing's new," she said.

Annie gave up on both the Spanish lesson and any hope for an explanation for Mag's panicked call. "Smells good," she murmured.

Dina nodded and patted the black head of the poodle sitting at her feet, ever hopeful for a handout. *"Huele rico,"* she agreed.

Annie closed the kitchen door. Outside in the hall she could hear the Momentum club infomercial on the Golf Channel coming from the den. She'd heard it a hundred times and still didn't know what the club was for. She didn't think it was actually usable on the golf course. She took a deep breath and opened the door. Ben, her husband and former partner, was supine on the sofa watching golf shows that he'd seen many times before. He was dressed in wrinkled khaki shorts and a T-shirt. His cheeks had at least a five-day stubble on them, his graying hair hadn't been cut in a while, and he was playing with the item being promoted on the screen as much as one could play with a golf club while lying on a sofa. He wasn't swinging the thing or anything like that. He was just sort of holding it as if at any moment he *might* spring into action and smack one of those little bumpy balls right through the window. Annie would have liked to see that.

The room was dark, but not so dark that she couldn't make out the discarded shoes and piles of paper—old newspapers and magazines that Ben used to discourage his family from entering his space.

"Hi. How was your day?" she asked.

"I have a headache. How about you?"

"Oh, I have a situation. Carol Mack persuaded me to start an account for her parents." Annie stopped there at the expression on his face.

In the old days it had been inconceivable to men in the office that a woman could be a stockbroker star on her own merits. They'd thought Annie got and kept her accounts by sleeping with her clients. How else could a cute but smallish woman beat out a bunch of meaty, fast-talking men? After all the years of proving herself, Annie saw a flicker of the same irritation in her husband's eyes. *So she's gotten a new account. Big deal.* Immediately his attention returned to the TV screen, and he seemed to forget her.

For a second she teetered on the fine line between sympathy and rage. Okay, it was clear that Ben was unhappy, but frankly, so was she. Even though she lacked his excuse of having escaped a falling building three (count them, three) years ago, the stress of being the sole caretaker of the family was killing her. She didn't want to go there, though, so she left him to his thoughts.

The good news was that although MTV was playing some offensive music video, no funny smoke emanated from her younger daughter's room. Annie exhaled in relief. "Hey baby, what's going on?"

"Nothing."

Barbara, known as Bebe, was sitting on the floor dressed only in a hip-length T-shirt and hot pink bikini panties. She was coloring an astonishing pattern of flowers and angels on her knee and thigh. Marking pens were scattered all over the floor around her. Annie couldn't help admiring the artwork. The designs on her daughter's legs were every bit as fantastical and skilled as the primitive Day of the Dead sculptures from Mexico and South America that sold for thousands. "That's cool," she murmured.

"Thanks." Bebe surveyed her work with pride.

Annie would have expressed more enthusiasm if she weren't terrified that the colorful artwork on Bebe's knees might soon evolve into a bunch of permanent tattoos. Or if the backpack abandoned by the door wasn't still bulging with unopened books.

Or . . . Annie frowned at two pairs of brand-new designer jeans laid out on the floor with the tags still on and the Bloomingdales receipt clearly visible. Bebe had been shredding them very carefully in strategic places so that when she walked and crossed her legs in school, bits of her body drawings would peek out. *Shit.* She'd gone shopping without permission, bought things she didn't need, and ripped them up right in the open. But at least she wasn't a sneak, a thief, or a liar. Annie smiled fondly at her daughter. Bebe was a beautiful girl. She had Annie's honey-colored hair, Annie's high cheekbones, hazel eyes, and a delicate mouth. But where Annie had always been an attractive woman, Bebe was eye-popping, and regularly stopped traffic in a city that was used to model-beautiful women. Her perfect looks were so soothing that Annie was reluctant to launch into the destruction of $150 jeans. She turned her attention to the abandoned backpack. "Have you done your homework?"

"Oh yeah, all done," Bebe said brightly.

Annie closed the door. In her older daughter's room an ancient *Friends* episode was playing on her TV.

"What are you doing still in bed?" Annie asked the lump, curled in a fetal position.

"I have a brain tumor," Mag announced.

"Oh no." Annie's own head throbbed with dismay.

"I've been throwing up all day. The pain is excruciating," Mag elaborated.

"Did you go to your job interview?"

"Mom, if I die, I won't need a job." Mag spoke to her mother as if she were a cretin.

Annie laughed to show how ridiculous *that* idea was. "Mag, you're not going to die. You're going to be terrifically successful at whatever you choose to do, get married, and have wonderful children."

Mag made a gagging sound.

"Oh gee, what did you do about the agency, just blow them off?"

"No, I'm sick, I'm not irresponsible. I called to reschedule for next week."

Next week? It was only Monday. Did she plan to have a brain tumor for a *whole week*? Despite all her good intentions, Annie lost it.

"Mag, you've been in bed for three months now. We had a deal. College, a job by Labor Day, or you're going into the military."

"Yeah, yeah, I know, and they rape girls in the army." Mag rolled away from her mother to face the wall. "I'm going to get a job. What's your problem?"

My problem is no one is home! No one is taking responsibility. I'm scared. Annie didn't want to tell her child that she was frightened and traumatize Mag with another breakable adult. So she tried another tack.

"Mag, you're my big girl, my only beacon of light. Please don't set a bad example for your sister. If she doesn't do her homework, she's going to flunk out."

"Oh no, don't start that." Mag put a pillow over her head.

"I mean it. You're her big sister. If you don't care about the future, how can she take anything seriously?"

Mag took the pillow off her head and rolled over. "Mom, she doesn't know when the Civil War was."

"That's not your problem," Annie replied.

"She doesn't know when World War Two was, either. She doesn't know shit. She's stupid. *That's* why she's going to flunk out."

Annie gasped. "Margaret! How can you say that?"

"You're always telling us to face reality. Well, haven't you heard the things that come out of her mouth? Have you taken a *look* at her recently?"

"I'm taking a look at *you*, Margaret," Annie said wildly. "We're talking about you! Sit up and look at me."

"Leave me alone," Mag whined.

"Well, I wish I could. I wish I could let you all rot in front of your stupid TVs. But I can't. You're my job, Maggie, I can't let you down. By the way, who's been smoking in the apartment?"

Mag bolted up to a sitting position. Finally visible, she was the very picture of her father with her thick dark hair, strong handsome features punctuated with striking dark eyes, and a perky nose. She had a good figure, too, but no one ever saw it. Ever since she'd graduated from high school in June, she'd retired to her bed.

"Nobody! Why do you ask?"

Annie shook her head. "I could swear I smelled smoke when I came in. You'd tell me if you were smoking dope, wouldn't you?"

"Are you crazy? We don't do that."

Annie shook her head. Why did everyone doubt her sanity?

ten

WHEN ANNIE RETURNED TO THE KITCHEN TO POUR
herself a restorative glass of merlot, Dina was out walking Curly. Before she got to the counter, however, the
temperature dropped about twenty degrees. Annie shivered as the distinctive whorl of Marlboro smoke rose
from the middle of the kitchen table and the ghost of her
mother materialized before her, as she had been doing at
will for a long time.

"Mom?" Annie said.

"Who else?" Brenda Flood was wearing a suit from
the 1960s with an ice blue velvet Lily Dache hat that
Annie knew for a fact was in a box somewhere in her
closet. Whenever her mother's spirit appeared from
nowhere like this, her face and hair were never fully
realized, but Annie could always tell her mood by the
way she lifted her hand, dragged deeply on her phantom
cigarette, and shook her head disapprovingly just the
way she had in life.

"Annie, you look terrible," she said now.

Coming from someone who'd been dead for almost
eighteen years, it seemed a pretty harsh assessment.

"Mom," Annie repeated, and tears came to her eyes
because even now her mother was a constant irritation.
The woman hadn't mellowed one little bit in death.

Annie remembered the first time the spirit had visited her. Brenda had been dead a month, and baby Maggie was only two weeks old. Annie was breast-feeding the newborn in the middle of the night, watching the city lights out the window, and thinking—at that very moment—how terrible it was that her precious daughter would never know her grandmother. Suddenly it got chilly in the room, and Annie smelled smoke. Then her mother appeared in her nightgown. Annie had been so frightened that she almost dropped the suckling baby. When the ghost spoke to her, she stifled a scream because although it looked like the mother she'd known, the ghost sounded like someone else.

"Yo doing that all wrong, honey chile. That baby gonna suck the skin right off yo nipple, and yo gonna get a breast infection so bayad yo'll wish you was dayed."

Annie did not happen to be one of those people who believed that the dead could talk to the living, but if she had believed in such a thing, she would have planned the conversation to run along a different course. Instead of an unpleasant warning, her mother would have made a more positive comment, like: *Nice baby, wish I were there.* Or *I love the way you've done the baby's room.* Or even, *I miss you.* Not, *You're doing it wrong, you're messing up. Again.*

Annie would have changed a few other things about being haunted. She would have preferred a nonsmoking ghost, especially since cigarettes had been the cause of her mother's death. Another thing she didn't like was her ghost's accent. It was dead wrong; her mother had been a New Yorker, and she hadn't said things like *honey chile.* One of the first things Annie learned, however, was that you didn't get any choices about this kind of thing. Visitations just occurred. If the spirit of her mother's ghost was correct, but her accent wasn't, so be it. You simply couldn't object to something beyond your control.

In any case, Brenda had appeared—not scary or threatening or unhappy or wanting to send regards, just plain old annoying Brenda exactly as she used to be. Then, as suddenly as the apparition had appeared that very first time, it had wandered off into the other room and disappeared. And sure enough, that same night the soreness that had been steadily developing in Annie's right nipple from the baby's long sessions of enthusiastic feeding became a noticeable and painful blister. The next day, after two more feedings, the deadly blister burst and Annie got the worst fever of her life. The infection was so bad that a burning red stripe started traveling down her arm to her hand, and Annie did indeed wish she were dead. Penicillin, however, saved her from that awful fate. That was the beginning. After that, Annie knew that whenever her mother appeared, she had a message.

Tonight her message was, "The end is coming."

"What? The end of the world?" Annie didn't want an inside track on that one. "Don't tell me."

"No," Brenda said impatiently. "The end of yo family. Yo work killing them."

Wait a minute. Her mother didn't know what she was talking about. Her work was *saving* her family. The last thing Annie needed right now was a conversation about feminism from a person who was stupid enough to smoke herself to death. "Look, I don't have a choice here. Ben was in the World Trade Center collapse. He can't work. He has PTSD. He almost died, okay?"

"Lordy me, that's hardly the *worst* thing in the world," Brenda shot back.

"It would have been for us!" Death was permanent. Annie was an orphan because of it.

"Lordy me, yo ignorant," the ghost said.

"I am not ignorant," Annie protested. That accent killed her. Had her mother just found a new way to drive her crazy, or had she gone to the other side and somehow landed in Mississippi instead? She wished she knew.

"Hush now and listen. That po woman gonna die. And yo gonna take the blame."

"Huh? What woman?"

"I tole you, working's no good for womens," Brenda intoned ominously.

"Oh Jesus."

Brenda blew smoke in her face. "I tole you. Husband no good."

"Whose husband?" That was another difficult thing about the ghost. Annie couldn't always tell which conversation they were having from which period of her life.

"It's just plain murder, honey chile. Better do something before it's too late."

"Mom! Could you clarify a little?" She hated begging for help from an apparition, but sometimes her mother really did know her apples. "Come on, whose end is coming?"

Just then Annie heard the front door open and the sound of Curly howling his head off. The feisty toy poodle always went ballistic when the ghost was in the house. Wa-wa-wa-wa-wa. *Let me at it.*

Dina opened the door. *"Que esta, Curlito?"*

The Spanish irritated Annie. Why did Dina have to speak it for the dog and refuse to speak it for her? When she turned back to her mother, the dog was still howling, but the ghost was gone. *Shit.*

eleven

CURLY CHARGED INTO THE KITCHEN, SNIFFING frantically. He skidded to a shuddering stop at the chair where Brenda's ghost had rested only seconds before. He shivered and snarled at it for a while. Then he raced around smelling the cabinets, the doors, even his bowl of water, to see where it had gone. He kept running and skidding, searching for the ghost's entry or exit path. When he couldn't find it, he sneezed his annoyance at Annie.

Dina hung the leash on the doorknob. "My daughter is pregnant." She said it simply without fanfare or defensiveness. She shed no tears of joy or sorrow as the women did on Spanish TV.

Annie shivered like the dog at her mother's spirit. This morning, another lifetime ago, Mag had hinted that something like this was in the wind. Rosalie, Dina's daughter, was Mag's age, the wrong side of eighteen. For a second she stood there watching the black poodle sneeze. How do you respond sensibly to such momentous news? The girl was still in high school. Annie didn't know much about her; nothing, in fact. Dina lived far away from her children, supporting them from abroad because it was too expensive to bring them stateside. Annie hesitated for a second, unsure what reaction would be welcome.

"Congratulations, what a thrill. When is the wedding?" she said finally.

Dina made a face. *Are you kidding?* "He's a very nice boy, but only sixteen. Very joung."

"Sixteen!" Annie reached for the bottle of wine. Sixteen was less than young. It was infantile. "Would you like a glass of wine to celebrate?" she offered, thinking Dina probably needed it more than she did.

Dina shook her head, deadpan. "He's not finished with school," she added.

"No." At sixteen he wouldn't be much of anything. Apparently he didn't even qualify for a name.

"They're not getting married right now, but he's coming to live in the house." Dina smiled shyly, as if this was a good first step.

Annie nodded some more. How nice, another mouth for her to feed. No, two more mouths. Two adolescents and an infant, what a prospect! "You must be very excited." She sipped the wine, trying to find an even keel for her emotions.

For her, a pregnant daughter with a boyfriend moving into the house would be a catastrophe of the highest order, a 7.5 on the Richter scale. Worse than a daughter who'd graduated from a first-rate high school, had gotten into a first-rate college, and then refused to get out of bed to go. But Dina was another person, and she was definitely smiling, not as upset as she could have been.

"I am exciting. I'm going home." She garbled just a little in her happiness. Suddenly Dina remembered the *arroz con pollo*. She quickly washed her hands, then hurried to the stove to check on it.

"Ah, for the birth . . . ?" When would that be? In eight, nine months? Annie's forehead furrowed with concentration.

"No, no, I'm going home to Arjhentina to take care of them now." Dina calmly folded a dish towel and hung it on the bar on the oven door. Then she found a treat to calm the still-sneezing dog.

Annie blinked. Take care of them now, that phantom family that always made her cry? Why? She held her hands apart a few inches. "For . . ." How long?

Dina shook both her head and the box of dog treats. Curly promptly sat and raised one paw without waiting for the command.

"Good boy." Dina rewarded him with a chunk of freeze-dried liver. The liver refocused the dog on the living. He shut up and performed a few more tricks. Dina patted his head. "I'm retiring. Are you okay?"

Annie gulped and found herself sitting at the kitchen table. Okay, so Rosalie was going to have neither an abortion nor a wedding. She could live with that. It wasn't her call. But to get her mother back for foolish behavior? *Good going, and congratulations, Rosalie,* she thought.

Life was so unfair. Like Ben, Dina was retiring at the ripe old age of forty. Annie didn't want to be small and selfish. It wasn't Dina's fault that her daughter got pregnant or that she wanted to go home to be with her. But the problem was, Dina was the only person in the whole world who really knew them—Mag, Bebe, Ben, and especially her. Dina was the only one who knew her every mood and sometimes even seemed to care about her well-being. She never forgot to make sure Annie had the things she needed: her bubbly water, her vitamins—all the foods she liked. Dina never complained about walking Curly when no one else wanted to. She was a perpetual smoother-over, a fixer no matter what was going wrong, the perfect mother, ever-forgiving. Annie was breathless at the prospect of such a loss.

"Dina, are you sure that's a good idea? I thought you were happy here." Annie said this slowly. Did she have enough money to retire?

"I yam happy here."

"Then why would you leave?"

"My daughter, she needs me."

"Can't your mother take care of her?"

"She'll help. She cooks," Dina said.

"That's good. But, Dina, if you quit, who will pay the bills?" Annie had always thought that as working mothers, they had something in common.

Dina paused, then inhaled and exhaled. Clearly she was concerned about it. "My family is very strong. They'll help."

Annie frowned. But wasn't this the same family that hadn't helped Dina when her husband died and left her with four boys, a girl, and two long-retired parents to support? Hadn't Dina catered parties, sewed wedding dresses, done alterations, and a bunch of other things back home to send her children to school, and still been unable to make ends meet? Hadn't she come to the United States six years ago just because she needed to support the family that wasn't helping her? Annie suddenly had the uncomfortable feeling that the real family Dina was counting on to help was her. To Dina, the Custers were still as *rico* as they used to be before all the disasters struck. Annie's headache worsened, and she felt a migraine coming on. She couldn't support her forty-year-old retired housekeeper and her family back in Argentina.

"My head hurts," she said in a small voice.

"Don't worry," Dina told her. "I'll get your *medicina*."

twelve

CAROL MACK COULD NOT FIND A COMFORTABLE
spot in her sleek living room to calm herself. Her panicked eyes darted around the carefully decorated room,
but none of the possessions that usually comforted her
soothed her now. Not the expensive, hard-to-sit-on con-
temporary sofas and chairs in muted colors. Not the
swathes of imported fabrics intricately tailored into costly
window dressings that highlighted the huge windows'
signature park views. Not the twentieth-century paintings that she and Matthew had purchased at so many
Christie's auctions during his firm's good years. Not the
diamonds around her throat or the diamond watch on
her wrist, the cashmere sweat suit she was wearing, or
even her lean, well-exercised body itself.

She had come a long way from her humble Staten Island beginnings, and she didn't intend to return to that
indignity again. Not having the toys and perks of the
children with whom she'd grown up had always hurt
and humiliated her, and she could not bear the idea of
being powerless again. Tonight, after she thought she
was finally safe, her father turned everything around
again and had even gone so far as to make terrifying ac-
cusations. Carol couldn't even put her lawyer husband
on the case. Matthew was at his office not answering the

phone. Carol felt like the victim in an old movie, tied to the railroad tracks with a train rushing toward her and no one to save her from a terrible fate. She saw a train wreck in the imminent death of her mother, the senility of her father, and Matthew's firm's financial woes. She had no control over any of it, and never had. It was the old and painful story of her life.

Ever since she was little, Carol had been confused by things that couldn't be explained. As a child she'd known that the contrasting images in her home weren't right. There were shabby furnishings in the tiny house, but it also contained her mother's collection of very good jewelry as well as some vintage clothing from the 1930s that included several perfectly preserved alligator clutch bags and shoes, designer dresses, and a sable stole. Her mother laughingly called herself *nouveau pauvre.* New poor, the opposite of new rich. Carol gathered that her mother had been driven to school in a chauffeured limousine, and her circumstances had changed after her parents died mysteriously. Then she'd married Dean Teath, a young dentist who didn't like his profession.

The story was vague at best, but it didn't have a happy ending. Mamie knew all about opera and ballet and expensive restaurants in Manhattan, but Carol had never been taken to them. Children's concerts at Carnegie Hall, the Christmas displays at Rockefeller Center and Saks Fifth Avenue. The Rockettes. None of that. It was almost as if the Teaths spent the forty-five years of their marriage years hiding out. No going out, no special lessons like riding and tennis and piano that her mother had enjoyed.

Her parents had lived a skeletal life. Carol shuddered with embarrassment whenever she thought of the skimpiness and scrimping. The endless repairing of old appliances and furniture that had been there long before she was born and were never replaced. It had felt as if the family lived off the very air they breathed, and someday even that might stop coming in. The fear of purchasing any unnecessary thing was so palpable that she'd fled to Hunter College, taken a training job in retail, met Matthew—a law student at Fordham—and married him as soon as she could. Matthew's family had some money out West. They weren't the Macks of the Mack Truck fortune, but they were comfortable. Matthew was a hard worker and an equally liberal spender. That had appealed to her. She'd been proud that her first job as a buyer and his as a lawyer allowed the two of them to pay for their own wedding. They'd proven early that they were competent in every way. Carol had scoured the city for a suitable, affordable gown, and they'd done the whole thing both nicely and cheaply. She was so proud of that. She could take care of herself.

But soon after that the bomb had dropped. A year or so later, Mamie told her about the money—the thousands of dollars that had come in regularly every year and was relentlessly rolled over. It was like an assault with a knife, a doubly devastating blow. The wealth Carol had so desperately craved had been there all along, hostage to future needs that, no matter how pressing, had never been met. She'd gotten nothing. When she'd heard this news, Carol's whole young life suddenly read to her like a familiar fairy tale: She was Snow White, she was Cinderella, she was Gretel, lost in the forest. All those years she'd suffered and gone without, she'd been one of those heroines, those should-be princesses that had been denied their heritage. She was the pauper who should have been a princess all along. She had lived a fairy tale.

Carol had believed that her parents had done a terrible thing to themselves—but also to her—for no good reason. And she couldn't find a way to make it right. They wouldn't move. They wouldn't change. And they wouldn't give it to her to safeguard! She'd been left to rely on Matthew's abilities to make the big money. There had been no way to recover her own legacy. For one thing, she didn't know where it was. Her parents wouldn't leave the house long enough for her to search it. They didn't like to go out to dinner. A vacation was out of the question; they didn't know how to be with people. The tantalizing carrot of their fortune had been dangled out of her reach for many years. Carol didn't even know how much it was. And now her father was resisting again. She should have expected this, but she hadn't.

She needed to discuss it with Matthew, and he was out of the loop as usual. Carol didn't know what Matthew was doing behind closed doors right now—maybe some court case or a desperate scramble to keep the firm together—but he'd always worked late. Her frustration in trying to reach him was nothing new. He told her the firm was failing, and he didn't answer the phone. But now her father wanted his fortune—whatever it was—back in his grasp. She paced her living room, thinking dark thoughts and avoiding the view that had always sustained her.

The park was smack in the middle of the city. The majestic sweep of eight-hundred-plus acres of grass and trees, boulders, paths, lakes, the zoo, the skating rink, and the merry-go-round was a symbol not only of New York's greatness, but of America's greatness, too. During daylight hours the splendid view from her window stretched from one end to another, taking in the lavish buildings that circled it and held it tight. At night it was nothing less than spectacular. The light show at Tavern on the Green, the necklace of sparklers along the park drive, the dark masses of trees and boulders that indicated the kind of wide-open space Carol hadn't had in her childhood. Central Park was her own personal mark of distinction; it stood for the end of deprivation.

But tonight the park and its views, the fortune spent on her apartment and its accoutrements, were nothing in the face of her stubborn mother dying at home. There was only her best friend to call for solace. She reached out for Annie.

thirteen

AT BARELY EIGHT P.M. ANNIE RETREATED TO HER room with a pounding head. When she reached her bedroom door, Curly was beside her, sneezing and growling. It was freezing in there, and once again Annie felt the presence.

"Mom?" she said softly.

One of the lightbulbs in the lamp on her side of the bed flickered, and she tripped on the edge of the carpet. *Don't do this to me twice in one day,* she thought. She didn't see the ghost and stifled the impulse to check for it under the bed. Sometimes it liked to tease and didn't show itself, just pulled off a few tricks with the electricity to get her attention. Annie approached the bed slowly. It was covered with a quilt she'd made back in the days when she'd been a big producer at work but still did old-fashioned homemaker kinds of things. The quilt was red, white, and blue. All those months during her mother's illness she'd worked on it frantically. As she'd sewed the patriotic pieces together, she'd prayed that all the tiny stitches she took would somehow bind her mother to her and keep her spirit alive, so she wouldn't be alone. Since then, she'd bought new sheets and pillowcases to change the look, but the bedspread remained. And so, alas, had her mother. Her prayers had been answered.

Annie lay down on her four-poster bed, and all her troubles crowded her brain at once. She was worried about Carol Mack's mother. She was worried about what Brian might do to her if something was wrong with the securities. If he tried to cover up, where did that leave her? A criminal in the first degree, a co-criminal? She was sweating as she moved down her line of worries back to those of her family. Why were her children still throwing bread at each other and chewing with their mouths wide open to annoy their father? Why couldn't they be regular kids who read the classics (or even Harry Potter), and played sports and musical instruments, and were interested in current events? Why didn't Ben wake up to their decline and get useful? She knew exactly what would happen when Dina left. Ben would expect her to hire someone else to wash and iron the clothes, keep the refrigerator well stocked, run the errands, and walk the dog. And she was not going to do that. She'd kept Dina on despite the family's financial crunch because she hadn't wanted to be responsible for one more person out of work in this country. The truth was that Dina's leaving was a good thing. They couldn't afford help, and they didn't need it. They'd have to take care of themselves.

A few minutes later the phone rang. She was in bed, but not yet groggy enough from the headache pill that was supposed to knock her out. She didn't move to answer it. Seconds later Ben yelled at her from inside the den down the long hall.

"Annie, Carol's on the phone."

She rolled over and played dead, hoping that he would come looking for her, see that she was sleeping, and quietly go away to deal with the phone call. He didn't do that. Instead he yelled louder.

"Annnnie, it's Carrolllllll."

Then she heard other sounds. From the left, a rerun of *Six Feet Under,* from the right, a music video. From the den, Larry King. It had to be after nine. She groaned. What could Carol want at this hour?

"Where arrrrre you?" Ben kept calling her even though there weren't a lot of places for her to be. After a long pause, he finally opened the bedroom door. "What are you doing?" he demanded.

The lights were off. She wasn't reading or watching TV. Her head was on the pillow, and her eyes were closed. It seemed clear enough to her what she was doing.

"Didn't you hear me calling you?" He wasn't going to go away, so she opened her eyes.

"I'm sleeping. What can't wait until tomorrow?"

"Carol's on the phone."

"Honey, I'm sleeping. Will you tell her I'll talk to her in the morning?"

He bristled and started to walk away. "I'm not your secretary. Tell her yourself."

Annie bolted up as if she'd been electrocuted. Blood

raged behind her eyes. She was so angry that she thought her head would explode. How dare he talk to her like that? "What's the matter with you? Can't you see I'm sleeping?" she said sharply.

He was almost out of the room. He spun around in the doorway. "Hey, get ahold of yourself. I came all the way in here to be helpful. You don't have to fucking bite my head off."

"Helpful! Helpful! Wait a minute! I never get a break. I never run away. I'm always here for you. Tonight I don't feel well. Why can't you do one fucking thing for me?"

Saying the word she hated more than any other, Annie was startled into silence. What was she doing? What was her problem? Why did she put up with this? For fifteen years she and Ben had been partners and taken each other's messages. Now it was beneath him to field a call while she was sleeping? Furious with him, she reached for the phone and quickly switched into broker mode. "Hi, Carol," she said in her sweetest voice.

Carol, however, didn't reply in hers. "Why didn't you call me, Annie? Why didn't you tell me what happened?" she demanded angrily.

"It's been a long day. Everything went fine," Annie lied. "Your father brought out the contents of his mattress. We set up the account. You're safe now. But you did leave out a few things, Carol. You didn't tell me everything."

"That's not the way I heard it."

"What do you mean?" Annie's migraine struck like an ice pick through her eyeball.

"My dad is upset. He wants everything back right now."

"Right now?"

"Yeah, he wants to alert the authorities. He says you robbed him."

A second bolt of lightning struck home. Annie sputtered with indignation and fear. "Oh Jesus. I can't believe I'm hearing this. Carol, you have to help me out here. You insisted that I go out there. You put me in a tough spot. And now I'm exhausted. I'm in bed now. Why don't I call you back in the morning?" She wasn't doing this now. She just couldn't.

"Well, excuse me. You've been trying to get this account for years. I gave you the opportunity for a big one. It's not my fault that you messed it up."

Messed up! She didn't mess up. "Carol! I can't believe you're saying this to me. I did you a big fat favor today. Your family fortune was piled up on the kitchen counter. Your father had no idea what he had. No idea at all. Do you think it's usual for brokers to handle dynamite like this? I put myself on the line for you."

There was a pause on Carol's end. "How much is it?" she said finally.

Oh, so now she was interested. Annie wished she could put Carol on hold for a while to stew. She was hurt. What was it with these Macks? She didn't like being threatened.

"The reason I'm asking is that my mother is leaving it to me. All of it will be mine when she dies," Carol said.

"I know, she told me."

"So how much is it?" Carol asked.

"The computer will have to come up with the values. There are a lot of small positions in companies that have merged, or don't even exist anymore. It has to be sorted out. We'll know in a few days. But it's significant. I'd guess between three and four million." There. She'd said it. Carol had a fortune after all.

"What? You walked away with four million dollars?" Carol shrieked.

"Well, I don't know for sure it's that much, but how about a thanks? You asked me to do what you couldn't do yourself. I saved your ass."

"I never told you to take it, Annie. I told you to talk to him. And now he's hysterical. He says you took it from him against his will and he's going to call the authorities."

"Jesus, Carol. The accountant was with me. He saw it all. And, Carol, you begged me this morning."

"I don't remember that," she said.

"You have that short a memory? How about, your dad is difficult, and you're scared to death of him?"

"Well, I think he has Alzheimer's," Carol admitted. "Sometimes he gets a little paranoid."

"A *little* paranoid?" Annie yelped.

"Well, he doesn't want to be taken advantage of, but who does?"

Annie thought she heard a reference to Ben and Matthew, old friends who were now bitter enemies. Annie let the remark go for the sake of their friendship. She'd let a lot of things go for Carol. Carol had stuck by her, so she changed the subject.

"Carol, you put me in a tough place today. Why didn't you hire a lawyer to take care of this?"

"How could I do that to my father?" Carol replied indignantly. "He wants it back. What can I say?"

"Let's get one thing straight. It's your mother's money. She wanted it out of the house."

"Well, I think I need to take charge of this myself. I want the stuff now, Annie. Right this minute."

Carol on the rampage. Just what she needed. Annie sighed. "You can't have it tonight. Everything's locked in the vault."

There was another long pause. "Then I'll come and get it in the morning," Carol retorted.

Annie gulped. "This is really unusual, Carol. There are procedures for this kind of thing . . ." She just didn't know what they were. She sat up and put her head between her knees.

"Don't give me that shit. You took it. You'll have to give it back." Carol was ranting now. She had a little weakness, a little crack in her façade that caused her to explode whenever she was under stress. It wasn't a pretty sight.

"Okay, calm down. Of course you'll have it back. I just have to ask my manager how to handle it. I'll call you in the morning." Annie hung up and bolted for the toilet. She had a little crack in her façade, too. Migraines wrecked her.

fourteen

ANNIE WALKED INTO BRIAN REDFIELD'S OFFICE AT eight A.M. on the dot. He glanced up from his morning ritual. "Thanks for coming in early."

"It wasn't a problem getting up. I never went to sleep," Annie told him.

"Have a seat. Do you want something to drink?" Brian had a line of capsules on his desk, was drinking hot chocolate, and had the news on low volume. The chocolate was too hot, so he was waiting for it to cool off a little before using it to down his assortment of dietary supplements. He rearranged the vitamins so he could take them in the correct order. He had to have both C and ester C, alpha lipoic acid, DMAE, all the B's and E. He couldn't swallow huge horse pills, he had to have the capsule version, and he wouldn't down them with water, either. He liked taking the supplements with his breakfast: chocolate. He wasn't drinking coffee anymore because the skin doctor on TV said it promoted fat, and Brian wanted to be trim, trim, trim. His wife had called him an old woman about his habits and rituals, but since they didn't hurt anybody, he'd never bothered changing for her. Now she was gone, and he was an anxious man.

"No, I had coffee at home," Annie said.

"Shouldn't drink coffee, you know, just makes you thick in the waist," Brian said, testing his chocolate to see if it was cool enough.

Annie put her lips together as if her lipstick needed blotting. She wasn't thick in the waist.

"Don't look at me that way, it's a fact," he told her.

"Look, I have only one cup." Her expression asked him where this was going.

"Doesn't matter how much you have. Perricone says one cup stays in your system a full twenty-four hours. Don't think I don't care about you. I have your best interests at heart."

"Brian, I couldn't sleep last night. Why don't you just tell me what you have to tell me?" she said impatiently.

"Plus, it makes you jazzed." Still on the coffee, Brian was in his manager mode. His index fingers formed a steeple. He hadn't slept much the night before, either. He'd been thinking about Annie Custer even more than usual.

Annie was a good person. She'd been one of the first ones to switch from a commission-based income to a flat fee that reflected only her performance in each account. Many brokers in the office had been reluctant to do so, and still resisted. In the lean years such a move had been heroic, but almost suicidal. The impact of the flat rate was that she had to work a lot harder for a third of the money. By doing it, however, she'd held on to a loyal client base and was still a good producer for the branch, if not herself. He admired her for that.

In addition, Annie was cute and sexy, and she usually made a lot of sense. Brian enjoyed looking at her and listening to her. Her common sense and lack of selfishness, and her interest in his life, were especially important to him. Everybody needed a woman to evaluate other women, and she counseled him about the women he was dating. At work he monopolized her time. He knew she liked him, and secretly he'd been waiting for the moment to get her for himself. He did not consider this a sneaky thing at all.

"Jazzed?" she said, questioningly now.

He studied her outfit. Yesterday she'd worn a navy business suit with a pencil skirt. He never failed to notice her great legs. Today she was wearing a black pantsuit, and her limbs were covered. Annie didn't usually wear black. She said her clients preferred seeing her wear lighter colors. She thought their confidence was boosted by upbeat clothing. She counseled him never to wear brown, so he never did.

"Jazzed?" she repeated, frowning at him.

"Okay, okay. You don't have a weight problem, but you know what I mean." He dropped the caffeine issue. He didn't want her to think he thought she was fat.

"Sit down. You're making me nervous," he added.

"Fine." She sat down and crossed her legs.

Ooohh, he turned away. Something had happened to him since yesterday. Annie had gotten into the place in his mind that he'd always reserved for other women. He didn't know how it had happened. Yesterday, she'd made a deadly mistake, and suddenly he was attracted to her as never before. Even though the Yankees had beaten the Red Sox in the tenth inning last night, the victory didn't engage him one bit. He'd stayed until the bitter end, which was rare for him. Usually by the fifth inning he'd had enough, especially if his team was losing and he didn't have a date.

Last night, however, with a lap full of peanut shells and a couple of low-carb Michelobs in his belly, he realized he was truly sorry that Annie hadn't joined them. Three men drinking beer alone in the firm's excellent box seats was not that much fun after a long summer of it. Annie could be the life of the party when she wanted to, and four of them together made a kind of office gang—everybody coming out of a failed marriage and each one a loser in his own particular way. Even though Annie was not quite out of hers yet, Brian saw all the signs of a marital endgame. He saw it coming. She was almost one of them. And now she was in trouble. This was an exhilarating combination. He tossed down an ester C 500 and a DMAE 250, looking away so Annie couldn't see what he was thinking. She was a smart girl, and he had to be careful.

She tossed her head to dismiss his nonsense. "I got a call from Carol last night. She wants to come in and pick up the securities today."

"What!" A torpedo-shaped E1000 flipped out of Brian's fingers. He struggled to catch it before it rolled off the shiny surface of his desk and onto the rug beneath. He caught it just in time.

"Yeah, she says she's coming in to take it back to her father, but I don't believe her."

"Jesus freaking Christ! Did you tell her no way?" Brian almost jumped out of his leather chair.

"No, Brian. I didn't tell her anything."

"Jesus, Annie, this is very tricky. Where's your brain?"

"My brain is in my head, where it always is." She glared at him.

"Uh-oh, don't look at me like that. This is your mess," he said mildly, sensing victory already.

She didn't say anything as he finished the last of his vitamins and wiped cocoa from his lips. That took care of breakfast. Then he wiped his fingers and raked them through his hair. Although he felt pretty old today, he was still a young man, and there was no gray in his hair at all. "Do you think Carol's taking it to another broker?" he asked.

"Brian, I don't know. Yesterday she wanted the account to come here. Last night when it got here, she wanted it out of here. It's all very strange. You wouldn't believe where it came from. A tiny falling-down house. No security. It's hard to imagine that Carol would want it to go back there, especially with her mother dying and her father in charge of the assets. It just doesn't make sense."

Brian made another steeple. "And most of the securities are in Mrs. Teath's name?"

Annie nodded. "All of them."

"Mrs. Teath signed the powers of attorney, and we have them here?" Brian said.

"Yes again. So it seems to me that the owner of the stocks will have to request their return and not anybody else."

Brian clapped his hands. "Good thinking. We'll have to ask Frisk. But my guess is we have her there."

"We do have her there. When I spoke to Carol last night, she was shocked by the value of the account. Maybe she just wants to get her hands on it." Annie hesitated. "Let's get to the point. You scared me to death last night. Is something missing?"

"Look, you know I'll take care of you." He gave her a little look that he meant to be reassuring.

She made a face. "Jesus, Brian. What does that mean?"

He raised a warning finger to his lips as Darian came in. She was carrying a large mug of coffee with the Hall Stale logo on it. Today she was dressed in orange and black, all set for Halloween.

"God, I'm scared already," Brian muttered.

"I heard that. Morning, all. Where do you want to work? Conference room?" Darian was perky. She was a woman who loved her work.

Frisk followed her in, rubbing his hands together. He did, too. "Yankees won in the tenth, nice, huh?" he said, then: "Ready to go?"

"We have an issue. Annie got a call from the daughter last night. They want it all back."

Darian, Frisk, and Brian exchanged glances.

"No shit!" Frisk said.

"Is something the matter?" Annie asked. "Don't keep me in the dark."

"Why does she want it back?" Darian turned to Annie for an explanation.

Annie lifted her shoulders. "It's not entirely clear to me." There was the old Matthew scandal, of course. But she didn't want to go there.

Petra stuck her head in and knocked on the door-frame. "Carol's on the phone, do you want to take it?" she said.

Brian shook his head at Annie. "Not yet," he said.

Annie turned to her assistant. "Will you tell her I'm in a meeting, and I'll call her back soon? Thanks."

Petra wagged her finger and disappeared.

Brian returned to the subject. "Frisk, here's the question for you. If Mrs. Teath is the owner and she signed the stock powers over to us—"

"Then she has to be the one to request their return. If that's what you're asking, the answer is yes," Frisk said.

"The daughter can't just take possession?" Brian said.

"No."

"The husband can't take possession?"

Frisk shook his head. "No, we have the powers. She has to make the request. She could fax us a request with her signature on it. That would do it."

"Wait a minute," Darian cut in. "We can't let this go without a thorough investigation. We should have done this last night. We took the certificates in. We should have checked it all out then, and recorded what we had."

Brian put his hand up and shook his head. *No grumbling. No second-guessing.* He didn't want to take any shit about what they didn't do yesterday.

Darian wouldn't stop, though. "We don't want to have this come back and smack us in the face. We have to list it all, check all the numbers against those on Annie's list. We can't return anything until that's all done." She crossed her arms across her chest. She was the branch watchdog. There were too many lawsuits out there. She wasn't taking any chances.

"We heard you last night, Darian, and we hear you now," Brian replied. But he was the boss, he was the one to say what they would do.

"This is for our protection. I'm not trying to be difficult." For a second, she looked like a porcupine.

"Calm down, everybody. Let's just figure this out. What do you want me to tell Carol?" Annie asked.

Brian inhaled and rocked back and forth in his chair. "The Teaths have a perfect right to change their minds," he said.

"Of course. No one is disputing that."

"And if they had executed this correctly in the first place, we wouldn't have had a problem. But they didn't—"

"Well, Mrs. Teath is terminally ill," Annie cut in. "She couldn't come in. And I took the stock powers to her. I did it properly. She wanted me to take it."

"What about the bearer bonds?"

"I didn't know there would be bearer bonds when I went out there," she said slowly. Awareness that taking them could cost her this job showed in her face. Brian liked that.

"Look, I understand. You're preaching to the choir. But now we have to go through a process, Annie. You're the account manager on this. You'll have to talk to Carol. Tell her we're documenting the items now. I want to talk to Dr. Teath— Jesus, what a name." He shook his head, then turned to Frisk. "We'll work in the conference room."

"She's waiting. Do you want me to call her now?" Annie asked.

Brian nodded, smiling benignly. He wanted his message to read, *We'll work this out*. He deliberately didn't tell her that $260,000 in bearer bonds was missing. Despite her claim of ignorance on the subject, he thought she already knew that.

fifteen

MAG WOKE UP EVEN MORE PANICKED THAN USUAL. Her body felt every negative vibration, and she knew things were not right. Nothing was right. She'd gotten up only an hour after her mother left and had gone into the kitchen for solace from Dina. She didn't want to lose Dina the way she'd lost her whole class from school, the way she'd lost Carol after Matthew fucked her father. Without Dina, there'd be no one to talk to. No one at all.

She sat at the kitchen table with Curly on her lap, mournfully watching Dina clean up the kitchen. "Dina, what are you going to do in Argentina all day? Won't you miss us?"

"Same things I do here, *niña,*" Dina said.

"Do they have TV there?"

Mag was joking, but Dina didn't take offense. "Oh jsure. Lots." She took a minute to build her weird drink concoction—the very last ounce of ancient coffee, a packet of flavored oatmeal, and two cups of boiling water. After it was made she let it sit on the counter to cool off while she washed out the coffeepot and put it in the sink. Then she joined Mag at the table.

"Jyou want something?" she asked.

"No thanks . . . I can't believe you're going home because your daughter is having a baby." It seemed so strange. Mag couldn't get her mind around it.

"Chyes, why not? She's my only girl."

Mag gave her head a little shake. She knew if she got pregnant right now, the very last thing her mother would do was stay home and hold her hand. Kill her and leave town to escape the law would be more like it. The contrast between Dina's loving response to her daughter's trouble and her mother's critical response to her really hurt. Mag's mother didn't give her any credit for the bad things she *didn't* do. Mag didn't stay out drinking all night. She didn't take drugs and get pregnant. Was she really a total fuckup if she took a few months off after high school like her mother seemed to think? She didn't tattoo or pierce her body in a dozen places, either. Getting wasted and pregnant; now, *that* would be fucking up.

Feeling seriously misunderstood about the first unscheduled summer of her entire life, Maggie knew she was nobody's girl. Curly had a snaggletooth that made him look like he was always smiling. He smiled right then and licked the back of her hand. He was the only one happy to have her home.

"*Pero,* I'll miss you, if that's what you're asking," Dina said.

"But I don't understand why you *want* to go back. You said it's terrible there."

"Thas true. Not so good as here, but I'm old, *niña,* I need a rest."

"You're not any older than Mom. She doesn't need a rest," Mag sputtered. "God!"

"Chyes. Everybody needs a rest. Even you."

Mag smiled. She didn't love Dina for no reason.

The door opened. Mag watched the housekeeper

hastily jump to her feet before her father could enter the
room and catch her resting. He was kind of old-
fashioned that way and didn't like anybody in a state of
repose but himself.

He registered that Mag was out of bed and glanced at
the clock to see what time she'd surfaced. She countered
by doing the same. Today both were up by nine. Dina
melted into the background, taking her oatmeal drink
with her to the sink.

"What's going on?" Dad asked, giving Maggie a keen
once-over.

"Nothing." She avoided his eyes by looking down
and patting the dog. Good old Curly. His head bobbed
with appreciation.

"You going to look for that job today?"

Dina looked away, trying to become invisible. She
began scrubbing the sink for the second time even though
it hadn't needed cleaning the first time. Spanish TV was
on without the sound. She appeared to be ignoring
them, but she was listening to every word.

"That's next week, Dad," Mag reminded him.

He sat down in Dina's place, scratching his head as if
he hadn't washed his hair recently. "What are you doing
this week?"

"A lot of things. I'm working on it." She didn't want
him to start reciting her mother's list of what she should
be doing to find a job. The sheet of positive steps was
lame. Mag wasn't doing them to appease her mother,
or her father, and she certainly wasn't going to pander to
her father by appearing to take an interest in the subject.

"Well, why don't you go over to the Gap and get a
part-time job there while you're waiting for the right
thing to come along?" he suggested.

Mag concentrated on the dog's ears. Her dad was out

of work, too. If it was such a great idea, why didn't *he* do it? The light over their heads flickered. Curly growled and leaped to his feet. The flashing lights always got to him. "Shhh, it's okay," she said, shivering. She didn't like being reminded there was a ghost in the house.

"Do we have any coffee left?" he asked Dina.

Dina didn't answer, just smiled and glanced pointedly at the coffeepot drying on the counter. Any idiot could see that the coffee was all gone.

"I guess not; will you make some?" he asked, lifting his nose slightly in the air at the snub. *Who did she think she was?*

"Why don't you do it yourself, Dad?" Mag said innocently.

"Make the coffee?" he said blankly, as if he had no idea what that meant.

"Yeah."

He looked puzzled. "What aren't I getting here?"

Mag rolled her eyes as Dina grabbed the bag of Starbucks out of the refrigerator and squeezed it flat. There was only a tiny bit left.

"Better get some more today. Jesus!" He put his hands to his ears when Mag turned on the grinder.

He was wearing a freshly pressed shirt and shorts, and loafers with no socks. He had that vague looking-for-trouble expression on his face that usually meant a fight was coming. She hated him the most when he was like that.

"What are you doing today?" he asked.

"I have a headache," Maggie said.

"Oh, PMS. Is that why you're so bitchy?"

She threw her hands up. "What are you *talking* about?"

"That remark about my making the coffee. Why should

I make the coffee? You're not doing anything. Why can't you do something useful? Be a checkout girl in the grocery store. Anything but a parasite."

Tears sprang into Mag's eyes at the direct hit. "All my friends are in college, Dad. I can't do that."

"Why can't you?"

"They're in *college*." She gave him a look. It wasn't a hard one.

"So they're in college," he said. "You could be in college."

She threw up her hands again. She wanted to punch him. "People don't take a year off from school to work at the Food Emporium."

"Then volunteer at a hospital or somewhere."

Mag thought this was the most unfair thing she'd ever heard. For a second she was sorely tempted to tell him that Bebe was smoking dope. Very sorely tempted. "You can't even make a cup of coffee for yourself, Dad. Why do I have to be Miss Perfect?"

"No one said you had to be perfect."

"Well, I don't see you volunteering at a hospital, or working at the Gap. You're the grown-up, for God's sake."

"I worked for twenty years," he said angrily.

"So did Mom, so did Dina. What's your point?"

The coffee was ready. Dina put a cup of fresh coffee at his place. She had foamed some milk for him and set the table with a spoon and napkin. At times like this she pretended she didn't speak English.

"Thanks, Dina, that's perfect." He focused on the cappuccino. "Look at that. Why should I do it when it's so much nicer to be served?"

Maggie had no response to that level of insensitivity. She got up and left him there to drink it alone. About half an hour later he came into her room without knocking.

"You want to go with me to the pier and hit a few golf balls?" he asked as if nothing had happened.

Sure, Dad, when pigs fly. She pulled the covers over her head and didn't answer.

sixteen

ANNIE DIALED CAROL'S NUMBER, AND SHE PICKED UP on the first ring. "Annie, I'm coming right over," she said. "Have everything ready for me. I'm taking it with me."

"And hello to you, Carol. How are you doing?" Annie replied, as coolly as she could. This was going to be a very hard call.

"I didn't sleep a wink last night," Carol said.

"That makes two of us. Yesterday was a terrible day. I'm very worried about your parents." And that was the truth.

"I'm so upset I can't eat, either," Carol went on. "I had no idea my parents had so much money."

"Well, it's not surprising you can't eat or sleep with your mother so sick. How is she today?" *Stick to the subject,* Annie told herself.

"Ahh . . ." The question caught Carol off guard. She didn't answer.

"Have you talked to her, seen her?" Annie asked. It

wasn't a self-serving question. Yesterday the scene had disturbed her very much. She couldn't help identifying with the old woman whose daughter seemed to care only about her inheritance. And there were other things, too. Annie needed some specific answers about what was going on in that household.

"Of course I've seen her," Carol exploded. "I see her all the time. Why do you ask?"

"Have you talked to her about this? About her illness? What exactly does she have?" Annie waded into the quicksand cautiously.

"What's going on? Why are you grilling me, Annie?" Carol demanded.

"Your mother's wishes are relevant. Have you talked with her about this?"

"Stop asking me that. My father pretty much takes care of everything. You know that."

Annie played with a paper clip, one of a hundred in a lumpy bubblegum-pink mug that Bebe had made for her in kindergarten. "Is he also in charge of the shopping and the food?"

"What are you getting at?" Carol's voice held a little whimper of fear.

"Don't get paranoid on me. I just asked about your mother's health," Annie said gently.

"Well, you sound threatening to me, kiddo. I don't like being questioned about my own family."

"I don't mean to sound critical in any way, but I've seen your mother more recently than you have. She's dehydrated; she's not eating well enough. She needs a nurse and a lot more care than she's getting. She needs you, Carol."

"What are you, a doctor now?" Carol replied furiously.

"It's just what I saw." Annie's voice took on an edge. "You told me yourself that your father is confused. He's not a nurse, Carol. The whole thing is highly unusual. Things are not in order there."

Then suddenly, like thunder in a clear sky, Annie heard her mother's words from the night before and realized that Mamie was the woman her mother had warned her about. *Mamie* was going to die. And—Jesus, she was being set up somehow by Carol's father. She saw it in a flash and knew she had to do something about it.

"The woman has cancer. She can't eat," Carol was saying huffily.

"I don't think so, Carol. I know what cancer is," Annie said slowly. "I lived through it with my own mother for two years. I know what it looks like." Every stage of it, every short high, every bitter defeat—every cell's death. She knew it intimately. She'd been with her mother every day of that battle. And she suspected that Mamie Teath was not dying of cancer. Annie swallowed the idea whole, like a fish with the bait, just as Carol started ranting the way she always did when someone told her something she didn't want to hear.

"All right. I know, you sat with Brenda every day, but not all of us can be Saint Annie!" Carol said bitterly.

Saint Annie, where did that come from? Annie was stung by the words, but they didn't stop her.

"Don't let your mother die like this, Carol. Believe me, you'll be sorry later," she said. Somehow she knew that Mamie wouldn't be coming back as a ghost. The poor woman didn't know the way to the city.

"Look, it's none of your business how my mother chooses to die. You don't know anything about us," Carol sputtered.

Oh, but I do, Annie didn't say. *I see what you can't see.* "It's a complicated situation," she murmured.

"What are you *talking* about? I don't see how it can be so complicated. You took their fortune from them, and now you'll have to give it back. That's the extent of it."

With that, Annie's resolve stiffened. "That's the smallest part of it," she said slowly.

"What are you saying?" Carol yelled. "What are you doing to me?"

"Think about it for a moment. Your father never gave up his stash before. Why did he give it up yesterday? And why is he asking for it back today?" There, she'd dropped the hint. Something was off. Way off.

"Shit, I don't know. What difference does it make?" Carol blustered. "Shit."

Annie took a deep breath. She didn't want to think that Carol and her father were setting her up just as Matthew had set Ben up. She exhaled.

"This is your mother's money, Carol, so we can't just hand it over to you on your say-so."

"Jesus. I told you my *father* wants it back."

"It doesn't matter who wants it back. The stash belongs exclusively to your mom. Her name is on the certificates. Yesterday, while her accountant and I were in the room, she signed stock powers on all of those certificates over to Hall Stale to be deposited in an account in her name. To have it returned she would have to make a written request to us."

"This is ridiculous," Carol erupted. "This is outrageous."

"And, of course, my manager wants to talk to both your father and mother about this. It's not a comfortable situation."

"But you know how they are. They're nuts!"

"They're more than nuts. Your mother is being starved to death." Annie didn't soften the accusation.

"You don't know what you're talking about!" Carol screamed.

"How do you know she has cancer?" Annie retorted just as angrily. "What kind of cancer does she have? What doctors treated her? Have you visited her in the hospital?"

Carol gasped. "You fucking bitch! You have no right—"

Annie cut her off. "There's a lot of money involved here. There are estate questions, legal questions. I think your father knows that he won't be able to cash any coupons with your mother's name on them if she dies."

Carol was silent.

"The IRS closes accounts of the deceased," she added. She guessed that this was the reason Teath was willing to let the stock certificates go. What she didn't understand yet was why he'd turned over the bearer bonds that he would have had no trouble cashing. No one knew he had them.

"Jesus!" Carol said finally.

"I can take care of this for you. But I want you to get your mother out of that house."

At that Carol actually growled. "Don't you understand this is none of your business? You have no right to threaten me like this."

"My manager says we have to have the paperwork. And he wants to talk to your father and your mother. We can sort it out, but we have to do it properly."

Carol hung up without replying. Annie sat back in her chair, trembling because Carol had not responded to the important question. She could be wrong, but a number of unusual things about the Teaths had bothered her all night. First, there had been almost no food in their house. And second, there hadn't been any pill bottles. It was a house without even an aspirin. Annie knew from personal experience that medications were part of the scene when someone had a terminal illness. A home filled up with them. Pain and nausea pills, steroids for swelling, and God only knew what else. Brenda had taken literally thousands of medications in the last year of her life. And something else bothered Annie. Cancer treatments showed. If Mamie had had radiation or chemotherapy in the last year, there would probably be some sign of it. Mamie looked like a concentration camp victim, not a cancer patient. Of course, she knew that not all chemo made hair fall out, but it bothered her anyway. Mamie had more than a year's growth on her head. She had long, stringy hair. Annie felt certain that Carol had not been visiting her mother regularly. She did not know what was going on at home, and it was so unlike the thoughtful and generous Carol she knew that Annie felt she had no choice. She had to alert Carol to her mother's perilous situation.

seventeen

BRIAN CALLED DEAN TEATH AT ELEVEN FORTY-FIVE. HE couldn't put the difficult task off any longer. He sat at his desk knowing that a lot of money was missing, and if the old man still had some gray cells functioning in his brain, Hall Stale was going to be in trouble one way or another. He braced himself and dialed. The phone rang five times before someone finally picked up.

"Yes?" came a crackly voice.

"Dr. Teath, this is Brian Redfield, branch manager at Hall Stale."

"I don't want any." The phone went dead.

"Jesus." Brian frowned at the receiver in his hand, then dialed the number again. It took the same five rings for the same cracked voice to come on and say "Yes" again.

"Dr. Teath, this is not a solicitation. I'm the branch manager of Hall Stale. We received some stock certificates from you at our office yesterday."

"Okay, why didn't you say so?" the old man said grumpily.

Brian went ahead without answering. "As instructed by your wife, we opened an account for her. The securities are being checked right now. We'll have a receipt for you by the end of the day."

"I don't want a receipt. I want it back."

Either the phone line was full of static, or the old man was actually laughing. It was an unnerving sound.

"Well, I'd like to talk with you a little about that."

"Talk as much as you want. I have plenty of time, but when you're finished I'm going to call the authorities."

Brian sucked in his breath. "There's no need for that. All I want to do is talk to you about the wisdom of keeping those certificates in your home in a time of family crisis."

"Family crisis! Don't try to sell me a bill of goods. I wasn't born yesterday."

"Dr. Teath. There are good reasons to consider what I have to say."

"Can't you hear, young man? I said we want it back."

"Well, I know you've done a superb job building an impressive portfolio, but people don't keep their precious assets in their homes anymore. It's not the best way to assure your future, or the future of your daughter—"

"And don't talk to me about my precious assets. Everybody lost money but me. I know what I'm doing."

"Well, I'm sure you do, but this is different—"

Dr. Teath interrupted. "I bet I did better in this market than you did. I still have every stock I bought." He chortled.

"I'm not sure what you mean." Brian simmered quietly.

"I kept every single thing I bought. I have excellent records. I know what I have," Teath said.

"I understand that, but the value of every portfolio fluctuates with the market. Even yours is affected in down markets."

"I still have it," he said furiously. "I still have every share. I didn't sell a thing."

"But when the market goes down, the value goes down. It happens to everybody."

"Not in my house," Teath insisted.

"I see. But what I'm trying to tell you is that your house is not the safest place for them. Here, they're insured. You can't lose them, no matter what."

"I already lost them. That young woman took them from me. You have them now."

"No, no, no. We don't have them. We're just custodians for them." Brian didn't seem to be getting through.

"That's not good enough," the old man insisted.

"Well, we can give you printed readouts every day if you'd like."

"I can get the scores in the newspaper," Teath countered quickly.

"But this is not a sports game." Brian watched the numbers run across his screen.

"Don't try to confuse me, young man. I know what I'm doing."

"I just want to be sure that we're talking about the same things. I'd be delighted to come out to your home to talk to you about this."

"We did that already. I'm done making coffee. I want my portfolio. I want it all, and I want it now."

Brian could hear him pound on a hard surface. He'd dealt with old people before, hundreds of them. This was hardly his first encounter with a muddled mind, but he had a feeling that something was different here.

"There are legal implications," he said slowly. "You are aware that this is your wife's account."

"Her father was a bootlegger, did you know that?"

"Ah, no." Brian was startled. He didn't know anything about this.

"Quite a colorful character in his time. He was shot to death in his bed. His wife, too. They didn't find the money, though. So don't tell me what's safe. And don't you go telling my daughter, either. Carol doesn't know this."

"Ah." Brian tried opening his mouth again, but Teath had the upper hand. It didn't matter whether the story was true or not, it was upsetting. The old man had a way of shifting things that was very disconcerting.

"The money probably belongs to the government. For all I know, he was a bank robber, too."

"Her father?" Brian was confused. He didn't know if this was relevant to the conversation.

"No, her grandfather."

Brian started worrying about other regulations—the feds, the statute of limitations. Dr. Teath was in his

eighties. Maybe he was talking Prohibition. That was
back in the 1920s. A lot of people had made their for-
tunes then. If what he said was true, then Dean Teath
might have laundered his wife's money, and its value had
compounded dozens of times since then. If it had dou-
bled every seven years . . . Brian tried to stay on track.
But he didn't know his liability here. Was he responsible
for tracking money back seventy-five, eighty years or
more to make sure it hadn't been stolen from some
Staten Island bank? He decided not to go there.

"Dr. Teath," he said after a moment, "no one cares
anymore where the money came from. The real issue for
the family is that you won't be able to deal with the
name transfers on your own after your wife passes on.
There are regulations about everything."

"I'm not interested. That's Carol's problem."

"But we can take care of all that for you."

"I said I'm not interested."

Brian persevered with Dean Teath for nearly an hour.
Finally, after going around and around in circles, he
said, "Since the stock powers were signed by your wife,
I'm going to need a written request from her and from
Carol to get them back to you." He threw Carol in for
good measure. He thought she might be able to stop
this.

"Fine, write the letter, I'll get it signed," he said.

Brian, however, planned to do no such thing.

eighteen

A FEW MINUTES LATER BRIAN CALLED ANNIE OUT OF the conference room. When she appeared in his office, her face was white.

"Something's wrong," she told him. "Something's wildly, wildly off. I had those bearer bonds. I know I had them, but they're just not here."

"Annie, I would stop saying that if I were you," he said softly.

"What?" Annie sat down with a thump in her usual green plaid wing chair. She crossed her legs, and he tried not to think of her knees under the somber black pants.

"Don't say you had them."

"I did have them," she said.

"Well, I never saw them." He enunciated every word carefully. "Frisk never saw them. Darian never saw them. Read my lips, Annie. Don't say you had them ever again. Look, I talked to that old man. Wacko."

Her eyes bulged.

"He wouldn't listen to a word I said. That man can make trouble for us." Brian did not look at her knees or heaving chest. He shrugged. "But Carol is your friend. Maybe she can help."

"Oh God, this is terrible," Annie blurted. "This is all my fault."

"Right, but let's not go there. Did he have a list of his holdings?"

"I'm telling you, the stuff was stacked all over the place. On the counters, on the floor. For all I know, the attic is still full of it. We may not even have it all. I can't describe what the place was like. Like something out of Hitchcock. Like an ancient motel. It was so creepy."

Brian looked up at the ceiling. "Could you have counted something and then left it at the house?"

"Oh God, could I have? I don't know. I tried to keep my eyes on those bearer bonds. That young accountant made me so nervous. The minute I realized how many there were, I kept my eye on them the whole time. But they're not in the shopping bag. They're not in the cage. I called the car service. The guy was an idiot, but he swears I didn't leave anything in the car. I know I didn't, anyway. I checked before I got out. I called the accountant. He doesn't know what I'm talking about. I don't think he knows what a bearer bond is. But I was in the bathroom when—" She stopped.

"So you could have left them at the house?"

Her eyebrows shot up.

"See?" he said simply.

Annie crossed her legs the other way, pressing her knees together. He wondered if she had something to hide.

"Hey, we've been friends for a long time."

She nodded.

"I don't consider you just a good producer or a good pair of legs."

"Huh?" She looked startled.

Oops, he hadn't meant to say that. "You have great legs. It's not exactly a secret. I only meant, we're friends." He stumbled a little on the word.

She looked at him as if he were speaking in tongues at a revival meeting.

"We've been through a lot together. My divorce. Your problems with Ben. We've always been there for each other, right?"

"I guess," she said slowly.

"So who else can I trust for the truth? You've been straight with me. You told me my wife was all wrong for me years before she left me."

"She dropped some clues," Annie murmured.

"And I'd say Ben is dropping a few himself."

"Where are you going with this, Brian? Did I miss something? What's going on?" Annie said suddenly.

"I just want you to know I care about you, Annie. I'm going to be there for you. We'll fix this."

Her frown deepened. "I didn't do anything wrong, Bry. Why would I list those bearer bonds if I intended to take them?"

Brian coughed delicately. "We've been through this before, Annie."

"Don't give me the you'll-be-there-for-me baloney. The three of you were in the room with them when I left to take a call—you and Frisk and Darian. You could have taken them."

"Hey!" Brian was alarmed at the way things were going. This wasn't what he meant to do at all. "Calm down. We'll fix this."

"How?" she demanded.

"We'll start by fully documenting every security we have, return them all, and hope that your list of bearer bonds is the only list." This wasn't what he intended to do, but it was what he said.

"What?" Annie's hand flew to her mouth.

"Don't worry about it." He got up and reached for his suit jacket. "We'll talk about it over lunch."

"Lunch?" She sat there for a moment, looking too stunned to move.

nineteen

CAROL MACK DIDN'T LIKE TO SIT DOWN. AT TWO P.M. she was pacing the waiting room of Hall Stale, nervously consulting her watch. Her mother had cancer. Her mother had cancer. How could Annie hurt her by making her doubt her own parents like this? Carol hated her best friend and wanted to cry. It had been a long night and a long morning, and now Annie was keeping her waiting in a terrible place.

For more than twenty minutes she'd had to endure a room that had always given her the most terrible creeps. Carol had her sensitivities in this area, and Hall Stale offended every one. The brown and beige Oriental carpet, coffee-colored leather wing chairs, brown and beige tweedy sofas, coffee tables and brass lamps in the reception area—which were copied at every Hall Stale office throughout the country—were anesthetics chosen to subdue and reassure rather than stimulate and encourage.

Carol was a furniture fashionista. Even at a time like this she couldn't help thinking about the decorations. She knew how to charge a room with accessories so creative and original, they knocked the eyes out. Or pare a room down to elegant Zen. To her, the Hall Stale decorating palette was as chilling as a torture chamber. As her watch ticked away precious minutes of the busy workday, she tried to shut her eyes to her surroundings. All this office meant to her was the loss of friendship and trust. Her mother had cancer. She was sure she did.

"Would you *please* page Annie again? I've been waiting more than half an hour," she complained to the gray-haired receptionist.

The woman gave her a cheerful smile. "I tried them several times. They're probably still at lunch."

They, who *they?* Carol stiffened at the thought of more treachery. Annie had promised she'd be there with the stocks. What was she up to? Carol felt her whole life twisting out of control as she waited. Every bad thing tumbled around in her mind, worsening the more she thought about it—her crumbling marriage to Matthew, their shattered friendship with Ben and Annie. The decline of her parents. What had happened to them?

It was impossible for her to be at Hall Stale without remembering how the two couples used to be in the good old days when the money had rolled in. Only a few years ago, it had seemed as if nothing could go wrong, nothing could fail, and even an unhappy past could be erased with success and plenty to spend. She was wondering where happiness had gone when Annie got off the elevator.

Annie didn't see her at first. She was with a handsome young man and turned to smile at him as if she didn't have a care in the world. Carol was shocked by that intimate smile. Annie looked so comfortable—indeed, so almost *happy*—that Carol instantly suspected the two of them were a couple. It was a devastating moment for her. Instantly Carol was reminded of her absent husband, Matthew, who showed no signs of loving her, and

Annie's husband, Ben, who no doubt still loved Annie. Treachery on every front! Carol began to hyperventilate with dismay, and simultaneously the couple in question caught sight of her. They suddenly looked grave.

"Carol, I didn't expect you. Why didn't you call?" Annie's eyes seemed full of concern, but Carol was too upset to care.

"I told you I was coming," she said angrily.

"This is Brian Redfield, our manager." Annie introduced them.

"Really!" Carol scowled at him as he held out his hand.

"Delighted," he chirped. "I've heard so much about you over the years." The man gave her a thorough appraisal and seemed to like what he saw.

"You have?"

Carol's withering look softened. She may have been deeply upset, but she was still a good-looking, elegant woman with a long-term commitment to maintenance. Her shoulder-length hair was a deep and shiny black. Her arresting china blue eyes were carefully made up. For the Hall Stale meeting, she'd chosen a pearl gray Armani pantsuit, a silk blouse that shimmered a blend of subtle pastels, a pink scarf soft as gossamer with a long fringe, a vintage alligator purse, and up-to-the-minute Stuart Weitzman pumps. Suddenly she was glad that the time she'd spent putting herself together this morning had not been wasted. A handsome man can have that effect even on a woman in the middle of a breakdown.

"Yes, I've heard you have fabulous taste. But of course, you don't need to be told that. Please, come into my office where we can talk." He led the way.

Scowling, Carol turned to her treacherous friend. "He's the manager? How old is he?"

"Almost as old as you are," Annie retorted. "Why didn't you call?"

"Annie, I called you *five* times. You've been avoiding me."

"Carol, I have not. You put me in a shitty position. God knows we're doing our best."

Carol wanted to talk about a hundred things. Her mother and the cancer accusation. Everything. But the young manager had distracted her. She couldn't help herself. "Are you and he . . . ?" She wiggled two fingers.

"Are you crazy? He's my manager." Annie edged Carol down the hall.

"Oh yeah, what does he manage?" Carol just couldn't help getting off the subject. He was that cute.

She entered his office and quickly scanned it for more aesthetic offense. Hmmmm. She was surprised to find the room wholly acceptable except for the fabric on the wing chairs, the same awful plaid as Annie's. His curved windows were on the downtown side, and his great view was only moderately shrouded in autumnal haze. A TV and computer monitor were on one desk facing the wall. His large glass-topped desk and coffee table were scattered with a valuable collection of obelisks in natural crystal and marble. He also had a number of miniature columns from Roman ruins that had been all the rage as souvenirs at the end of the nineteenth century. Carol lifted an eyebrow. He had a penis fixation. She wondered about that. Amazing how a Tom Cruise look-alike could cause the mind to wander. She planted herself in one of his wing chairs, considerably softened.

"What does a manager do?" she asked.

"Oh, I supervise and deal with all controversy regarding personnel and operations in this office."

"What does that mean exactly?" She propped her chin in her hand coyly.

"Whenever there's a question about anything, I'm the person who helps find the answers." His face was open, his expression just self-deprecating enough to be convincing. His gaze was steady. He looked at Carol as if she was the only person on earth—and also as if she was extremely attractive, which caused her to sit up even straighter in her chair.

"Annie tells me that you've been struggling with this problem with your father for a long time," he went on.

Carol's eyes misted. She had indeed. Ever since she was a little girl. Brian laced his hands together on the desk and tapped his index fingers.

"I'm sorry we didn't have a chance to talk about this earlier. We've had quite a bit of experience dealing with family matters of this nature."

Matthew never used this soft tone of voice with her. Carol glanced at Annie. Annie gave her an encouraging smile.

"It's hard to take control from fiercely independent people," Carol said softly. *And liars,* she thought.

"I know how it is," Brian said. "I spoke to your father a little while ago."

"You did?" Carol was shocked.

"He has some pretty strong opinions. Of course, everybody's been traumatized by the performance of the market, and I know how much you want your father's legacy preserved."

"My mother's," Carol corrected.

"Of course." Brian's gaze did not waver.

Her eyes misted some more. Yes, she did want to preserve the legacy. She also wanted someone nice to care about her.

"Annie told me your father wants the assets returned to him. Are you certain this is the right thing to do?"

"No," Carol said flatly. "He's not rational."

"Is this what your mother wants?"

"I have no way of knowing what my mother wants. She's not a communicator."

"Well, what do you want?" the manager asked.

"Me?" She wanted her husband to be a sweet and loving man who was interested in her. She wanted her mother to be a regular mother. She wanted her father to be a regular father. She wanted Annie to be a good best friend. She wanted to be really close with Annie's girls again. Her eyes puddled with tears because she knew none of those wishes was going to come true.

Brian tapped his fingers while she composed herself. "Are you dissatisfied with Annie's performance?"

Carol dabbed at her eyes with an expensive handkerchief and crossed her legs the other way. "It's not a pleasure to lose my money," she said angrily.

"I didn't lose your money, so let's not go there," Annie retorted.

Carol held up her hand. "Fine, let's not talk about it."

Brian stopped the exchange from going any further. "Look, I'm just trying to facilitate what's right for you. If you want to move the account to another broker, that's your prerogative. Of course I'll do everything I can to help you do that. Is that your plan today?"

Carol flushed, because it was.

"Well, let's go over the situation. What's changed since yesterday?"

"My dad is a very controlling man. My guess is he feels naked without his money. He wants it with him." Carol, however, had no intention of giving it to him.

Brian smiled and laced his fingers up again. "Assets can be quite warming. I understand your father's feelings, but as your mother's principal heir, I'm sure you're aware that there will be more difficulties down the road sorting out the estate if we don't set up the account properly while she's able to do it."

Carol frowned at the thought of probate, lawyers, lawyers' fees, years of waiting for the government to have its way with her mother's estate. New York City. New York State. Everybody who could take a piece would take a piece. They'd eat up her inheritance—not that she was waiting for her mother to die. She let out a little sob at the whole situation and studied the manager's face.

She suspected that he was not just interested in helping her deal with a difficult situation. Hall Stale had lost Matthew as a client. Now they didn't want to lose her. She wasn't naïve about these things. She thought he was a very attractive man, and he *seemed* sincere. His intense focus on her actually helped her calm down. She glanced at Annie out of the corner of her eye.

Annie tended to make her hysteria level rise. Annie had a husband who loved her no matter what; she had two great children and a whole world that Carol didn't have. The contents of Carol's IN basket in the life department were two crazy parents (one a zombie and the other a compulsive liar) and a litigating husband who hurt people for a living. She had a moment of stabbing loneliness at the thought of how bitter and self-involved Matthew had become. He hardly ever even bothered to come home. Then she glanced back at Brian. He seemed like a nice man who was truly interested in her problems. She wondered if he liked her.

"I can help you if you'll let me," he said earnestly. "I suggest that you let us continue with the plan you had in place yesterday. In a matter of weeks we can get your account properly set up. Whatever happens with your family situation, one thing will be off your plate. You won't have to worry about this."

Carol shifted in her chair. It was hard to argue with the proposition. He didn't push the fact that her father was demented and her mother was badly cared for, as Annie had. He didn't say she owed it to the firm, which she herself felt she did. He just made sense.

"My dad expects me out there with the stuff now," she said, checking her watch. "But what the hell. I'll just tell him it can't be done."

"It might be better to tell him the truth, considering his litigious nature," Brian suggested gently.

twenty

DESPITE BRIAN'S ADMONITION TO BE TOTALLY TRUTH-ful with her father, Carol arrived at her parents' house still undecided how she would proceed. Then she saw the Christmas sled and icicle lights on the roof. The last time she'd visited, her father had promised that he would finally have the wretched things removed. As a reassurance to her that he was capable of remembering simple tasks, he'd sworn that he would clean up the yard and mow the lawn, get rid of the Christmas decorations, and a bunch of other things. He hadn't done them, just as he hadn't had the house painted, or the bathrooms re-modeled, or the kitchen appliances upgraded.

Ever since she could remember, he'd been making all

kinds of promises and had never fulfilled any of them. Each new time he broke a promise she was disappointed all over again. This time was much worse. The Christmas lights still on the roof had been seen by Annie. No wonder she and that handsome boss of hers thought the worst about her. She shook her head and got out of the limo that Hall Stale had ordered to bring her out here. She walked up the weedy front path and unlocked the door of the place her parents called home. "Dad?"

Dean Teath was in the living room with broken reading glasses taped on the bridge of his nose. He was sitting under a dim light studying a giveaway paper from the grocery store. He looked like a homeless person.

"What took so long? It's almost time for supper." A crooked grin creased his cheeks as he lurched to his feet and lumbered toward her.

"Hi, Dad," Carol said weakly.

Her father the millionaire was dressed in the same old clothes that he'd been wearing on her last visit. They looked as if they hadn't been washed since. His slippers were so full of holes, they could only be holding together through habit. She regarded him with a profound feeling of sadness. It just didn't jibe with the stash that Annie and Brian had shown her. The folders full of securities could have given them a wonderful life. Something had gone very wrong a long time ago, and he'd never let her fix it.

"What?" He touched the white hair curling on his neck. He wouldn't even get a haircut.

Carol's teary eyes suddenly focused on the expensive gold watch he was wearing. It was from her mother's jewelry box and had been her grandfather's. Something else caught her attention. A very unusual stickpin with rubies and a huge diamond in it was threaded into the collar of his frayed and faded plaid shirt. She wondered where that had come from. His lopsided grin widened at her interest in it.

"My baby." He opened his arms.

She gave him a quick hug and was overcome by the odor of mold. Mold was in the house to be sure, but it also reeked in his clothes and even seemed to be coming from his skin. Her gorge rose, and she backed gently away. She didn't want to think that Annie was right about her *neglecting* her parents.

"How's it going, Dad?"

"Great." He patted her back with a big-knuckled hand. "Everything is just great except for your mother's damn cancer. You look good." He'd dispatched the subject quickly and tilted his head to examine her more carefully.

"Thanks." Unlike her father, who smelled of mold, Carol moved in a cloud of Joy. "Tell me about Mom."

He shrugged. "What's there to tell?"

"Pretty much everything," she said coolly. "You've hinted and hinted, but you know I don't know a damn thing, really."

His eyes did that funny evasive shimmy they always did when he didn't want to talk about something important. "Honey, I don't want to upset you."

"Go ahead and upset me. What kind of cancer is it? And I don't want to hear one more time that it's some woman's thing."

"It's in her stomach," he said vaguely. "But she thinks she's going to be all right, so don't go upsetting the applecart."

Applecart? Her mother's health wasn't some applecart. "People don't hide these things anymore, Dad. People face them straight on," she said gently.

"I know what's best for my wife," he said stubbornly.

"I don't think you do. I'm going to have to take her away, Dad," Carol said, shaking her head.

"She won't go," he replied smugly. "Now where's my stash?" He rubbed his hands together expectantly. With the shabby clothes, the neglected air, the expensive watch, and the garish stickpin, he no longer looked eccentric to her. He looked just plain crazy. She didn't know why she hadn't accepted it before.

"I brought food," she replied.

"Oh, food." He waved it away impatiently, as if food didn't interest him. "You didn't need to. We do just fine."

As a child Carol had read *A Little Princess* many times. She'd always wanted to be saved by a rich gentleman from India who would give her beautiful presents and wonderful food. As a grown-up she'd fulfilled her own secret wish by sending her parents a weekly supply of expensive prepared foods from Zabar's. In this role reversal, she became the nurturing parent for parents who hadn't nurtured her. Every week she spent some time and a small fortune doing it, and every week her father pretended they didn't need it. Annie had been way off base on that one.

Carol shook her head again. "Dad, you know you're not fine. Look at you, you're wearing rags. You haven't had a bath in a while." She held her nose to demonstrate how he smelled. "You're a mess."

"Now, don't start that. I had a shower this morning."

She checked under the shade of the lamp where he'd been sitting. Two of the three bulbs were out. He couldn't even change a lightbulb.

"I love you, Daddy, but it isn't working anymore. You don't have the basics. You can't do it," she said softly.

He'd hoarded a fortune. He wasn't in his right mind. She'd read about people like this.

"Don't start criticizing. All your life, nothing but criticism. Every time you come here. Why can't we have a conversation, a nice visit for a change? Why don't you sit down, have a meal with your mother and me? Why isn't this place good enough for you? Big shot," he muttered.

"I'm not criticizing. I'm talking facts. You can't take care of yourself. You're not taking care of Mom. You both need help."

"I don't need help," he protested.

"Dad, your car has a flat tire. How do you get to the doctor?"

He looked surprised. "It does?"

"When did you use it last?"

"This morning. I went to get the paper."

She shook her head some more. "Wearing all your jewelry?"

The crooked grin returned. "No, I put that on for you. Someday all of this is going to be yours."

"Well, I'm not in a hurry."

"Oh yes, missy. You're in a hurry. Why else would you come all the way out here? And why bring us food?"

"Dad, I send you food all the time."

He waved his hand. Food was nothing.

"Where did you get the pin?" she asked. She couldn't stop staring at it. She had an eye for these things, and that huge diamond actually looked real.

"It was your grandfather's. He was a pirate."

She snorted with frustration. See, they couldn't have a real conversation. Everything was a smoke screen. He made things up all the time. Every day there was a new story. "I'll be back in a minute," she told him.

She went through the door into the kitchen to check the refrigerator for the Zabar's. She opened the ancient fridge door and gasped. There was half a package of hot dogs. Some cottage cheese. Not much else, certainly no Zabar's containers. Where was the food she'd sent only a few days ago? Soup, a roast chicken, lasagne, couscous, and vegetables? She hurried down the hall to see her mother.

As she cracked open the door to her parents' tiny bedroom and peeked into the darkened space, her throat closed up and didn't want to let her breathe. The sight of the two single beds separated by a table with an ornate lamp took her a long way back, to the many afternoons when she'd come home from school to find her mother just like this, lying in bed with the lights off and the blackout shade on the window drawn way down past the sill.

"Mom?"

Mamie Teath looked tiny under the covers, only a little lump, hardly bigger than a pillow. The sheets rustled like dry leaves in the wind. "Who is it?"

"It's me, Carol."

"Carol? Why aren't you at school?"

"I don't go to school anymore, Mom. I'm a grown-up."

Mamie Teath struggled onto her back and stared up at her daughter. "Carol," she said. "You are grown-up. I was dreaming of the old days. Weren't we happy then?"

"Mom, what's the matter with you?" She looked so much worse than she had only a few weeks ago.

"You look pretty, sweetheart," she said conversationally.

"Mom, tell me what's happening. Have you been to the doctor this week?"

"What for? I'm not sick." She turned her head toward the clock. "Is it Saturday already?"

"No, it was Saturday a few days ago. I sent you a lot of food. What happened to the food?"

"I thought you were coming this Saturday."

"Well, I was, but something happened. I'm here early."

Mamie sat up. "What happened, honey? Did you forget your books?"

Carol sat on the side of the bed, tearful again. This was a scene she'd lived many times before. Her mother couldn't focus; she'd never been able to focus. "What happened to the food?" Carol asked.

"What food, honey?"

"I sent you food. I sent you cake. Why aren't you eating it?"

Mamie looked at her blankly.

"Mom, do you go to the doctor? Where's your medicine?"

She didn't answer. Carol changed the subject. "Mom, do you remember the people who came to visit you yesterday?"

"There's nothing wrong with my memory," she said sharply. "Your pretty friend came, and I signed the papers. There were a lot of them, but I signed them all."

"Right." Carol took one of her hands. "Good. That's exactly right. Do you remember why?"

"To get the stocks to you, Carol. I don't want your father to have them." She didn't have to whisper. Her voice didn't carry far.

"He didn't tell me this."

"Oh, let's face it. He's been waiting for years to see me go. He's an interesting man, but a do-nothing. You know he was the only man I ever kissed. Never had another date. Never had anybody." She turned her head to the wall.

"Oh geez. Mom, you had me." Carol started to cry.

"Well, sure. So the stocks are for you, honey. Don't let him change your mind. He'll take everything if he gets a chance. He's tried it before." She shut her mouth.

"Oh God, why didn't you tell me?" Carol sobbed.

Mamie didn't have an answer for that. Her head moved a little on the pillow. "You know, I don't think about food anymore."

Carol blew her nose and tried to pull herself together. "You have to start thinking about it. You have to start eating again."

Mamie didn't respond for a long time. Carol thought she'd fallen asleep when her mouth finally opened. "Don't forget to take my daddy's watch. I want you to have that . . . and his stickpin."

"His stickpin?"

"I was going to make it into a diamond ring for you, but I never got around to it. I have pretty jewelry, don't I, baby?" she said.

"Yes, Mom, beautiful jewelry."

"You're my baby."

"I brought you a chicken," Carol murmured. But her mother only shook her head.

After a few minutes of silence, Carol returned to the living room. Her father was sitting in his armchair with the paper propped up in front of him.

"Dad, I'm taking Mom out of here."

"I'm taking care of my own wife. This isn't your business."

Carol shook her head. "You've had your turn. You've done it long enough. It's my turn now."

"Well, she hasn't been that great a wife, but she's mine. I'm going to do what I have to do to take care of her. Where are my assets? You said you'd bring them back."

"You know they're not safe here." Carol wasn't going to discuss it with him anymore. He was too tricky. "You shouldn't have gold watches and diamond pins here, either," she added.

"I'm not giving them up," he said.

"Okay. Where's the food I sent this weekend?" She couldn't help returning to the subject of the food. Annie had accused her of letting her parents starve. That was the one thing she knew she hadn't done.

"Oh please, we don't need all that food. I give it away to the homeless."

Carol's jaw dropped. It was the last thing she'd expected to hear.

twenty-one

THE DRIVING RANGE AT CHELSEA PIERS WAS LIKE A narrow field on the edge of an abyss. Mag followed her father out the door on the third floor of the building that housed the golf school, where a strip of unprotected roof served as the tee for fifteen practice drivers. Through the glass door she caught a glimpse of video equipment, a mini sand bunker, putting and chipping greens. She scowled with disdain.

Her father had insisted that she come with him, so she was here against her will, and deeply angry at herself for giving in. The whole thing made her skin crawl. Just the *idea* of physical proximity to such an empty and elitist sport had always disgusted her. Now actually being on the site for the first time was almost more than she could bear. She hated her father for being such a dork when he used to be a regular guy. He used to care about real things, about them. Now this ridiculous sport (which didn't seem to her like a real sport at all) was the only thing that interested him. And she had gone along with it. She didn't know what she'd been thinking.

Mag scuffed her sneaker against the floor, overwhelmed by her plight. Everyone she knew was in college. She alone had been thrown back into the hell of childhood, her whole life abandoned. And she knew somehow she'd done this to herself. From K through twelve she'd performed every task that had been expected of her. After graduation, all she'd wanted was to rest for a while. But instead of taking a few weeks off, she'd fallen like a rock. She'd crashed into total paralysis, like her dad. Now she was afraid she'd never get out.

Mag was further put off by the trio of yellow-haired little boys sitting in a row of chairs swinging sneakered feet that wouldn't touch the ground for some time. They seemed to be waiting for a lesson. Jesus. Wasn't starting them that young *sick*? Mag had a well-known expression on her face. It was the leaden look of a put-upon offspring dragged along on an outing only because it couldn't be left home alone. She always made the most of her misery. Long ago, from close study of the fixed stares of drug-addled models in fashion magazines, she'd cultivated the daunting expression of disaffection. She'd forged the terrifying face of pain in the fire of adolescent rage. It was still effective against aggressively helpful, unwanted parental advice.

Mag had honed a talent for rudeness that often sent her parents scurrying away like crabs on a beach, at least for a while. Unfortunately, the maneuver hadn't worked today. Recently her father had developed some tactics of his own. In an unpleasant role reversal, he'd become the child who wouldn't go out alone. He couldn't get in the elevator; couldn't go out on the street and hail a cab. It was totally annoying and upsetting to Mag that he had to have his own way in everything. Today he'd wanted to come here, and needed her support so badly that even the frightful fit she'd pulled hadn't stopped him from forcing her to accompany him.

Everybody told Mag she had a good heart. Indeed, if she'd seen herself acting miserable, she almost certainly would have been alarmed by her behavior. She never did see herself acting like a miserable brat. Facing herself in the mirror after she'd grudgingly accommodated someone else's wishes, she always felt like Mother Teresa, practically a saint for her generosity of spirit. Now she was wearing a loose sweatshirt and cargo pants with pockets and zippers enough to pack for an entire weekend. As she sucked from a huge ice-clogged container of Diet Coke, her face was locked in a thick pall of resentment for her selfish father who no longer thought of anyone but himself. Muttering obscenities to herself, she pushed through the door after him and staggered at the sight that greeted her. She was on a totally deserted ledge, only a few feet from certain death.

"Oh shit!" she muttered.

Mag had a bad reaction to heights, which she attributed to the brain tumor that was not killing her nearly fast enough. Even the escalator in the Trump Tower atrium caused a terrifying loss of equilibrium. Just the fountain of water cascading from thirty feet above was sometimes enough to bring it on. She hadn't known what to expect today, but she was not prepared for a sudden exposure to a vast open space that plummeted unchecked to the hard ground below. Then she was smacked by the afternoon sun and couldn't see a thing. At four P.M. the sun had not yet begun its steep descent into the New Jersey side of the Hudson River. The fireball hung in the sky just low enough to create a blinding glare on Manhattan's West Side. Abruptly, Mag felt ill. She needed to heave her guts up, or at least sit down, but she didn't want to throw up and there was no place to sit. Furthermore, no one was out there to notice her distress.

She clutched her cup of ice with the terrible feeling that she was so alone in the world, she might as well be dead. Her mother was wrapped up in her stupid work. Every single one of her friends had abandoned her. They were spread all over the country. Everyone was gone. Her father had no interest in anything but golf. She couldn't even think about where Bebe was headed. She asked herself the same question she posed a hundred times a day. She had to die sometime. Why couldn't she just die now and get it over with?

That day her feelings had teetered between the homicidal and suicidal. One minute she wanted to obliterate everyone she knew with an assault rifle. The next minute she wanted to kill herself. Right then it was murder again. Trust her idiot father to drag her from the relative safety of her bed to a place that made her so sick, she wished even more passionately than usual that she were dead. She struggled with the nausea. Then, as it slowly began to subside, it struck her that this actually was a good place for an accident. She looked at the sky above and the ground below and realized that this was her first real opportunity all summer to end it all.

Stunned by the new possibility, she turned to watch

her father. He was dressed in his preppy khaki shorts and navy Lacoste shirt. He was carrying a plastic bucket full of golf balls. He was lugging his forty-pound Callaway golf bag filled with expensive golf clubs, some of which were covered with fuzzy hats. He was wearing saddle shoes similar to the ones her mother made her wear before she was old enough to object. Oblivious to the incapacitating sun, he was carrying all his gear, trudging down the line of tees looking for exactly the right one to use. Each little golfer's area had a patch of fake green grass and a swathe of net hardly strong enough to stop a golf ball. To Mag all the tees in the line appeared the same, but her father kept going until he got almost to the very end. Finally he picked the second spot from the last, very far from her.

She watched him prop the huge golf bag against the stand provided for it and carefully search through his precious collection of clubs until he found the exact one he wanted. He slipped it behind his neck so that it rested on his shoulders, raised his hands to grasp each end, and twisted back and forth. He'd begged her to come with him, and now he seemed to have forgotten she was there. She hated him. He was a total alien, a person from a world she couldn't begin to comprehend.

Then something caught her eye. A bird in the sky, a reflection, she didn't know what. She turned her head. The sun hit her squarely in the face, and she was overcome with vertigo again. Nausea seeped down from the sick place in her brain and rose up from her chest. Death was a siren song, calling to her. She was sure she wanted to go.

Straight ahead on the Hudson River, boats glided soundlessly. To her left were the massive smokestacks of a cruise ship preparing to depart. Seagulls swooped low in the sky, and three stories down a field studded with bull's-eye distance markers swam in and out of focus. She couldn't make out the number on a single marker, or see the human form of the driver inside the cage of the ball catcher as it lazily zigzagged back and forth, collecting balls earlier golfers had launched out there.

She swayed toward the edge of the roof, where no safety net would catch her. A clumsy person could spin right off the edge into all eternity. Her cheeks were hot, and water filled her mouth. No one understood how sick she was. She swallowed and stepped closer to the edge. At that moment her life felt like a thin line that she could cross with no consequences—but only if her death looked like an accident. She'd been brooding about escape all summer. An obvious suicide was out of the question. She couldn't devastate her mother or sister with a suicide. Even if they didn't like her, they wouldn't be able to get over it. Bebe might even follow her. No, her death had to be caused by a fatal illness. Or an accident that would be perceived by everyone as no-fault. Her stomach heaved. A fall from vertigo. That was it, the perfect answer to all her problems.

At that moment she was distracted by a *ping* from down the line at her father's tee. The sound was unlike anything she had heard before—a solid *thwack* with a metallic ring. A few lacy clouds appeared from nowhere in the previously uncluttered sky. In a nanosecond they misted the sun, clearing Mag's vision just long enough for her to see the flight of the ball her father had hit . . . absolutely perfectly. The ball arched in the air high above where they stood and sailed far, far out into the field below, until it disappeared altogether. It was almost magical the way it lifted off, hooking slightly to the left and soaring long and effortlessly over the open field toward the Hudson River.

Amazed, Mag felt her heart lifting with the ball. As it

arched and fell, she searched the ground past at least four of the markers for the place her father's first ball had landed. All she could see in the deep distance was a tiny flag flapping gently in the breezy September afternoon, marking the target at which he'd aimed.

twenty-two

ANNIE WAS IN TROUBLE. AFTER CAROL LEFT IN THE limo, she reviewed the situation. She hadn't wanted to go to lunch with Brian. He'd insisted. She wanted to tell Carol about the missing bearer bonds herself. He'd resisted. Over a mountain of rainbow sushi at a Japanese restaurant, he told her to keep her mouth shut in the meeting.

"I'm going to fix this," he assured her. He was particularly adamant about not burdening Carol with knowledge of missing assets. "Believe me, she'll flee if she finds out. Who wouldn't?" he argued. Annie agreed he had a point there, but it still didn't seem right to her.

Then, after agreeing to come much later in the day, Carol had surprised them by arriving early. They'd ended up keeping her waiting. That was an unfortunate accident, but it was no accident that Carol was in a crazy mood by the time they got there. Annie hadn't anticipated how bitterly angry Carol was about so many things. To make matters worse, Brian worked his magic on Carol just as he said he would. He flattered and charmed and calmed her down so that she changed her mind about taking the account away. While this was going on, every fiber of Annie's being screamed at her to come clean and tell the truth. Someone, most likely Carol's own father, had taken a quarter of a million dollars in bearer bonds that belonged to Carol. She should be aware of it. She should be told.

As Annie walked Carol down the hall to the elevator, and finally outside to the curb where the car was waiting, she debated telling her right then. She knew she had to do it sometime, but after practically accusing Carol's father of lying about cancer, how could she now accuse him of stealing Carol's money, too? Maybe it was too much for Carol to handle in twenty-four hours. And Brian had urged her to wait. Maybe she should wait.

She didn't say anything when they got to the door of the office because Frisk and Darian were standing there. Downstairs was even more crowded. For Annie it was a particularly tough moment. This was the kind of thing that had to be done gently, and there were so many people around . . .

In the end she just couldn't tell her friend she'd let her down. She felt like a coward. After everything that had happened between Ben and Matthew, she didn't want to lose Carol's high regard. She couldn't bear to let the friendship go in a second. They could argue on the phone, bitch at each other, and feel resentment, but the two women had known each other for a long time. They'd talked about pretty much everything. Carol had been loyal to her despite Matthew's complaint against Ben. And the two women had another bond, too—the girls. Mag and Bebe had no other adult woman in their lives. Carol was like their aunt. Annie couldn't take that away from them.

There was too much history, and Carol didn't have

children of her own. She'd always been close to Mag and Bebe. As soon as the girls had gotten old enough to sit like grown-ups at the table, Carol used to take them to lunch at Serendipity on Saturdays. Every Christmas she'd taken them to *The Nutcracker,* the Big Apple Circus, and all the animated Disney films. She had little birthday parties for them and always bought them great gifts. How could Annie return Carol's trust, loyalty, and friendship with such terrible news? Someone was a thief, and it was probably her dad. She decided to tell Carol tonight, after she'd had a chance to calm down.

Still, as Annie returned to her office, her sin of omission felt like a tightening noose around her neck. Nothing like this had ever happened to her. She didn't play games with her clients. She'd always been honest no matter how tough the truth was. Now there was a hole somewhere inside her where honesty used to reign. She closed the door in her office. Never had she felt so alone. Brian had promised that he would continue to investigate, but Annie knew that since he'd never seen the bonds, he was going to take the position that they'd never been out of the owner's possession. In a wall of offices across the street, Annie could see a woman hurrying to her desk with a huge bowl of popcorn. Every day at this time, the large woman gave herself this particular treat. It always meant the stock market had closed.

Annie's phone rang, and since Petra was already gone, she answered it herself. "This is Annie Custer." She twirled in her chair to face the window.

"Annie Custard, it's Vartan."

"Who?" Static on the line prevented her from hearing the name.

"Vartan Vole. I'm calling from Stockholm. I have something very big coming in."

"Oh, Vartan." Annie's heart spiked with anxiety. She'd hoped her day was over.

"What time is it there? My Rolex says it's nearly four your time."

"Well, it's after four." She knew this by the popcorn eater across the street, but she checked her watch anyway. Annie's watch was a watch. It didn't have a fancy name. She thought Vartan Vole was a weird duck, but sometimes weird ducks came through with the goods. "Where are you, Vartan?"

"I'm on the way to the airport in my Mercedes. I'm flying first-class to Stockholm. I talked to Alan this morning. He told me the economy still had room for stimulation."

"Uh-huh." Vartan always had a different story about where he was, but Annie knew when he said *Alan,* he meant Alan Greenspan.

"That means rates might go lower," he added.

"I know what it means, Vartan." It was what the head of the Federal Reserve Bank had said in his press conference that morning. Nothing new there. She didn't think he'd actually spoken to Greenspan at all. "What can I do for you?"

"Baby, didn't you get my message that I have a transaction coming through? I'm putting big business in your lap. Pay attention."

"I always pay attention." Annie needed big business in her lap, but she didn't like being called *baby.*

"Didn't your girl tell you that we're wire-transferring two hundred million into the account? The bank in London has just confirmed the transfer."

"Yes, Vartan. Petra gave me the message yesterday. But nothing came in."

"What? I can't believe it. Hornbill Financial assured me it would be there today. Are you sure you have the

accounts set up correctly for the Canadian corporation?"

Annie swiveled back and forth in her chair. "Vartan, I
told you last week that we can't open an account for a
Canadian corporation. It's not an option."

"No, no. Annie, I told you to forget that International
Northern account. We opted to open the account in *my*
name and flow the funds through me to the charities involved. Do you have my list of transfers?"

"Well, I have the account in your name. But what
does that have to do with this Canadian deal?"

"It's not a Canadian deal. International Northern rep-
resents a pension fund."

"Is that where the money is coming from, the pension
fund?"

"And insurance companies, of course. They've man-
dated a sale of commercial paper for this particular
transaction. Why are you asking me this?"

"We need to know where the money is coming from
to make sure everything is legal," Annie told him.

"Well, I told you Hornbill Financial is handling this,"
he said irritably. "What's your problem? Do I need to go
somewhere else?"

Annie sighed and let him stew. She'd never heard of
Hornbill Financial. It hadn't come up on her Web search.
That didn't necessarily mean it didn't exist: Money traveled around the world along strange pathways all the
time. However, they couldn't do things the old way anymore. They had to know who was sending it and what
the money was for. She thought of Ben's overseas customer and shuddered.

Back in late 2000, a young man from Egypt had been
extremely active. He'd wired a hundred, two hundred
thousand dollars in and out of his account every week.
He was forever on the phone moving money, and they

hadn't thought anything of it. People moved money around all the time—it was how business got done. Even after 9/11, she hadn't thought much about it. But accounts that behave like that are flagged by compliance people and regulators—those anonymous watchers who are supposed to keep things legal. Ben's client was called Habib. As soon as the FBI got involved in Habib's investigation, the accounts were frozen and Habib disappeared from the face of the earth. The FBI had investigated Ben, and that was strike two. Maybe it was his strike three in his own mind, who knew?

Annie sighed again because the money business was being watched by several different agencies, and she didn't know anything about Vartan Vole except that he was the son-in-law of a friend. It didn't make him good or bad, but these issues were complicated. It wasn't always easy to decipher who were the good guys and who were the bad guys. Annie would never do anything illegal, but if Hornbill Financial existed, if it was on the up-and-up, and if it had two hundred million to throw her way, it would make her one of the most important brokers on Wall Street. In her present financial crunch, she was hardly going to let that opportunity get away.

"Didn't Petra open the account for me?" Vartan asked.

"Yes, of course she did," Annie assured him.

"Then the money should have hit," he insisted.

If that much money had hit one of her customer's accounts, Annie would know about it. She swiveled back to look up the account number, then punched it into her computer just in case. But no, the balance stood at a thousand dollars—nine thousand less than the amount he'd deposited to open it. He just didn't look or act like the big player he said he was. "No, Vartan. It hasn't hit," she told him.

"I can't believe this. There must be some explanation."

She gazed sadly at the balance in the account. "Give me the tracking number, I'll check it out for you," she said pleasantly.

"This transaction is being cleared through London. I don't know what the tracking numbers are. I gave them the transfer information you gave me. Let me assure you. We'll be moving the funds around the world for humanitarian causes, but at least one-third will always be held in your hands. I want you to profit from this, so call me back. My Mercedes is going through a tunnel."

"Look, Vartan, I'm going to have to talk to my manager about all this. We need to clear a few things up."

"Good, good. Clear it up." He hung up.

It was after four P.M, and the Dow had closed a meager four points up. It had been a scary day. Annie knew that Brian was anxious about having the account of another Mack to worry about, and now there was this whole Vartan thing. He wasn't going to like this. She was exhausted. She slipped her shoes off and put her head back against the shiny leather of her chair to watch the woman across the street. The poor woman didn't know she looked like a gorilla in the zoo.

Annie closed her eyes for some relief. She wished Carol had the guts to uncover the truth about her mother. She wished the bonds weren't missing after all, that Vartan Vole really had big money, and that she could go home and have a pleasant evening with Ben and her girls. All those things were just dreams, but she dreamed them anyway. Then she heard a voice.

"Annie, listen. It's been a tough day. Let's go out for a drink and talk this over."

She opened her eyes. Brian stood in the doorway. He had loosened his tie and opened his shirt collar. With his worked-out body and dark hair, he looked a lot like a movie-star version of a banker, or a lawyer, or a stock-broker. She glanced at her watch, which read four fifteen. The last thing she wanted to do was to go home and face the particular music playing there. For the first time ever, it occurred to her that a drink with Brian after work could buffer the pain.

"Great idea," she said, shuffling her feet around under her desk for her shoes. That's how it started.

twenty-three

ANNIE DRANK MARTINIS AND FLIRTED FOR TWO hours. She was flying high when she got home. Then she saw the golf bag and her bubble burst. The bag was filled with brand-new clubs that didn't look like they'd been used even once. It was much smaller than Ben's, and far less pretentious. Three of the clubs had cute covers, one of which was a poodle with a puffy white pom-pom on its head. Annie was horrified by those kitschy covers, and she knew from experience that Ben bought only very expensive equipment.

Wondering what he was up to, she threw her jacket on a chair. Sounds of the evening news came from the den. She crossed the marble floor and opened the door. As usual, the room was in blackout, and the only light came from the TV. Ben was lying on the sofa and didn't stir at her arrival.

"Hi. What's going on?"

"Nothing much." He glanced up from the screen and gave her one of his martyr smiles.

"Who got new clubs?" she asked, hoping against hope that they weren't for her.

"Maggie," he said happily.

Maggie? Annie was stunned.

"She wanted to go to the pier with me. I thought it was a good sign." He gave her a sly smile.

"She *wanted* to go?" Annie found that hard to believe.

"Well, she was a little grumpy at first. You know our Mags, but as soon as she got there, she got right into it. Her lesson went great."

"She had a *lesson*?" Impossible. Annie hung on to the doorframe, a little drunk, as she tried to adjust to the idea of her elder daughter having a golf lesson.

Ben nodded. "With Chuck. She loved him, of course. He had her hitting the ball in five minutes. You want to see her video?"

Annie took a step backward, teetering just a little on her heels. "Her video? Why did they make a video?"

"She needed to see the problems in her swing. But she got it right away. She swings like a pro already. The girl is a natural athlete. Like me," Ben said proudly.

Annie had a hard time digesting this, too. Her daughter didn't like to get out of bed. How could she be a natural athlete? "Is that why you bought her a set of golf clubs?" Annie struggled to maintain her cool.

Ben scratched his neck. "Well, I put it on the Master-Card."

She gasped. "That's *my* card."

"God, it was great out there. You should have seen Maggie. You would have been so proud—"

"I'd be proud of her if she got a job." Annie cut in faster and with more bite than she meant to.

"Ouch."

"I don't have the luxury of golf. I'm watching our world fall apart." She waved her arms.

"Oh please." Ben rolled his eyes at the drama.

"How could you be so selfish? How could you spend money when we're struggling so hard to stay afloat?"

"What are you talking about? We're fine."

"Oh. My. God."

It was clear Ben actually believed what he was saying. Annie could see that his transformation was complete. He'd turned into someone who couldn't understand that less income meant less money coming in.

"Maggie needs to go to work. She doesn't need to keep you company at the driving range," she said furiously.

His face hardened. "She wanted to go. What was I going to say, no? I thought it would be good for her to get out."

"Well, you didn't have to get her a ninety-dollar lesson for her to get out. She could have taken Curly to the park."

"Who said they cost ninety? They're a hundred now, and I got her ten," he corrected.

"You got her *ten* lessons?" Annie's blood pressure spiked off the chart, and she heard her mother's disapproving voice in her ear.

"Shhh," she told the air, as if it had spoken out loud.

"Don't *shhh* me. I have a right to say anything I want," Ben said sharply.

"Not *you*," she barked.

"Well, Mag is thrilled. She couldn't be happier." He finished the argument with a wave of his hand. "We're going out on a course as soon as she's completed her first set of lessons. I told her we could join a club when she gets good enough."

Annie stared at him. They didn't have a car. How were they going to get there?

"Don't look at me like that. You said yourself she needed to be socialized."

"What she needs is to go to *college*, Ben!"

"All they do in college is drink," Ben retorted.

"Oh, are you against college now?" Annie cried.

"I'm right here." Mag walked past Annie in her bare feet. "I can hear every evil word you're saying, and I don't have to go to college to drink. There's enough to get hammered right here—"

"Mag, tell your mother you love golf," Ben interrupted.

Annie whipped around to see her daughter's face. The face said it all.

"Oh, it was great," Mag said listlessly. "Did you see those lame shoes?"

"He bought you *shoes*, too?" Would the offenses never end?

"She had to have the shoes," Ben said.

To stand on a New York City pier? Annie didn't trust herself to comment, so she changed the subject. "Where's Dina?"

"Dina didn't come back today. She had to go to the lawyers about her papers."

Annie's eyes narrowed even more. She now had a new horrible thought. "Anybody take Curly out?"

"I didn't." Mag slunk off into the kitchen.

"Jesus. Where is he?" Suddenly Annie realized that Curly hadn't come to greet her.

She hurried into the bedroom. "Curly? Curly, baby. Where are you?" Curly was under the bed, trembling at the sound of his name.

"Poor baby, come on, I'll take you out."

He sneezed and wouldn't come out.

Then she smelled it wafting in from Bebe's room, and saw the whole picture. The dog had taken his dump in Bebe's room. And if it was still there, that meant Bebe wasn't home yet. Where the hell was Bebe? Furious about yet another thing, she went into Bebe's room and looked quickly around. In a futile attempt to hide his offense, Curly had gone in the corners. All of them. He must have been frantic in his abandonment and dumped everywhere.

Annie cleaned up the messes, then grabbed her jacket and headed for her bedroom. It was colder in there than usual. In fact, it was freezing. Curly was still hiding under the bed. She called to him. "Curly, come here. It's not your fault."

He wouldn't come out. She had to coax him out with his favorite liver treats. "I still love you," she assured him as he emerged for the snack. She sat cross-legged on the floor and hauled him onto her lap. After about a second of love, the dog began to howl and struggle to get away.

"What's up, Curly?"

For a second she thought it might be a mouse or a cockroach. Despite her aversion to both, she held on to the dog with one hand while she lowered her chin to the floor to see what was bothering him. The lower she got, the more it felt as if a freezer door had opened on her.

Annie closed her eyes and stood up. When she opened her eyes, her mother was sitting on her side of the bed. "Oh, Mom. What are you doing there?"

"Mamie Teath is coming home tonight," the ghost said.

"To Carol?"

"No, honey, to God."

Annie held the struggling dog in her arms. "Oh God, are you serious?" She relaxed her grip for just a second, and Curly wiggled out of her grasp. He leaped onto the bed to attack Annie's pillow, but by the time he got there, Brenda had gone home, too.

twenty-four

A FEW MINUTES LATER ANNIE WAS HALFWAY TO THE kitchen.

"Anniiieee, Carol's on the phone," Ben yelled.

She hurried the rest of the way and almost fell over Curly, who'd sacked out by the door after his ordeal. "So drunk I can't see," she muttered to the dog. She grabbed the phone, hoping she wouldn't slur her words.

"Carol, it's Annie. What's up?"

"I bet you're thinking I'm pretty crazy right now," Carol said.

"Ah, no." Actually Annie was thinking everybody was a little crazy right now.

"I know you too well for that. Tell the truth," Carol demanded. "I had a terrible day. I want to straighten things out."

"Well, me, too," Annie said cautiously. "I certainly don't think you're crazy." She sat on a stool and eyed the half-empty bottle of red wine on the counter. The wine tempted her. She needed something to take the edge off, something to help her deal with her volatile

friend. Then she reminded herself she'd already taken
the edge off. Several times.

"Matthew thinks I'm crazy," Carol said.

Ah, it was confession time. Carol sounded as if she,
too, had taken the edge off.

"Is he there with you now?" Annie asked slowly. She
didn't trust Matthew.

"Are you kidding? He won't be home for hours."

Annie hesitated; then all the alcohol in her system
loosened her tongue. "Well, we've got opposite husbands. Yours never comes home. Mine never leaves, and
they think *we're* the crazy ones."

The ice broken, they both laughed softly. Annie
prayed that Matthew, the litigator, was far away and not
setting any traps to ensnare her.

"I've thought it over. I'm absolutely certain now. I
want you to keep the account," Carol said suddenly.

"Oh. Well, thank you. I appreciate your trust." Annie
was silenced by the real warmth in her friend's voice. It
made her feel the burden of the missing bonds and want
to tell Carol about them immediately. She didn't have
time, though, before Carol changed the subject.

"Look, I'm sorry I got so mad at you about the cancer. I love my dad, but he doesn't always tell the truth,"
she said.

Oh really. Annie was on the alert again. She wished
she had a tape recorder, because that statement would
save her ass if it came to a dispute. She tried to fight off
her alcohol fog. "What does he lie about?"

"Oh, anything and everything. What he had for lunch.
Where things came from. The weather. He can't help it,"
Carol said.

Maybe, maybe not. In any case, Carol admitted there
was a problem, and Annie breathed easier. She'd tell this
to Brian and be off the hook for any accusation of theft.

"Here's a case in point," Carol went on. "I haven't been neglecting them like you said. I've been sending food from Zabar's for three years. They didn't eat it. Dad's been giving it away. He told me they didn't need it."

"Wow," Annie muttered. More ammunition to support her innocence.

"You wouldn't believe all the stuff I sent them. But I have to hand it to you, Annie. You were right. When I got there today, the refrigerator was empty. You can't trust anybody, can you?" Carol let out a little sob, and Annie had a feeling she was thinking of her husband.

"I'm really sorry. Carol—" Once again Carol cut her off before she had a chance to talk about the bonds.

"My mother wanted me to have the certificates," Carol told her.

"That's what she told me yesterday, Carol. Did she tell you anything else?" Just a few minutes ago Brenda had said Mamie was coming home. Maybe Annie had dreamed it. Maybe she was going off her rocker. Annie didn't know.

"She just wanted me to take everything valuable out of the house. I wanted to take *her* out of the house, but she didn't want to go." Carol's voice broke.

The bonds forgotten, Annie reached for the wine. There wasn't a glass handy, so she took a swig from the bottle. Fortified, she made a suggestion.

"Listen, Carol, let's go back out there and get her now. I'll go with you. We can bring her home tonight."

"You'd do that?" Carol sounded surprised.

"Of course. I'll call a car." Annie took another swig of wine. She wouldn't mind a nice long drive to nowhere and back. Yes, that was what Brenda meant. They had to take Mamie home.

"But, Annie. I was planning to get her on Saturday when I have more time . . ."

"I think we should do it now," Annie pressed. "Tonight," she repeated.

"Why?" Carol sounded irritated.

"A little bird told me it would be a good idea." Annie slurred slightly. She knew it wouldn't be a good idea to say who.

"Jesus, Annie, have you been drinking?"

"I had a glass of wine. I wouldn't exactly call it *drinking*. What do you say? We could make an outing of it."

"I already went out there today. I don't want another outing," Carol said peevishly.

"Let's not take a chance." Annie wanted so badly to come clean about everything. Her suspicion about the bonds, Carol's mother being at risk, her father even further off the deep end than she'd thought. Oh yeah, and Brian's manipulation.

She had a lot on her mind. People did all kinds of terrible things for money. She saw it every day. Look at what had happened between Ben and Matthew; a war over money had destroyed their friendship. And Carol's parents were not just eccentric: They'd been fighting some weird money war for decades, not spending a thing possibly just to spite each other. Annie suspected they were fighting their war to the death.

Can't you see, he's throwing out her food? she longed to say. But how could she tell Carol that her father might be starving her mother, and claiming she had cancer to cover it up? Annie held her breath. This wasn't her job. She wasn't a cop. Just because it was clear to her didn't mean she was right.

"Carol, this is a dangerous situation. Don't play with fire. You might be sorry later." That was all she could say.

"Don't freak me out, Annie. I have a busy week. She'll be fine for three more days. That's it. Call me tomorrow." And just like that Carol hung up.

Should I call her back? Should I let it go? Shivering, Annie slid off the stool. It was too much to bear. There was too much history between them. She couldn't push. Shit. She realized it was freezing. She wasn't trembling with anxiety and frustration. Her mother was back. She could feel the disapproval ooze through the walls. It was frigid in there. Curly shuddered in his sleep. Then a snort shook him all over and he was awake, growling at two pale shadows moving across the room. *Oh God, it couldn't be.* Annie staggered to bed.

twenty-five

THE FAX HAD COME INTO HALL STALE AT FOUR A.M. With a hangover, Annie saw it at eight twenty the next morning. Like many of Vartan's faxes, it was long and full of complicated instructions. Annie read it four times. Beyond the huge amounts of money cited in it, a number of other things were extremely odd. Yesterday Vartan had talked about transferring $200 million; today he was alerting her to a wire transfer of $1.547 *billion*. He was trying to deposit all this into his personal account at Hall Stale because the Canadian corporate account he'd tried on them last week wouldn't fly. Furthermore, he was instructing her to immediately transfer

$315 million to a bank in Australia, two banks in Illinois, one in Norway, and one in Georgia. The source of the money and the purposes for which it was to be used were about as clear as mud. On the other hand, even if that amount of money came in and went out, the lion's share of a billion dollars would still be left in her hands at Hall Stale. She had a hangover. She wanted to laugh. She wanted to cry.

Vole seemed to be something of a nut, but entrepreneurs were often eccentric. And rich people were very demanding and volatile. Look at Carol. Easy come, easy go, easy come again. Annie knew she could never count on anything. Still, if the seemingly crazy Vartan Vole came through with one-tenth of what he promised, she'd be sitting pretty. The cliché made her smile.

One of her old managers had been a real fan of platitudes. He used to say, "You have to take the good with the bad." His repertoire consisted of about five inane sayings, which he used in a wide range of situations.

"If you listen to me, Annie Custer, you'll be sitting pretty," he'd told her.

She had to listen to him repeat those phrases over and over until she wanted to scream. Years later they'd come unbidden to her mind like advice from her mother. When he'd come due for retirement, he'd transferred to the Boca Raton office, and she'd lost track of him. Since then her branch had seen a number of managers come and go, never lasting very long. After a few years they moved up the corporate ladder or out to smaller branches around the country. Or they retired. Brian had been there three years and was due for a change. Annie had been thinking all evening about how she longed for a change. Boca Raton was looking pretty good to her.

That morning she was still thinking about it as she'd made her special cappuccino, showered and dressed, given a pep talk to Bebe, walked Curly, and made sure Bebe got on the bus with her backpack containing everything she needed for school. Then she returned to the apartment and yelled at Mag to get up and start being productive by noon. She didn't bother to communicate with Ben. What was the point?

Something had changed overnight, and by morning it wasn't just a hangover. A deep cold had seeped all the way into her bones, and by dawn she realized she didn't have to accept her life the way it was anymore. She didn't think the martinis she'd drunk with Brian had anything to do with it. She just saw everything in a new light. The mist had cleared on her marriage. All the hurtful things that had happened between her and Ben since 9/11 had shaken her, but not turned her off to him. The golf clubs for Maggie had done what nothing else could do. He'd flipped the switch, and she was done with loyalty.

As she left for the office and strode down Third Avenue, she felt like a ship setting off from port, slipping away from land on a high tide. With the new thought that she could be free if she wanted to be, she simply walked out of her cage. Her plan, after twenty years of marriage, was to return to her natural self. It was such a liberating thought it almost made her dizzy. Just to think of a life in which she could do whatever she wanted, whenever she felt like it, and never worry a second about Ben, was a thrill.

Then she got to the office and saw Vartan's fax. By eight thirty her second cup of coffee was nearly empty, and she was finished studying his instructions for the disbursement of the funds that he claimed would hit his account by ten. She took the fax and went into Brian's office. He'd just walked in and looked the very opposite of her slug of a husband, who no doubt was still in bed. Brian was wearing a yellow tie, a knockout new gray suit, and a pale blue shirt with a white collar. His hair looked wet from his morning shower. She remembered the long looks and sly smiles of last night and knew she was smitten.

"Hey, beautiful. You look like the cat that got the cream," he said.

"Carol called to confirm that we're keeping the account," she told him. "We don't have to worry about it anymore." Nor had Carol's mother died in the night. So much for the intelligence of ghosts.

"Well, good for you. She could have taken it somewhere else. It does you credit. Really." He grinned at her, and she knew it wasn't about the three million. She was pretty happy, too.

"I didn't tell her about the bonds. She confessed that her father is a compulsive liar. I think it pretty much makes our case." She smiled as he started his cocoa ritual. Before, it had seemed idiotic to her. Now it was charming.

"Great. I'm glad it all worked out, and I don't want you ever to tell her, okay? Now how about some cocoa? I was just about to have mine."

"Ah no, thanks." Never tell her? Annie hesitated. She had to tell her, but she wasn't going to bother Brian with the issue now. "Brian, I have something else to bring to your attention." She moved closer to the desk and held out the fax from Vartan. "Vartan Vole is back. How do you want me to handle this?"

"Geez, this guy is like the proverbial bad penny."

Annie frowned at Brian's using a second cliché in less than ten minutes.

"What's the matter?"

Cats and cream, bad pennies. She decided to let it go. "Oh, nothing. Just take a look."

He read the fax once. "Fuck. I don't believe this." He read it again and scratched the side of his face. "The money hasn't hit yet . . . ?" He glanced at her with raised eyebrows.

"No."

"Well, send him a fax asking him all the basic questions: who all these people are, what they do, where they're located, why the money is going to them, and what they're going to do with it. Let's see what he comes up with."

He gave her another grin, this one even warmer. "Where do you want to go to lunch?"

She had a lot to do and didn't answer.

twenty-six

LATE IN THE EVENING MATTHEW TOOK OFF FOR A morning meeting in Chicago, and Carol tossed and turned in their big bed all night. She was used to being left alone in the evenings, but tonight she felt so sad about her mother's condition that she couldn't calm down. She'd debated calling Annie a dozen times to yell at her for scaring her with more upsetting warnings. She'd even considered going out to Staten Island to check on her mother. Many unanswered questions bothered her. How could her father lie to her about a thing like cancer? She couldn't find a satisfactory explanation, and her mother hadn't told her anything. Some people were like lockboxes and never talked. Mamie Teath never said anything about herself. Carol didn't even know where she'd come from. Staten Island somewhere, for sure. But what house, what street, who had been their friends, where had they worshiped? She knew about the chauffeur-driven car, but she didn't know any of the important things.

She'd tried to imagine what Staten Island had been like in the 1930s when her mother was a young woman. Much of it had been marshes and dunes, but there was criminal lore, too. Even now it was home to cops and the Mafia alike. Yesterday her father had told her that her grandfather had been a pirate. This was the first she'd heard of it. The stickpin with the diamond in it struck her as an improbable family treasure, but what did she know? All she knew was that her mother was frozen in some other dimension. And unlike Staten Island where she lived, there wasn't any ferry to reach it. Carol didn't know the story or the secrets her mother didn't want revealed. It hadn't been surprising to her that her mother hadn't talked about any illness over the past year. Not talking was her MO. Carol couldn't blame herself for what happened. She'd had no reason to think anything was unusual until the certificates had turned up.

The stock certificates at Hall Stale were a complete surprise, like the blood she'd found in her underpants in sixth grade. The first event occurred before her twelfth birthday. Tiny budding breasts and a fuzz of pubic hair had been the only signs of impending womanhood. The blood in her white cotton underpants had terrified her. She'd been certain that she had a fatal illness, and she was afraid to go home and have to tell her mother. Her mother didn't like to leave the house, and didn't like going to the doctor. Problems were upsetting to her, so Carol had hung around in the girls' room for hours after school until a teacher found her hiding there and set her straight. Her mother hadn't told her it was coming. She hadn't told her about the food disappearing. She hadn't set her straight about anything.

Carol also brooded about her husband. Wasn't there something wrong with a man who didn't have time to talk to his wife, who never came home? It took her a long time to fall asleep. She dozed for a while in the early-morning hours, but she was already wide awake when her father called her at five.

"Mother's gone," he said without introduction. His voice was so low that Carol wasn't sure at first what he'd said. For a moment she actually thought her mother had run away.

"Where?" she asked.

"With the angels. Honey, it's over. You've got to bring me my bonds back now."

"Wait a minute. My mother is dead?" Carol was still processing angels.

"That's what I'm telling you," he said sadly. "She's gone."

"She's dead?" That just didn't make any sense. Her mother had been alive and frail yesterday, but not ready for any angels. And Carol certainly couldn't picture her mother in heaven. For one thing, she wouldn't fit in with the angels. What was he talking about now? Religion, like happiness, had not been a concept her mother had understood. Mamie Teath hadn't believed in God or heaven. Carol thought he was mixed up again. Maybe lying to get her attention. He certainly couldn't be telling the truth. That would be a first. He coughed, and it almost sounded like weeping, but she couldn't tell for sure.

"Honey, I'm all alone now. I need my stash. Mother said I could have it in case of need. I'm a poor man; I'm in need."

Then she got it. Her father wasn't talking about *her* mother being with the angels. He was talking about *his* mother. *His* mother had died a long time ago. She was a totally different lady. Carol breathed a sigh of relief. "It's okay, Dad. You'll be fine," she told him.

twenty-seven

AT ELEVEN, ANNIE FINISHED WITH ONE CALL AND Petra buzzed her with another. "It's Georgina."

"Thanks." Annie picked up. "Hi Georgie, what's the good word?"

"I need some money."

Oh gee, what else is new, Annie thought. "Okay, let's see what we can do," she said cheerfully.

She pulled up the girl's account and was not surprised by what she saw. Georgina had already spent her allowance for the year and had three serious shopping months left. She was the daughter of a wealthy client. Originally she had an account of about two hundred thousand, two-thirds in bonds and Fixed income, the rest in Blue-chip stocks. The deal Georgina had made with her parents was for her to use only the interest and thus preserve the principal until they died. However, she was now over eighteen, the account was in her own name, and she wasn't sticking to the agreement. She was eating through it as fast as she could. Annie couldn't and wouldn't tell on her, so she had to use her own methods to keep the girl in check.

"What do you need?" she asked.

"Five thousand," the girl said quickly.

"How about five hundred? Two dividends just hit. Brings your money market account to just over five hundred," Annie told her.

"Can't you sell a bond?" the girl wheedled.

"Well, let's see. We've already sold all your long terms and most of your short terms. Now is not the best moment to sell stocks, and I'm guessing you're going to need some cash around Christmas. You've got a bunch of dividends hitting around the end of the year. You don't want to sell those bonds, do you? And your birthday's coming up soon. Don't you get your ten thousand tax-free gift then?"

"Fine, I'll take the five hundred," the girl said cheerfully.

"Thanks," Annie said, as if the girl had done her a favor instead of the other way around. Ha, saved her four and a half grand.

Petra came in with some papers. "Incoming. Vole again."

"Great." Annie reached for the fax.

The four questions she'd asked only two hours ago had to do with the companies he'd named: Who is Hornbill Financial? Who is International Northern? What are the sources of the funds to be transferred? What will be done with the funds once received? She was very interested in Vartan's answers. Before she got very far, she started laughing. He'd misspelled her name again; he kept calling her *Ms. Custard*. After that, he cited some international treaty agreements and said that he hoped that would satisfy her due diligences. He got *due diligence* wrong, too. It meant vital information gathering, and he didn't do any. In fact, he hadn't answered a single one of her questions. She picked up the fax and headed for Brian's office. On her left was a bank of brokers in glass enclosures, and on her right were windowed offices overlooking the avenue. Many of them were empty. It was sad how many people were gone.

Darian caught up with her before she got halfway. "We have your printout for the Teath account," she said, handing it to Annie. "Here's everything we received."

Annie glanced at it. She hadn't expected to see the missing bonds from her list on the printout, but it gave her a jolt anyway to see only forty thousand in bearer bonds instead of the three hundred thousand she knew she'd tucked into the shopping bag.

"What are you doing about *my* list?" Annie said.

"Brian took it for the file. This is what's been approved. I'm starting the registering process. It should be done in a couple of weeks."

"What about Frisk? Does he have a copy?"

"You'll have to ask him."

"Well, thanks, Darian," Annie murmured. She was a little disturbed about everything going into Brian's file.

"It's what I'm paid for," Darian replied seriously.

"Still." Annie nodded, catching her reflection in a young broker's glass enclosure. She'd recently cut her hair pixie style and hardly looked thirty, much less the forty she was and the sixty she sometimes felt. Seeing the round cheeks, not yet creased into puppet lines around her mouth, simply amazed her. This was what forty looked like—not so different from the girl who'd started there before her twentieth birthday. Her eyes were the same quizzical hazel. If anything, worry kept her figure even leaner than it had been in easier times. Oh sure, she could see the fine lines around her eyes in the mirror and the beginnings of a double chin when she looked down. But here in the hall it seemed as if time had stopped. She'd heard that the big damage came after forty, though, and that gave her the sinking feeling she didn't have much time left for all she wanted to do.

Brian was shaking hands with a stocky man at the door of his office and waved at Annie to come in after he left.

"Getting hungry?" he asked.

"Brian, I want to talk about the printout of the Teath account."

"Yeah, it's going out today. Come in, but don't annoy me with this."

Annie handed him the printout, then sat in one of his wing chairs. "Is this what you're sending Carol and her father?"

He nodded without looking at it. "Don't tell me you have a problem with it."

"But I do. I have the serial numbers for a whole lot of missing bonds."

He shrugged and gave her the look that said she was irritating him. "So?"

"Well, if the old man took the bonds, he may try to cash them. With the serial numbers, we could catch him."

"Uhmmm." Brian tapped his fingers.

"On the other hand, if he keeps the bonds and hides them, Carol may never find them. Either way, we owe it to her to tell her they exist."

"That's too many problems, Annie."

"Like what?"

"Our liability. You may have your list, but some of it didn't get here. It may be your problem, but I'm not going to let it become ours."

"Brian." Annie laughed. "Assets went missing. We can't ignore it forever."

"Carol acknowledged that her father is a liar, so it's her problem. Sometimes, for the good of the company, you just have to let it go."

Annie frowned. "For the good of the company? How is lying for the good of the company?"

"Fine, I'll tell you. Do you know whose pocket got hit in the Matthew Mack case?"

Oh God. There it was, the Matthew Mack case, which also happened to be the Ben Custer case. Annie lifted a hand. She didn't want to talk about it.

"Listen to me. I'm responsible for this branch. Anything that goes wrong, okay? It comes out of my pocket. So your husband's settlement was taken out of my bonus." He hit his chest, and Annie shuddered.

Did she know this? She didn't think so.

"Once burned, your fault. Twice burned, my fault. You notice we got a similar amount of money here? You know what I'm thinking? I'm thinking that Matthew is behind this. I'm thinking they're doing this to us again. I'm thinking I'm not getting in the middle of another Custer–Mack fiasco. No way."

Annie whistled. Good performance. She decided this was not a good time to give him Vole's fax.

twenty-eight

CAROL GOT TO THE OFFICE AND PUNCHED IN HER parents' number on her phone. There was no answer. "Oh shit. Don't do this to me, Dad. Come on, pick up," she muttered.

Her parents didn't have an answering machine, so she hung up after nine rings and tried again. Still no answer. This was not entirely unusual. Her father didn't have caller ID and was paranoid about telemarketers. Sometimes he answered his phone and sometimes he didn't, but today she didn't like it. Whatever Carol said about Annie, she trusted her, and Annie had raised some very good questions. Why had her father suddenly asked to have Annie—and only Annie—take the fortune out of his house? Why did he demand to have it returned the minute it was gone? Certainly he had to know Carol would never let all those stock certificates return to his house.

What was he up to? Why pretend her mother had cancer when she didn't? Carol didn't ask herself why she bought his stories. For better or worse—mostly worse—she was his little girl. She had always bought them. Today he'd called her at five A.M. sounding nuttier than ever, but for the first time the story didn't ring true. It was too far-out, too upsetting. With the fortune finally revealed, Carol decided she wasn't going to let her father jerk her around any longer. She wasn't buying every crazy story he threw at her. She was an heiress now. Her mother had put her in control of her own life—at least it felt that way, and she was relieved that she could finally make the decisions.

She planned to retrieve her mother on Saturday, and she wasn't letting her father get in the way of that. Indecision, however, tore at her guts. Should she take her mother home? Once she was there, she'd need so much. A doctor, a nurse, a TV in her room, a nutritionist. Could she handle all that? She started making her mental list. She longed for a second cup of coffee, but her stomach couldn't take it.

Carol had always thought things would be different if she was an heiress, but things weren't different for her that morning. Her husband still paid no attention to her. Her assistant was late again. No one cared about her. Familiar gripes bubbled into searing heartburn. She had a mountain of work to do, a big presentation to prepare for the following week. A sick mother to care for. Everything coming down on her at the same time. She dialed Matthew's cell phone number for the seventh time since dawn. His voice came on with the same annoying message:

"This is Matthew Mack. I'm presently out of range. Please leave a message, and I will call you back."

Matthew's being presently out of range was pretty much the story of Carol's life. She tried his private number at the office, even though she knew he wasn't there.

"This is Julie," sang out the chirpy voice of Matthew's assistant.

"Hi, Julie. I need to talk to Matthew." Carol girded herself for an unpleasant exchange. Matthew was in the air. He was in transit. His Chicago meeting had just begun. He was on his way back. Whatever.

"Oh, Carol, he's behind closed doors right now. Do you want to leave a message?" Julie's birdie voice signaled no guile.

Behind closed doors? "He's there?" That was the very last thing Carol expected.

"Oh yes. He's with a client, but he should be out soon. Is there anything I can do for you right now?"

"Gee, Julie, I thought he flew to Chicago last night."

"Oh. That meeting . . . was . . . postponed—" Julie's voice slowed like an old record on the wrong speed. Then it stopped altogether, and Carol's heart hit the wall. She could actually feel her heart stop. Then after two long seconds, it kicked in again with a thud. It was the strangest feeling. She knew that lives ended just like that all the time. When the rhythm stopped, it was over.

"Ah . . ." *Thud, thud, thud.* Carol's heart felt like a drum. "I need to talk to him," she said.

Julie hesitated. "Well, you know how much he hates to be interrupted . . ."

"Fine, when he gets out of that meeting and has a free moment, tell him I'll never interrupt him again."

"Just a minute, Carol. I'll see what I can do."

And fuck you, too, Carol thought.

After a few seconds, Matthew came on the line. "What's the matter now, Carol?" he said irritably, as if nothing in the world could possibly be wrong.

She was hurt by the excuse that he'd gone to Chicago so he could stay out all night. Further, she was hurt by the way he'd callously ignored all her desperate calls that morning. She was so incensed by it all that she almost threw her three-million-dollar inheritance in his face. *Just who do you think I am? I'm not taking your shit anymore.* But before she could get the string of angry words out, a little voice told her that Matthew was just like her father. If he knew money was coming to her, he'd only try to take it away.

Instead of yelling at him, she hung up.

Hours later Carol was at lunch with two suppliers from out of town. They lived in Gary, Indiana, but their factory was in Hunan. The two chubby Hoosiers had wanted to go to Lutèce, but the old standard had closed, so Carol was hosting them in another fancy restaurant with a four-course lunch that was taking forever and no doubt costing more than one of their Chinese workers received in a year. So far she hadn't been able to swallow a bite. Halfway through the lunch her cell phone vibrated in her pocket, and she plucked it out to see if Matthew was still trying to reach her. No, it was an unfamiliar 718 number.

"Excuse me, I have to take this," she told her guests and pressed TALK. "Hello."

"Mrs. Mack?"

"Yes," Carol said tentatively.

"This is Gregory Walkom, from the Walkom Funeral Home."

Thud. Her heart did that scary thing again. Carol glanced at her guests. One of them had hair transplants. It hadn't clicked with her before, but now she could see the plugs carefully laid out on his baldpate, sprouting like new plants in a vast plowed field. Simultaneously, the other man's eyes happened to be rolling up to the ceiling as his tongue came in contact with his first bite of the lobster special. Everything was so vivid. The look and smell of the restaurant, her suppliers' obvious pleasure in the food. That was what she would remember: how life kept on around her at the same time that death made an entrance.

Without being aware of moving, she rose from her

chair and walked toward the door. Numbly she said the word "Yes."

"Mrs. Mack, I have your father here."

They didn't like cell phones in expensive restaurants. She pushed through to the street. The sun was blindingly bright. She couldn't see, and almost tripped on the curb. "My father," she said wildly, "my father is dead?"

"No, no. He's right here. He says you'll be responsible for your mother's funeral."

"My mother's funeral?"

"Yes." Gregory's voice was smooth.

"My mother's dead?" Carol said blankly.

"That's right. She passed on last night. I thought you were aware . . ."

Carol was having trouble breathing. This couldn't be. She wasn't ready. "Are you sure?" she said dumbly.

"Yes ma'am. Her remains are with us now."

"Her remains?" For a second Carol had the incongruous thought that her mother had been remaindered.

"Will you be able to meet with us soon?"

"Ah, of course. How late are you open?"

twenty-nine

ANNIE WAS DEALING WITH THE TRAUMAS IN HER LIFE by shopping at Victoria's Secret. No billion and a half dollars had been transferred into Vartan Vole's account that morning. Her manager blamed her husband for his bonus cut *three years ago*. She blamed her husband for being a do-nothing and purchasing useless items that were going to bankrupt them. And the big one—Carol had dragged her into another Mack mess.

Victoria's Secret was a great leveler, however. When her cell phone rang, she'd been trying to figure out how her adult body could possibly fit into the tiny thong in her hands. The thong was violet, her favorite color, but even in a Large there was hardly anything to it. Three strings and a tiny lacy patch the size of a fig leaf were about it. The photos of celebs wearing such things in *People* magazine didn't illustrate which leg went where. She figured the patch went in front, but how to get into it wasn't clear. Wearing only the matching violet bra, she kept turning the thong around in her hands searching for the correct entry point.

She was as startled by the ringing phone as she would have been if she'd been caught frolicking nude on a sports channel videotape. The phone kept ringing as she scrambled to find it in the bottom of her messy purse. Ah, there it was. She recognized Carol's number and picked up. "Hi."

"My mother died," Carol said frantically.

Annie dropped the thong. All she could think of was how. "How?" she asked.

"I don't know, in her sleep, I guess."

She didn't know? How could she not know? "When?" Annie asked.

"Don't bug me with all these questions, Annie. I don't know. I just got a call from the funeral home. She's gone, and I have to bury her. That's all I know."

Oh Jesus. Annie was horrified. She'd been in the room when her own mother had died. And she had known the cause of death. Cigarettes. Why hadn't Carol gone out and gotten her last night to save her? Terrible, it was ter-

rible news, and there she was shopping for sexy underwear. Guilt-stricken, she stuck one foot in her skirt, then
the other, and hurriedly zipped up her zipper for dignity.

"I'm so sorry, Carol. She was a lovely lady," she murmured, taking one last second to admire herself in the
lacy bra. *Not bad. Not bad at all.* She still had a good
waist, good lift . . .

"You really think so?" Carol asked.

"Of course. A wonderful woman." She pulled off the
bra and changed to her own, which happened to be gray
with age. She buttoned her suit blouse. Done.

"I need you, Annie," Carol wailed.

How did Annie guess she would say that?

"You're the closest thing I have to family."

"Of course, what can I do?" Annie asked.

"Come with me to the funeral home. You've done this
before. I haven't."

Annie groaned. Been there, done that. Twice. But she
didn't hesitate. "Of course. It's not a problem," she said,
even though everything Carol asked her to do turned
out to be a problem.

"I'll call for a car and pick you up," Carol promised.

Quickly Annie gathered up all the lingerie she'd chosen. She wasn't leaving those beauties behind. Forty-five
minutes later the two women were in another limo,
heading out to Staten Island. Carol looked gray.

"Honey, are you okay?" Annie asked.

"Is that manager of yours married?" Carol replied.

"What?" Annie thought she'd misheard.

"Brian, is he married?" Carol repeated.

"Ah . . . no. He's divorced. Why?"

Carol looked out the window. "Just wondering. He
seems nice."

"He is nice, but he has a girl a week."

"Really." Carol was silent for a few moments.

"Why do you ask?" Annie ventured cautiously.

"I'm thinking of leaving Matthew."

"Wow. Why?" That was a bombshell.

"Why? He told me he was going to Chicago yesterday, but it was just an excuse not to come home. Last night of all nights he did that. He shouldn't have left me alone like that." Carol took out a handkerchief and dabbed at her eyes.

"He didn't know your mother was going to die," Annie said automatically.

"That isn't the point. He's a prick. Let's face it."

Annie studied the view out the window.

"Come on, Annie, don't be such a fucking saint. Admit it, men suck."

"Ah, I don't want to get into it," Annie murmured.

"What do you mean you don't want to get into it? Look at what you put up with. Ben is living off you, giving a horrible example to the girls. When are you going to wake up?"

"Matthew chose a poor moment to be a jerk, but that doesn't mean—"

"He screwed your husband, Annie! It's okay to take sides. Everything's been shit ever since then."

Annie didn't say anything. It wasn't exactly a secret. Ben collapsed with the World Trade Center. The girls weren't doing well. All true.

"Did he ever grab your ass?" Carol asked.

"Huh?" Carol jumped from subject to subject like a bird from limb to limb. Annie shook her head.

"I'll bet he did," Carol said.

"Cut it out," Annie said sharply. That was the one thing Matthew hadn't done, but she wasn't going to defend him.

"It doesn't matter. I'm divorcing the bastard."

Annie's shocked expression felt almost comical. It was all coming down today. "This is really odd," she said after a moment.

"What's so fucking odd? Enough is enough."

Annie shook her head. "I was thinking exactly the same thing this morning."

It was Carol's turn to look surprised. "Are you going to divorce Ben?"

"As you said, enough is enough."

"Wow." The news silenced Carol for nearly ten blocks. Then she returned to her original subject. "What about Brian? Are you and he . . . ?"

"No way. I told you, he's my manager," Annie said angrily. The underwear in her Victoria's Secret bag told a different story.

"Well, you never know. You two looked pretty cozy the other day."

Annie could have said that she had her eye on him. She could have said the two had been flirting, and were leading up to something. But she didn't. Another sin of omission. "I've known him for a long time, but he's not viable that way," she said vaguely. Carol's interest in him was something Brian would have to deal with himself. She was not going to do it for him. The rest of the way there she let Carol do the talking.

The Walkom Funeral Home was the usual two-story white house, but quite modest as funeral homes went. Carol got out of the car slowly. "I've passed this place a thousand times and never thought I'd have to go in there," she said.

Annie asked the driver to wait and followed her into a parlor decorated entirely in brown. The lights were so dim it seemed like night. A small man with a black suit appeared in a doorway and came toward them bowing slightly from the waist.

"Mrs. Mack?"

"Yes, and this is my friend Annie Custer."

Annie could tell by her tone that she was put off by the place. A large funeral wouldn't be booked here. It would be like having a wedding at a diner.

"How do you do? I'm Gregory Walkom. We're going to take good care of your mother."

"Ohhh . . ." Carol clearly couldn't deal with that. She waved at Annie to speak for her.

"Is Dr. Teath here?" Annie asked.

"No, he left some time ago. Please come into my office."

The two women followed him into an office the size of a closet. There was barely enough room for three chairs. Carol started weeping.

"I'm sorry for your loss," Walkom said.

Carol didn't acknowledge the condolence.

"Carol, why don't you go outside for some air. Just for a minute, okay?" Annie suggested.

She took off without another word, and Annie turned to Walkom. "I have a few questions," she said.

He nodded. "Of course."

"How were you notified of the death? Was it the doctor, or the hospital?"

"We collected the remains from the hospital."

"She died in the hospital?"

"Ah, no. She passed away at home. Dr. Teath called nine-one-one. An ambulance came for her."

"Did the police come?"

"That's common procedure with any death."

"I see." Annie was quiet for a moment. She wondered how much checking would have been done to determine if an old woman's death had been natural. "And they released her to you?"

"Within a few hours, yes."

"How did Mrs. Teath seem?" Annie asked.

"She seemed very peaceful. It appears that Mrs. Teath died in her sleep."

"But is there any way to confirm that?"

"Not without an autopsy." He gave her a nervous look.

"Don't they do autopsies on all sudden deaths?"

"No, not unless one is requested. I hope you're not considering it, because the deceased has already been embalmed."

Annie's gorge rose. "Really?"

"Mm-hmmm." He nodded seriously.

Oh God, Carol's mother had been drained since that morning. Annie swallowed. "I gather that means there is none of her blood left to be tested for any kind of—"

"Toxins, no. What are you concerned about, some allergy?"

Annie shook her head. She knew this wasn't her place, but the circumstances were so suspicious, and she got the feeling that Carol wouldn't be able to ask any hard questions—or indeed, any questions at all. Annie could hear her sobbing in the parlor.

"Mrs. Teath died very suddenly, Mr. Walkom. She seemed malnourished. I just wondered if there was any way to reassure ourselves that she died a natural death." Or confirm the contrary.

"I can assure you that sometimes they lose their appetites and stop eating on their own. Or come to some kind of personal decision. I wouldn't mention that to her daughter. She could have had a heart attack." He lifted a shoulder.

"Are there any, like, marks on the body. Bruises . . . ?"

Walkom waved away the question. "Even an autopsy doesn't always show why a person suddenly stopped breathing. Mrs. Teath could have had a stroke. There are a number of possibilities. And, you know, it doesn't do to distress the family. What exactly is your relationship to the deceased?"

"I'm a—friend," Annie said after a pause. *I'm the broker* sounded . . . wrong.

He shrugged again. "Mrs. Mack is her daughter."

"Yes," Annie conceded. She wasn't happy with Walkom's answers, but didn't know what more she could do.

She found Carol weeping by the front door. "We need to choose a coffin," she told her gently.

thirty

LIKE SO MANY OTHER THINGS IN MAMIE TEATH'S life, her funeral was minimal. Her husband, daughter, and son-in-law buried her quietly in Staten Island where she'd lived in near seclusion all her life. She was finally interred on Monday morning nearly a week after she passed away. Annie sent flowers. So did Brian. Throughout the weekend, Annie had called Carol a number of times. Carol hadn't wanted to churn up the family waters, and didn't want to talk. She'd changed her mind once again and decided to keep the peace by sticking with her father, and reconciling with Matthew. Matthew wasn't speaking to Annie because she was married to Ben, so Annie wasn't invited to the funeral. She'd brooded about it all weekend and all day. Carol had banished her because she didn't want trouble. She'd let her mother be buried without asking a single difficult question. It was so sad.

Just before the bell ended the day at the stock exchange, Brian came into her office. "Annie, you seem down. Want to come over and give me some decorating advice?"

Brian had asked her this a hundred times. She'd always said no. Today she said, "Sure."

Half an hour later she was in Brian's office with her purse slung over her shoulder. The phone rang. It was the last call of Brian's day, and instead of leaving, he grabbed it.

"Brian Redfield." He listened for a minute, then glanced at Annie and hit SPEAKERPHONE. "Dr. Teath, let me convey my condolences," he murmured. Teath didn't let him get any further.

"That girl stole my bearer bonds." Dr. Teath's voice came out loud and ferocious.

"This is Brian Redfield," Brian said smoothly.

"I know who it is. I received your so-called statement. It's bullshit," came the angry reply.

"What's the problem?"

"I told you. My bonds are gone. I want them back."

It was cool in the office. The market was closed, and the day was over. Annie's forehead beaded with sweat. She'd known it wouldn't go away. She'd told Brian it wouldn't go away.

"Ah, Dr. Teath, we've recorded and deposited all of your wife's securities."

"Not all of them. I keep meticulous notes. I know what I had. I'm going to report you to the NASD. I'm going to take your company down," Teath threatened.

"Dr. Teath, four people documented the contents of the package that arrived at our office. Everything was duly recorded and deposited in your late wife's account. I personally supervised the process." He winked at Annie.

"Bullshit. It was stolen. I'm going to report you to Eliot Spitzer, too. I'm going to send that thief to jail."

Brian's voice remained as smooth as satin. "Can you give us documentation, serial numbers of the bonds in question?"

"What are you talking about? I know what I had. I know over a quarter of a million dollars is missing. Your young woman stole it."

Brian's expression sobered. "That is a very serious allegation," he said after a moment.

"You bet it is, and I want my money back. I can see what's happening here. I'm preparing my complaint immediately. That woman came into my house and stole my property. I will have her prosecuted—"

Brian stopped him quickly. "Dr. Teath. I understand your distress. Today has been difficult for you. I'm so sorry for your loss—"

"I'm not talking about my wife. I'm talking about that damn woman who stole my bonds!"

"We'll work this out. Let me assure you that we will begin a full investigation," Brian told him.

"I don't want an investigation. I want my bonds."

"If there's a discrepancy in your wife's account, adjustments will be made," Brian told him seriously. "We'll take care of it."

At the magic words, Teath calmed down immediately. "When?" he asked calmly. "I need to plan my future."

thirty-one

ANNIE WAS STILL TREMBLING WHEN SHE AND BRIAN got outside. He put his arm around her shoulders, but she didn't feel it.

"Calm down, Annie. He's a panicked old man. He buried his wife today. Think about it. This will pass."

"Oh, Brian, you know this won't pass. He set me up for this from the start."

"Don't get all worked up."

"He told me she was dying of cancer. She didn't have cancer. He was starving her."

"Annie, don't go there."

"Why did she die the night Carol confronted him, huh?"

He shook his head. "I'm not a cop. I can't get into this."

"I'll bet he put a pillow over her head."

"Annie," he said sharply.

"I can't help it. I can't get that poor woman out of my mind. Don't you see? She died because no one would take responsibility for what was happening to her."

Annie could see just how easy it had been for Teath to pull it off—as easy as drowning a kitten or thrashing a two-year-old. She was sure he'd killed her for the money. Money was the great corrupter. It had ruined Matthew and soured Ben. Even she was not immune to its power.

She let Vartan Vole jerk her around day after day in perpetual hope of the riches that would fix her life. She'd lost respect for her husband over money. She could go on and on.

"Sometimes you have to let things go." Brian kept saying it. He wouldn't take responsibility, either.

"Bry, Mamie cut him out of her will years ago. He must have taken revenge by stocking up on bearer bonds that didn't have her name on them."

"So?"

"So last week, she must have known the end was near. She was the one to insist that everything go. I may not even have it all. Carol and I didn't go there the day she died. There could be more. I wanted to search the place for the bonds, but Carol was a basket case. She isn't stupid. I'll bet she knows."

"You didn't tell her about the bonds, did you?" Brian asked, suddenly anxious.

"No, Bry. I couldn't."

"Well, good. You going to stand here all afternoon?"

Annie didn't care that she was standing in the middle of the sidewalk. "He watched as the accountant and I counted the bonds and put them in the bag. I'm guessing he took them out when I was in the bathroom searching for cancer medications. Don't you see? It's so clear. He's relying on us to double his money."

"Well, don't worry, I'm not going to do it," Brian assured her.

It didn't calm her down. Annie fumed on, "You were so right. This is just what Matthew did to Ben. I'll bet that's where the old man got the idea."

Brian wagged his finger at her. "And you let him. This is the reason we have rules about taking possession of securities outside the office. Same family, same story. Don't you ever learn?"

Annie stared at him. "Well, this one can't end like the last one. I'm not going down like Ben did."

"Don't worry, we can fix this." Brian used the arm he had around her shoulder to turn her around. When she was facing him, suddenly he leaned closer and sniffed her neck. "Are you wearing a new perfume?"

Huh? Annie was too startled by the sudden shift into her personal space to remember. She was being accused of stealing by her best friend's father. Eventually Carol would hear about it. Past history with Matthew made the whole thing doubly perilous. It was a huge important thing. How could he think of perfume now?

"Smells like . . . Paris."

The evening crowd swirled around them. Brian leaned closer and grazed her cheek with his lips. "Is it Paris?"

Ah . . . she nodded numbly and quickly started moving with the crowd. Paris it was. When she'd stood at the Bloomingdales counter trying on scents only a few days ago, she'd been thinking of Paris and her youth. She'd wanted a nice light fragrance, something with a distinct appeal, but nothing too strong and pushy. Brian guessed right. It was a new perfume for her. She'd just opened the bottle this morning.

Guilt closed in all around her. What was she doing? She had a husband. Brian was her branch manager. He was acting a little too smooth. It made her uncomfortable. He couldn't get her fired, but he could make life very difficult for her in a thousand different ways. How could she think about getting involved with him? She started walking north. She was going home after all.

"Come *on,* don't let this get you down, Annie. We'll go over to my place, have a nice martini. Hey, what's the matter?"

She'd picked up her pace, was almost running. She felt

like a recovering alcoholic who'd been dry for years and almost succumbed to a deadly temptation. How could she throw away almost twenty years of fidelity? Ben had let her down in the marriage department. She hadn't let him down. She held the moral high ground and wanted to keep it. If she was going to end the marriage, she had to do that first. She wanted to get home to scream at her husband for being such a jerk.

"Annie?"

She didn't respond. The light turned red. Cars started moving in front of her. She had to stop.

"Earth to Annie. Everything's going to be all right, honey."

He gave her a little squeeze, and she started to breathe again. "Look, I have to go home," she said.

"Why? I thought you hated it there," he said innocently.

"I do, but that's not the issue."

"I thought you were coming over."

"Well, not tonight."

"Oh Jesus, Annie. Don't be such a sissy. Nothing's going to happen. One drink. What's the big deal? Don't leave me alone now," he begged.

She was breathing again, nice and even. Don't leave him alone? That was ridiculous. He was a grown-up, not a puppy.

"I don't think this is a good idea," she told him.

He marched along stiffly beside her. "What happened? I just wanted to show you my place."

"I've seen your place."

"I know, but not since Sally took everything. I'm ready to furnish again. You're the only one I trust."

And there he said the magic word. Annie always responded well to the trust of others. She sneaked a look at him and saw the boy he'd been. Probably a very nice boy, although he was nearly forty now. God, they didn't change much, did they? Boys. She smiled, comfortable again now that he'd stopped sniffing around her ear. Okay, what harm was there in one drink and some decorating advice that Brian was certain not to take?

"Okay," she said. "One drink, but that's it."

thirty-two

MAG HAD PLANNED TO GET UP IN PLENTY OF TIME to wash her hair and dress for her second job interview, but her plan had changed when Stacy Golden called her from Stanford late the night before and kept her talking about college life until two thirty in the morning. Stacy had been a camp friend from the time she and Mag were seven. She'd always been the perfect kid, never any trouble. Last night, though, she'd sounded wasted. She didn't want to get off the phone and kept calling Mag *dude.*

"What's goin' on, dude?" she'd said.

"Oh, I'm playing a lot of golf with Chuck," Mag said, trying to sound offhand and cool.

"You, play golf? That's a new one, ha, ha, ha."

Stacy's stoned laughter traveled three thousand miles to Mag's room with the moldering ceiling. The third time she said *that's a new one,* it wasn't a new one anymore, and Mag knew she was pretty messed up. People who were really fucked up forgot they'd already covered a subject and kept repeating the same thing. Stacy didn't know what time it was, didn't care about the difference between New York and California, and she clearly didn't want to say goodbye.

"I have a job interview tomorrow," Mag hinted.

"What kind of job?"

"A magazine." Actually, it wasn't a magazine at all, and Chuck wasn't a boyfriend. He was her instructor, at least thirty and probably married.

"What a coincidence. I'm writin', too. I'm doin' a column for the paper," Stacy slurred. "Sss called Freshman Vices."

"Really?" Mag was not happy to hear that. She hadn't enjoyed hearing about Stacy's football-player boyfriend, either. Was he into vices, too? she wondered.

Still, she was so grateful that someone had finally called her, she didn't want to hang up on Stacy no matter how wasted and annoying she was. She was patient throughout a long and repetitive one-sided conversation, punctuated by a lot of drunken laughter. By the time Mag finally got off the phone, she was so depressed about all the fun Stacy was having at college that she had to take three Tylenol PMs to even think about getting to sleep. The Tylenols, of course, left her too tired to wake up before noon to get ready for her interview at two. In addition, she was still pretty nauseated about how badly the first interview had gone.

The week before, she'd applied to a temp agency where the waiting room was filled with a bunch of women who were a lot older than she and didn't look anything like her. She'd borrowed the use of her mother's car service to get her there, even though it was a straight run down Lexington Avenue. The minute she'd walked in, she'd known that none of the other job seekers had attended private school. They didn't look to her like the kind of people who went job hunting in limos, either. She didn't fit in and wanted to hide under her chair.

Worse, she'd gotten there a little early for her appointment, and was kept waiting for two hours before her number came up. She'd wanted to kill herself the whole time. When her name was finally called, a large woman gave her one test after another on the computer and almost no time at all to do them. Mag could speak French and Latin, had gotten A's in math and science, and had a combined thirteen hundred on her SATs, but she didn't know how to do Quicken. She couldn't do a spreadsheet or Excel, and she failed the copy-editing test. The last thing absolutely outraged her. How could anyone fail an English test? She refused to believe it and wanted to check the answers herself. No chance of that. The woman testing her whisked the test away before she could see it.

Then another woman, well dressed and not very old, who seemed very nice to Mag at first, had the audacity to look her over critically as if she were a cow at a state fair. Mag was so embarrassed in front of the other applicants she could hardly stand it. It was especially humiliating when the woman proclaimed Mag unfit even for the job of a receptionist.

"Why?" Mag asked, astounded.

"You need to work on your attitude." She threw Mag back on the street with the suggestion that she return and try again after she'd acquired some skills, thus ensuring that she never would.

Afterward, Mag had felt a stabbing pain in her chest and some numbness in her right arm. All the way home from the Empire State Building, where the temp agency's office was located, she was certain she was having a fatal heart attack. This time, however, she didn't call for a car. She slogged along trying to decide whether her chest pain, which was very severe, was severe enough to qualify for a trip to the emergency room.

What if she had a weak heart and shouldn't be looking for work at all? What if she fell off the curb and was hit by a speeding bus? That seemed like a very appealing no-fault kind of death until she remembered that her great-grandfather had once been hit by a bus. He used to think he was God and walked out into the street all the time without looking. Once, during the Christmas season when he was about ninety, he'd jauntily stepped off the curb and gotten knocked down, proving he wasn't God after all. Fortunately the bus hadn't actually run him over, and his major injury was to his pride. In the end he'd died in his sleep. Mag wouldn't want to fall off the curb and be hit by a bus unless it crushed her to death. She didn't want to wait until she was ninety. She wanted to get it over with and die in her sleep at eighteen.

She felt like absolute shit. How could she fail at computer? She'd been using a computer since she was three. How could she not qualify for a temp job? She'd thought anybody could get a temp job. The brain tumor made her body feel so heavy she didn't think she could take one more step. She stopped for a red light and almost vomited. She leaned her head against the light pole and hung her head. That was when she remembered the boots, good pants, and leather jacket that she'd borrowed from her mother. She didn't want to risk throwing up on her mother's outfit.

"You okay, honey?" A guy on a bicycle slowed down, eyeing the purse that dangled in the crook of her arm.

Alarmed, she stepped off the curb into the side street, where the light was green and a taxi sped toward her. She saw it too late and froze like an animal that didn't know which way to dodge.

"Jesus Christ!" An arm snaked out and grabbed her as the taxi missed her by an inch.

"Thanks." She turned toward the person who'd saved her, but no one was there. Only a woman pushing an infant in a stroller was behind her. No one else at all.

Shit, now she was imagining things.

Everything in her life was all messed up. She knew she'd looked terrific when she left home, and she thought she had a good attitude. Maybe it was the mean woman in that stupid office who had the attitude problem. What was wrong with her anyway? Mag wasn't a freak. She'd finished high school. She could more than read and write. She was confused by the weirdness all around her.

Musing over her near-death experience, she forgot how nauseated and dizzy she was and started walking home. She marched like the soldier her mother badly wanted her to be. She marched a mile and a half home and was still breathing when she got there. It was a miracle that she was still alive, so she went to bed to pamper her brain tumor.

Now, less than a week later, she had to do this horrible thing again. This time, instead of the four hours she needed to look her best, she had only an hour to get ready. Certain that she was too sick for another interview, she went into the bathroom to study herself in the mirror. She thought she looked pretty bad. She was hungover from the Tylenol PMs, and her brain tumor was on the rampage again. Nauseated beyond belief, she staggered out of her bathroom and right into her father, who had opened the door without knocking.

"How are you doing in there, Maggie?" he demanded. He was wearing a T-shirt and plaid boxer shorts, which offended her hugely because he was an adult and shouldn't wander around in his underwear.

"I feel like shit." She also hated it when he came into her room unannounced.

His eyes widened at her outfit. She was wearing the same thing he was—a pair of his boxer shorts and a white T-shirt. "Aren't those mine?"

"What do you want?" she asked rudely.

"I liked those shorts." He stared at them.

"Fine, I'll give them back. What do you *want,* Dad?" She used her most annoyed tone and watched him ignite.

"This is your forty-five-minute warning," he barked. "You'd better get going."

"Aw shit. I don't feel well. I don't think I can make it."

"You're making it, or no more golf lessons," he threatened.

"What?" What was wrong with him? She wasn't a kid who could be grounded. She tried staring him down. Her father had a five-day shadow that was threatening to become a real beard. In his bare feet and stubble, he looked like a patient in some mental ward. With absolutely no authority, his finger stabbed the air as he tried to take command.

"This is a client of your mother's so don't fuck up," he told her.

"Don't say *fuck,* it's not age-appropriate," she returned.

He snorted. "Get dressed, you're going."

"Fuck," she replied.

Mag happened to know for a fact that the company she was interviewing with, Gift Boxes of America, hadn't hired anyone in a year. Furthermore, all the news programs her father forced the family to watch during dinner said no companies were hiring college graduates. Even MBAs weren't getting entry-level jobs. She knew she wasn't going to get a job anywhere.

Her father left her room without closing the door. Fuck! Mag had to go and shut the door herself. She wanted to strike out at something. She saw her golf bag and picked out a club. Posing for a second, she swung with all her strength. As it slammed through the air, a piece of ceiling chose that moment to fall. Mag straightened up, horrified as more ceiling broke off and fell. What the—? She hadn't touched it.

Reminded of earthquakes in poor countries that toppled whole buildings, she imagined herself a tiny child caught in the end of the world. Maybe this was it. She stuck her golf club into the wet spot around her chandelier and poked around to see if the whole thing would come down on her. That would be a no-fault way out. A few tiny chunks came down, but not many. Fuck. She returned the golf club and flipped the light switch by the door. All five lights on the chandelier went off, then came on again.

She heard her father's voice calling to her. "Hurry up."

"Fuck you," she muttered as she headed down the hall to look in her mother's closet for something to wear. Dina disappeared into Bebe's room just ahead of her. Hadn't she heard the ceiling fall? Mag wondered, but didn't stop to ask.

She loved her parents' room. The ceiling was perfect in there. The bed was made up, and there was no clutter anywhere. Beyond the bedroom the bathroom was large, with two sinks and a Jacuzzi Mag much preferred to her own boring old bathtub. Even more wonderful was her mother's walk-in closet, which was the very opposite of hers in every way. Mag's much smaller closet contained everything she'd acquired since junior high. Jeans, sweats, coats, sweaters, socks, shoes, boots, backpacks, tennis shoes, rackets, a dozen party dresses from sweet-sixteen days—and the infamous prom dress that she never wanted to see again—were all shoved in on top of each other. She never got rid of anything.

Her mother's clothes, on the other hand, were clean and smelled of perfume. And she had a two-year rule: If she didn't wear something for two years, she purged it. The ones she favored were neatly arranged not only by season, but also according to status. She didn't wear her best clothes much anymore, which were all in see-through plastic covers. Their matching shoes were in boxes with plastic windows on the shelf above. Her favorite suits, all of them in beige and tones of gray, hung next to them. A rainbow array of blouses was carefully aligned above the matching skirts and trousers. Her sweater sets were stacked in even rows on the shelves. Built-in drawers contained her underwear, panty hose, nightgowns, and gym clothes. There was no dust in her mother's closet, and everything was fresh with floral sachets.

Among the mothers of Mag's friends were several who kept their closet doors and jewelry boxes locked, so their daughters couldn't go hunting there. One good thing about Annie was that she wasn't like that. For the most part she didn't mind when her daughters borrowed her clothes. At twelve thirty Mag was looking among many similar outfits for a particular gray blouse and matching gray flannel trousers. She flipped through the hangers quickly but didn't see what she was looking for. After a few minutes she started opening the drawers one by one. Same old shit, same old shit.

Then she got to the bottom drawer where her mother kept her oldest and least favorite things—the clothes that Mag could usually borrow without her mother's even noticing. She whistled. Here was something new. Lacy bras and thongs in lavender, pink, and baby blue were stuffed in the back, along with a few other enticing items of the sort her mother didn't usually wear—items that were meant for only one thing.

Mag pulled them out and examined them one by one. Skimpy little strings with heart-shaped fronts. Other than these, her mother didn't have any thongs. In fact, for the last several years, Dina had bought their panties and sleepwear in Wal-Mart whenever she thought replacements were needed. She'd come to work with stacks of cotton bikinis in pastel colors that she said she'd purchased for a dollar each. She'd distribute them among the three females in the house. After she washed them a few times, she'd forget which ones she'd given to whom. Neither Mag nor Bebe, nor even Annie, ever bothered very much about matching bras and panties.

Mag sat back on her heels and considered the new lingerie. She'd known for a long time that her mother was going to leave them one day, but here was evidence that her mother had a boyfriend. Mag was horrified. Her thoughts returned to prom night last June, which was the last time she'd worn anything that qualified as lingerie. It had not been a huge success. She'd spent the long and unpleasant night with someone she'd known practically since kindergarten, who extracted a high and painful price for the important date and then didn't call her afterward. The prick.

While it was easy to imagine her mother leaving them, it was a lot harder for Mag to imagine her mother buying these items, so she could do the disgusting things Mag never wanted to do again. For a moment she almost felt sorry for her father. Poor Dad didn't have a clue. Maybe she should give him a hint. She stuffed the things back in the drawer and grabbed the first pair of gray pants and sweater she could find. She glanced at her graduation watch. If she was lucky, she'd be too late for her interview.

thirty-three

BRIAN HAD A TWO-BEDROOM APARTMENT ON A low floor, in a fairly new building on Second Avenue. It was made of yellow brick, had small windows, and went up many stories. The lavish lobby had furniture and a fountain, but his apartment looked bare. There were no curtains in the living room or dining room. He had a leather sofa, a coffee table, and a recliner. A pile of *Forbes* magazines and *Wall Street Journal*s lay on the rug. The two glass paperweights that Annie had given him for the last two Christmases were lonely ornaments on the table. In the dining room, not even a fake flower arrangement graced the glass-topped table. The place had the feeling of recent occupancy even though Annie knew he'd lived there for more than a decade.

"Home sweet home." Brian went into the bedroom and returned a moment later without his jacket. "I love this place, but it needs a woman's touch. How about a drink? I have everything."

"Oh, I don't know." She couldn't think of anything she wanted.

"A martini?" He knew what she liked and gave her a wolfish smile.

"Well, maybe a short one. I can't stay." Annie followed him into the kitchen, where more piles of old newspapers and magazines covered most of the counter space. He was right; it did need a woman's touch.

It didn't take more than a few seconds for him to find what he needed in the cabinet. Assorted glasses and liquor bottles were neatly arranged in a place where most people kept their dishes. He chose the vodka and a bottle of olives wrapped in lemon peel.

Annie opened the refrigerator. Not even an old container of milk lived in there—just some aged jars of condiments that might have been old enough to go to kindergarten. "Doesn't look like anybody lives here," she murmured.

"Sally took everything while I was at work one day," he said, shrugging. "I don't have anything left." He opened the freezer for ice. He filled two huge martini glasses with ice to freeze the glasses, then grabbed two more handfuls for the shaker.

While he fussed over vodka, Annie wandered into the bedrooms. One had a desk with a phone and computer with a desert-island screen saver. A lamp on the desk was on, too. Double-bed mattresses, ringed with rumpled bedding, towels, clothes, and scented candles, were on the floor of the master bedroom. The scented candles were pretty much overpowered by the odor of sweaty gym clothes. The bareness of Brian's larder and his general lack of domestic organization kindled Annie's sympathy. Sally had been gone for several years.

With the beginning of a headache, Annie returned to the living room. She huddled miserably on the sofa, wishing she hadn't come. In a minute Brian joined her with two brimming martini glasses, carefully balanced not to spill a single drop.

"Cheers." He held out his glass.

She didn't feel very cheery, so she just clinked the

glass. After her first sip, however, she felt better. "You make a good martini. What's in this?"

"Tequila. It's called a martila. Annie, thank you for coming. You know how much I rely on your opinion." He gave her one of those deep male gazes that always made her feel important.

She lifted her hand to brush it away. She didn't want him relying on anything. She couldn't decorate his apartment or anything else. She had to go home.

"I really do," he said earnestly.

"Okay." She drank her cocktail and decided the tequila added a nice touch. Then she picked up a paperweight.

"See, you gave that to me," he said.

She nodded. Yes, she had.

"And I treasure it. I've got it on display." He put his hand on her knee. "We make a very good team, don't you think?"

Annie tried not to look at his lips as he spoke. Even though his apartment needed some attention, he had very desirable lips and pretty much desirable everything else. An excellent male body. She took another swig of martila and enjoyed the heat as it traveled down her throat. She also felt that furnace burning away much lower down. She could go home about now. Or . . . she could stay a little longer. She glanced around the room while she thought about it. There wasn't much to look at, so she checked out Brian's collection of cheap paintings. He had a rural scene with a cow in a pasture, a landscape in the kind of countryside he'd probably never seen himself. A seascape with what looked like a floundering sailboat. A windmill with some quaintly dressed Dutch people. No particular theme among the pictures emerged from closer scrutiny. It looked as if he'd bought a bunch of paintings in a five-for-twenty-five-dollar sale.

She jumped when his hand traveled across neutral territory and found her thigh.

"What do you say?" he murmured.

She crossed her legs and tugged at her skirt. "I'm very upset about this Teath situation. What are we going to do?" *And I have to go home now,* she didn't add. She could have moved away. She even thought about it for a moment, but she didn't. The truth was, she'd never done anything like this before and was curious about what he would do.

His fingers moved higher under her skirt, then paused there, letting her know he wasn't going away. He had something else in mind. "You'd have been fine if you hadn't listed everything," he murmured.

They'd been over this a dozen times. She made a disparaging noise.

"Do you have any other thoughts on the subject?" he asked.

"Is this an interview?" It occurred to her that even though two of his fingers were now circling her inner thigh, heading higher and higher, she might still be able to justify this meeting in Brian's apartment as work.

"No, no. Of course not." His lips touched her lips and set off some fireworks.

Annie felt hot all over. His lips touched hers again, and this time pressed a little. She wanted to return to the conversation, but forgot what they'd been talking about. What she did remember was her own admonition to the girls about this kind of thing: Do not go to boys' apartments. Do not pretend nothing is going on when they try to make out with you. Do not advance while holding off a decision about when to retreat. Suddenly she was back in high school.

"You have nice legs, Annie." Brian kissed her again, longer this time.

After a few seconds Annie turned her cheek and murmured, "Thank you."

He kissed her neck. He kissed her chin. "You know, you really have the best legs."

Annie was surprised. "Oh really, I always thought Darian had the best legs."

"She has nice legs, but yours are better." Brian stopped kissing to scrunch her skirt up higher and get a closer look at her thighs. "Very nice."

Pleased, Annie took the opportunity to drink some more martini. She suddenly realized that this was a lot more fun than being home. Brian explored the space between her legs, then freed his hands to untie his tie, pull it out of his shirt collar, and toss it on the floor. He started unbuttoning his shirt.

"Your turn," he said.

"What?"

"It's your turn, Annie. Blouse or skirt."

Ohhh, he meant she should take off her blouse or her skirt. Oh God, she was ambivalent.

"I'll give you a good time," he promised, leaning over to nuzzle her knee.

"Ah, Brian, the primary thing on my mind is this Teath case. I want to know what's going to happen." There, she got back on the subject. He moved away and started talking.

"Okay, okay. This is how I see it. If Dr. Teath makes a complaint to the NASD, the accusation against you will go on public record. You'll have it hanging over your head until the hearing, which may take as long as a year. You did break some rules, Annie, so a panel could easily rule for the old man. If they did, it could cost us penalties as well as the value of the missing bonds. Although I'd support you . . ." He shrugged about his bosses.

She didn't say anything.

"If you want to accuse a confused old man of fraud and murder, go for it." He made it seem like a poor idea. "Or else we won't go to arbitration. We'll save your hide, make a settlement, and do it really soon. How does that sound?"

Annie didn't answer. She was thinking of Ben—of the year he'd waited for arbitration, so sure all that time that he would win, only to lose in the end.

"Look, it happens all the time. A lot of clients make a lot of complaints of this nature. This is what I do. I manage these cases. If I want the Teath thing to go away, I can make it go away."

The fun was gone. Annie tugged at her skirt. "What about the consequences for me?" she asked slowly.

"This is what we have insurance for. There won't be any."

Annie wasn't sure she should believe him. "No personal liability?"

He shook his head. "If we settle, it doesn't become public, and no one but us will know."

"What if he doesn't want to settle?"

"Trust me, he'll settle." Brian smiled.

After that Annie wasn't sure exactly what happened. It certainly wasn't trust that happened. She took a moment to go to the bathroom. She washed her hands and face. She wondered at the possible reasons why Brian hadn't settled Matthew's case and saved them all a lot of pain. She considered going home. When she returned there was a fresh martila on the coffee table.

After that something changed. There was a moment when she was fully dressed and then a moment when her blouse was on the floor. Her skirt was on the floor. The

panty hose were on the floor. She was grappling with
Brian on the sofa wearing just the thong and matching
bra. The leather was cool and slippery and exciting on
her bare bottom. Then without her removing her bra it
was on the floor, too, and all she was wearing was the
thong. Brian stopped grappling and leaned back to stare
at her.

"Wow, Annie, you're so beautiful!"

"Really?" She was certain that her flesh had long ago
turned to cottage cheese.

"Are you kidding?" His lips found a nipple, and he
teased it with his tongue. "Oh God, you're perfect."

Me? Perfect? That was a totally new idea. Annie was
unused to the concept and also the narrowness of the
thong that had crept up so high it had become
the ultimate wedgie in the ultimate sensitive place. She
squirmed a little as Brian smiled at her from above, then
traced the curve of her waist and hips with the tips of his
fingers.

She liked the caress, but she didn't know what to do
with the smile. *I'm a married woman,* she thought. No
one but Ben knew how she looked naked. Brian's smile
made her uncomfortable. How could this end well? she
asked herself. It couldn't. But like every other woman in
a sticky position, she was conflicted. Part of her wanted
to get up and run. The other part of her wanted to see
what Brian would do. She wanted to see the bulge in his
blue plaid boxer shorts revealed for whatever it was.
What if it was a great one, better than Ben's?

Frankly she half believed that she deserved to see it.
She hadn't been anywhere near another man's penis for
half her life—more than half, because the first sixteen
years didn't count as life. How many men had she had
before Ben? Only a few. One in high school, two in col-

lege. Ben ever since. Didn't she deserve some time off for good behavior?

Smiling at her, Brian played with the strings circling her hips. Still debating, Annie realized she had to make a choice. She was there with her bare buttocks on the sofa and a really good-looking man hovering over her, kissing her breasts, then her lips. It felt good. Then, while kissing with his tongue deep in her mouth, he slipped his finger under the string.

Ah, relief from the pressure. Annie groaned with pleasure. After that she didn't have the will to think about anything. Brian knew where he was going, and he knew how to get there, and she stopped worrying about anything but feeling as the thong came off, and the real fun began.

thirty-four

"WOULD YOU DROP ME AT THE OFFICE?" MATTHEW made the request without any preliminary discussion. Already he had his office paraphernalia gathered around him. Umbrella, *Times*, briefcase. The funeral was over, and he was finished being nice for the day.

Even though his face had changed back to his work mode about an hour before, Carol wasn't prepared for such a quick defection. He'd read the paper on the way to her mother's funeral. He'd taken notes during lunch. Now that all the unpleasant business of the burial and two measly prayers was over, she'd expected him to spend at least a few hours of recovery time with her. Instead, he was going back to the office. Even though that kind of thing was par for the course for him, she was flabbergasted that he'd revert to type so soon after she'd so plainly told him she couldn't go on like this anymore.

"What?" Matthew said with that look of complete innocence that made her think his brain was missing some important gray matter. She'd read him the riot act. If he couldn't be a real husband to her he'd have to find another place to live.

"You don't go back to work after a funeral. It's disrespectful," she said.

"Your mother's gone. She won't care." He was so offhand about it he almost laughed at the idea.

They were in a limo on the way back from Staten Island. They'd taken her father to lunch in his favorite diner, then returned him to his house. He planned to stay there only for a few weeks before heading south to Florida. He'd refused such a move for years, but now he couldn't wait to go.

Matthew had been detached throughout the process of burying his late mother-in-law, but Carol was more connected to her past than she'd been in years. The final separation turned out not to be easy for her. The death of her mother changed her life in some important ways. Memories that no one else had were gone. Her childhood—unhappy as she'd felt it had been—was gone. Now neglectful Matthew didn't seem enough anymore.

"I didn't mean disrespectful to her. I meant disrespectful to me," she said softly.

"Oh, honey. I'm just going in for a few hours. I have a deposition tomorrow." Matthew gave her the rueful, half-apologetic shrug that always used to do the trick.

Carol shook her head. "We buried my mother today. Couldn't you spend a few hours with me so I can mourn with someone who loves me?" Ha ha, she wasn't so sure about that.

"Well, it's not as though you weren't prepared. You knew it was coming," he argued.

"Matthew, I need you to spend some time with me."

He looked out the window as they traveled across the Brooklyn Bridge. "I've got a lot to do. Maybe I'll be more on top of things this weekend. We can plan something for then."

"No, Matt, I need attention now." She didn't want to seem controlling. She didn't want to *be* controlling, but he was her husband. This was his job, too.

He smiled and squeezed her hand, then let it go. "I spent the morning with you," he told her in a voice that sounded eminently reasonable. He was a lawyer; he knew how to talk.

"You spent the morning with the newspaper," she corrected. She'd lived with a lawyer. She knew how to talk back.

"Oh Jesus. What do you want?" He rattled the newspaper with his knee, annoyed at being challenged about something he thought was petty.

"We need to be together. There are times people need to be together. We're never together."

"I don't know what you're talking about. I can't go over and over the same things with you," he said impatiently. "I just can't."

She stared at him and knew that this was how marriages ended. How many times could she let something important go?

"What?" he said again.

"Give me an example. What do we go over and over?" she asked.

He thought about it for a second, then resorted to his sheepish expression. "Okay. Look, I have a lot on my mind right now."

"I know you do, but I want to be the first thing on your mind."

"What are you talking about? Everything I do is for you."

She made an impatient sound. "You say that, but everything you do is for you. What's going on? Do you have a girlfriend?"

"Oh Jesus." He hugged his briefcase, rolled his eyes, looking panicked.

"Is that a yes? Is that a no? I never see you. You stay out all night and lie about it. My mother died. You didn't rush home to be with me. It's not normal, Matthew."

"You never liked your mother. That's not normal, either," he countered quickly.

"That's not the point. My life has changed. I can't go on the same way. I don't have any children. Without you, I'm alone."

"What is this, some crazy midlife crisis?"

"Matthew, what are your priorities?"

He shook his head. "Okay, okay. Your life has changed. I'll come home early. We'll go out to dinner. How about it?" He looked down at her hand and patted it perfunctorily. "There, that's the building," he told the driver.

Carol glanced at it. It was one of those big downtown buildings, official and imposing, looking nothing like the funky places where she went on her buying expeditions, nor like the stylish stores where her items were sold. Matthew worked in a monolith. He'd gotten so important. He was always doing some hugely vital deal that took precedence over everything. She hadn't had children because he never wanted any getting in the way. He didn't want her getting in the way. Her life had been absorbed into his. Pretty as the arrangement looked on the outside, it wasn't much of a life. She was nearly forty. Her mother was gone. She felt as if the belt on her treadmill had simply worn out. She didn't have to run for him or anyone else anymore.

The car slowed to a stop. She had one more moment to speak. She took it. "I don't think you love me," she said.

"Oh God, don't do this to me. I haven't got time for your moods. I have work today."

Moods? He called her feelings *moods*?

"Matthew, I don't think you love me," she said firmly. She glanced at his face but he gave her only his profile. She saw the jowls. She saw his middle-aged paunch. Matthew ate whatever he wanted, drank a lot, and didn't exercise. And now he wouldn't look at her.

"You've accused me of neglecting you, of having a girlfriend. What do you expect?" He got out of the car, leaned in, and added, "I'll see you later," as if that covered it all.

She didn't reply or show any sign that she'd heard. The car door slammed, and her heart hardened with the sound. All he had to do was say he loved her. That was all he had to do, and he couldn't do it. It was a half-hour ride home to the Upper West Side. As the car threaded its way through traffic, she thought about Annie Custer and Ben. She didn't know what she would have done if Matthew had had a breakdown and stopped working. She knew betrayal from a friend wouldn't have sunk his ship. Clearly he didn't care much for friendship. This wasn't the ending the four friends had planned for themselves. The men had fallen away from them like sand on an eroding beach.

Then Carol had a new idea. If she divorced Matt and Annie divorced Ben, they would have each other again, in the old comfortable way. She'd have the comfort of the two wonderful girls. Carol knew she would not get much money from her divorce. Matthew had no soul. He was a lawyer first. He would hurt her as he'd hurt Ben. He would bully and lawyer her to the death. He would win, right or wrong. It gave her a stomachache to think this was the kind of man she'd married.

As she neared Midtown, it occurred to her that although Matthew hadn't taken his fists to her, in his own way he'd been abusive. He didn't care about her point of view. He couldn't listen. Carol signed the receipt for the long day's use of the car and went home to her apartment with the grand view of Central Park. She put her purse down in the foyer and walked around the apartment, made so spare because Matthew had wanted it that way. No beads on the lamp shades, no funky colors. Just fashion-forward in the modern Italian manner. She tilted her head one way, then the other, and realized that she hated it. What the place needed was some really comfortable furniture, some clutter—colors that inspired a better mood. She started pondering a renovation. She wandered from room to room, measuring the spaces, and thinking about giving the furniture to Matthew for his new home. The bastard. She grew excited by the opportunity to re-create her world in her own vision, and even though she was alone, the afternoon flew by.

When the phone rang, she was surprised by how late it was. She was even more surprised by her caller.

"Carol, it's me."

"Hi, Dad."

When she heard his voice, she felt bad for him. He'd buried his wife only hours ago. He probably wasn't as pleased with his solitude as she was with hers. While she'd never had much of Matthew's attention, her father was alone for the first time in almost fifty years. She wondered what she should do for him. Maybe she should go get him, bring him back with her to the guest room where no guests ever stayed, cook him a meal, and let him chill out until he left for wherever he was going. Matthew had told her she wasn't normal. Taking care of her old dad would be the normal thing to do.

"I'm not good, baby," he said.

"I know. It was tough saying goodbye to Mommy." Carol was in a nostalgic mood.

"Oh, let's face it. Your mother wasn't so great."

"What?" Carol was jerked out of her warm feelings by the cold words.

"And that friend of yours stole my money. I'm going to the authorities."

"No, Daddy." She groaned. Oh God, he was back on the money.

"I have to sue them. That quarter of a million was all I had. I can eat dog food if I have to. But that money was mine."

"You won't have to eat dog food, Dad, all the securities are right there in the account. You'll have whatever you need, I promise."

"I'm not talking about the securities. I'm talking about the bonds. Those bonds were mine, and they're gone."

"Daddy, nothing's gone. It's all there. You'll see when the statement comes in."

"I saw the statement. The bonds were stolen."

"No." Carol was not sitting still for this.

"Don't tell me no. You don't know anything about it. You left home, and I don't blame you. Everybody has to grow up. But I had to stay, and let me tell you, I went through hell with your mother."

"I thought you were happy," she said faintly.

"Now I'm just an old man. And what do I have left? Dog food."

"Calm down, you're not going to eat dog food," she said sharply. She was stunned by the vicious attack on her poor mother, whose life she'd always suspected was a misery entirely because of him.

He cut in before she finished assuring him that he wouldn't starve. "There's nothing wrong with dog food. Pedigree is not so bad. I've eaten dog food from the day I married your mother. You don't know what that's about," he said venomously.

"Dad, I sent you Zabar's. You didn't eat dog food." She wanted to set the record straight.

"Never mind Zabar's. Your mother was a bossy woman. She was a shrew."

Carol had been pacing back and forth in front of the view. Lights sparkled all the way up to Harlem. This was too much. She sat with a *thud* on the hard Italian sofa. Her mother, bossy? Impossible. The woman couldn't bully a dust bunny. He should know, there were plenty of them around.

"Well, I know you miss her," she said, sounding feeble even to herself.

"Hell I do."

"Dad, you're just in a bad mood."

"No, little missy, I want my bonds. That's what I want."

"Dad, do you want to come into the city and spend some time with me?" she asked nervously.

"No, I do not. I will not live under the thumb of another woman if I live to be a million. Give me my money back so I can take care of myself."

Carol exhaled with relief. She didn't realize that she'd

been holding her breath, terrified that he might take her up on her offer.

"I'm on the rampage," he added.

"I can see that," Carol said glumly. "What do you need tonight?"

"I told that manager I was going to sue, and I will. That's what I need tonight. A good lawyer. Let me talk to Matthew."

"You had all morning to talk to Matthew," she reminded him. Now it was too late.

"I know, but I hadn't decided then. I want him now."

"Well, you'll have to find another lawyer. Matthew and I are getting a divorce."

There was silence for a moment, then a satisfied grunt. "Well, he wasn't so great, either."

"What!" Carol was stunned by all these pronouncements. Her mother wasn't so great. Her husband wasn't so great. Her best friend was a thief. It was too much to digest.

"What manager are you talking about?" she asked slowly. He wasn't talking about that cute guy at Hall Stale, was he? She didn't want to hear he was a bad guy, too.

"Don't be funny with me, young lady. You know who I mean. At that Stale company. What a terrible name. Wouldn't you think they'd get a better name for a stock house?"

"Dad, did you talk to the branch manager? Is that who you're talking about?"

"I talked to him. I told him I'm sending that woman to prison."

Carol pressed her lips together to prevent herself from screaming. What was he thinking? What was he doing? He was a crazy man. She'd always thought so. No wonder she'd left home. She'd had to get away. Now she had to set things straight. "Nobody stole anything. You have to stop this," she told him.

"I will not. I know what I know."

"Please, Dad, don't embarrass me with this. Just let it go."

"I'm not letting a quarter of a million dollars go out the window. Just ask her, go ahead, I dare you. Ask that Annie Custer where the money went. Right in her pocket, I'll bet."

"Okay, that's it." Carol got her father off the phone and called Annie at home. By then it was dinnertime, even for a lawyer, but Matthew hadn't called. Once again he'd broken his promise to come home early and take her out. More surprisingly, however, Annie wasn't home, either. Carol talked for some time to Mag. Mag was sympathetic about her mother's passing on and told her about her disastrous interview at Gift Boxes of America. She made it sound funny, but Carol knew she was deeply upset.

"Why don't you and I go out for lunch?" she suggested.

"I'd like that." Maggie sounded pleased. "It's creepy here. You know Dina's leaving. All she does is run around taking pictures."

"I heard. It must be upsetting with your dad hanging around all the time, too. I have an idea. Let's make an afternoon of it. I'll take a few hours off. Where do you want to go?" Carol asked.

"Paris. I haven't been anywhere since . . ."

"Oh yeah." Carol knew she meant 9/11. She had been to a lot of places since then, dozens of places. It occurred to her that traveling with someone would be a lot of fun. Why not Mag?

"Yes, you need to go somewhere," Carol told her, and wondered where that place should be.

thirty-five

WHAT DID PEOPLE FEEL WHEN THEY WENT HOME
after cheating on a spouse? Annie felt like shit. The
minute she was out of Brian's apartment and down on
the street she was running. She ran to the corner and
raised her hand for a taxi. She couldn't find one, so she
ran the six blocks home.

It was way past eight, and Dina's last supper was already in progress. Annie came into the kitchen and
found her family all seated at the table with the candles
burning and the food already served. Shit, she'd forgotten it was Dina's last night.

"Hi," she said, her cheeks flushed with shame.

No one returned the greeting.

"Sorry I'm late. I got tied up. God, it's freezing in
here." She shivered, then looked guiltily around the
table.

Mag had her suspicious face on. Very suspicious, but
that didn't worry her. Bebe looked a little spacey. That
did worry her. Ben was scarfing down chicken paillard
and risotto with wild mushrooms, oblivious to everything. Nothing short of a bomb blast would get to him.
Dina was all dressed up and fussing with her very last
cake for the Custer family. The cake said HAPPY BIRTH-
DAY A TODO, covering all the birthdays she would miss
down the road. Over there in Annie's place at the chilly

end of the table sat Brenda, calmly smoking a cigarette while everyone ate around her. Annie gasped at the ghost sitting in her chair. "What are you doing?"

"Eating. You didn't expect us to wait, did you?" Mag glanced pointedly at the kitchen clock.

"Where have you been?" Brenda asked.

"I was in a meeting." Annie shook her head at the ghost. *Beat it.*

"That makes every day this week." Brenda wasn't going.

Curly cowered under the table, growling angrily from the back of his throat.

"Oh please, I don't want to hear about it." Annie patted Dina on the shoulder. "What a beautiful cake. What kind?" she asked.

"Low-fat coconut from *Cooking Light*," Dina said.

"My favorite. Happy birthday to you, *también.*"

"You don't want to hear about what?" Mag demanded.

"I didn't mean you. Somebody's been smoking in here. I smell smoke."

"Don't look at me," Bebe said, even though a new pink stripe in her hair said the opposite. Annie ignored the stripe and pointed at her own occupied chair.

"Right there. Someone's smoking. Can't you smell it?"

"Nope," Mag said. "Did you see Bebe's dye job?"

"She's smoking right there," Annie insisted.

"Oh Jesus, not that again." Mag rolled her eyes. "There's no one there, Mom."

"I'm telling you she's right there," Annie said, as if vehement repetition would convince them.

"I'm guessing you were with your boyfriend," Brenda said.

"I don't have a boyfriend," Annie gasped.

Ben glanced up from his eating for the first time. "What about me?" he demanded. "Aren't I your boy-friend?"

So he was alive after all. "Oh, you," she said. That was a thing of the past.

"What do you mean, *Oh, you*?"

Bebe sniggered, and Mag frowned at her sister. "What's *your* problem?"

Bebe snickered some more.

"Where have you been?" Ben asked Annie with inno-cent eyes.

She lifted an eyebrow. "Have you been drinking?" she asked.

"No, but you have," he said, still looking at the chicken.

Uh-oh. "Ah, I did have a drink. One." She went over to her chair and put her hand right through her mother to wave away the smoke. "I want to sit here, please."

"Go ahead, who's stopping you?" Mag muttered.

The ghost didn't move. Dina turned around with the family camera in her hand. Dina clearly wanted to get a picture of that cake for her collection.

"Oh, good idea. Take some pictures." Annie pointed at her mother with the smoke rising from her cigarette.

Dina snapped the picture.

"I hope it comes out," Annie murmured, wishing that proof of her haunting could finally be established.

"I think she's been more than drinking." Bebe pulled on the pink section of her hair. *Look at me.* "The least she could do is share."

Three of the kitchen lights went off just then, and everybody looked up.

"She's gone now," Annie said with satisfaction and sat down in her seat.

thirty-six

AN HOUR LATER MAG REMEMBERED THAT CAROL
Mack had phoned ages ago urgently wanting to speak
to her mother. "Mom, did Carol reach you?"

"No, when did she call?"

"About eight. She said it was urgent."

"Okay." Annie hurried into her room to return the
call. She closed the door and lay down on her bed. Despite the stress at dinner, she now felt a secret guilty
pleasure at having something separate from her family,
something all her own. Something a little wild that
somehow didn't feel so terrible now that she was back in
the hell of family chaos.

She dialed Carol's number, and Carol picked up right
away. "Hello, Annie."

"How did it go? Are you all right?" Annie asked
slowly, remembering that it was funeral day and that she
hadn't been invited.

"Thanks for calling back tonight. It was tough. I'll
miss her . . ." Carol's voice trailed off.

"Of course. I've been thinking about you all day."
Annie heard a note in her friend's voice. Something was
up. "Are you all right?" she asked again.

"Not really. I think Matthew has a girlfriend."

How odd to hear that tonight of all nights. Somehow
it wasn't surprising. The man was never home, and he'd

been horribly disloyal to Ben. Disloyalty seemed to be a character flaw that spread wherever self-interest led it.

"I don't know for sure, but it will help in the divorce, won't it?" It sounded like Carol was fishing.

"Oh, Carol, are you breaking up again?" Annie wouldn't be unhappy about it. Two bad marriages going down at the same time.

"This time I mean it," she said.

"Did he go with you to the funeral today?"

"Oh yeah, he went. But he wasn't really there and he didn't help me with it. He didn't talk to Dad at all. He didn't even want to look at the will or anything. He told me I'm the executor, so I have to do the work."

"How much is there to do?"

"Not that much. Dad owns the house and contents. He has to deal with that . . ." She paused. "Annie, I want you to know that I've really missed you these last months. I guess we drifted apart."

The husbands and their differences had taken care of that. "I know. Me, too," Annie said.

"I miss the girls. Mag sounds so unhappy."

"Well, her whole class went to college, and she went to bed. How else could she feel?" Annie made herself more comfortable against the pillows. She felt both sad and angry at her daughter, and pushed away her own guilt for what had happened with Brian.

"What about therapy for her?" Carol suggested. She sounded so nice and concerned that Annie was lulled into a conversation that usually made her too anxious to explore.

"Ben has strong opposition. He doesn't think it works," she said slowly. "Mag follows her father's lead on things like this."

There was a long silence on the other end.

"Are you there?" Annie asked.

"Well, my mother never had therapy," Carol said slowly. "She was a depressive if I ever saw one, and look what happened to her. You have to nip this in the bud, Annie. Maybe medicine would help."

"Maybe." Annie was noncommittal. She knew that Carol was talking about Mag's depression, not Ben's, but she wondered if she could put Prozac in all their food. Bebe's, too. If she couldn't force them into treatment, how about tricking them into taking happy pills?

There was another long silence. Annie was upset about receiving a suggestion she couldn't take. She didn't know what to say to lighten the moment. But Carol's mother was dead. She was the one who needed consoling.

"Annie, I'm really sorry to have to tell you this." Carol said this so slowly and with such weight that Annie knew the subject had changed to business. Despite every effort to remain calm, she actually felt the ax begin to fall.

"My dad wants to sue Hall Stale."

There it was. Annie gulped. "Oh God," she murmured.

"He called Brian and told him you stole some bonds. I'm really sorry, Annie. I had no idea he'd do this."

"Oh *God*," Annie said again.

"Annie, please don't be mad at me. I'm going to take care of this. I know he's crazy."

Annie's mouth was as dry as a desert. Once again Carol surprised her with a generosity she hadn't expected. Carol had buried her mother. She was getting a divorce, but instead of thinking about herself she was thinking about Mag's depression and the trouble her father might cause Annie.

Everything evil that she'd done suddenly crashed in on Annie like a tsunami. She'd committed adultery. Worse, she'd slept with a colleague. Worse than that, she hadn't been honest with a friend. She hadn't told Carol about the missing bonds right away. And even worse than all *that,* her children were floundering. She had to take action. She had to come clean.

"Carol, your father's right," she blurted out.

"What?"

"There are some missing bonds."

"Missing bonds?" Carol sounded amazed. "Really? When did they go missing? How did it happen? Why didn't you tell me?" The questions tumbled out.

"Nothing like this has ever happened to me. Last week when I went to see your parents, it was—traumatic to say the least. I wasn't expecting—"

"—them to be living in such a place," Carol finished. "I know I should have warned you. I owe you an apology."

"And then there were so many certificates! It took hours to count them all."

"I'm sorry about that, too. I had no idea there was so much. Maybe you made a mistake about what was there."

Annie could hear Carol desperately trying to help her out, just as she'd stuck with her when Matthew accused Ben of purchasing stock without his permission. Matthew had lost money from a number of transactions he'd made, and accused his friend of making them without his consent. It had been his only hope of getting his money back. He'd sacrificed his friend for money, then lost far more money when he'd moved to another brokerage firm. Annie knew she had to tell the truth.

"No, there's no mistake. I made a list of everything that went into the shopping bag I took. The only problem occurred when I got back to the office after four. Everything went into the vault without being recorded. That night you called me and wanted it all back. I was so upset about your mother's condition I wasn't even thinking about the bonds."

"But what *happened*?" Carol's voice had the brittle edge of panic. She hated to lose money as much as her husband did.

"The compliance people wouldn't let anything out of the office until we'd recorded everything that had come in. So the next day we started counting it and two hundred and sixty thousand dollars' worth of bearer bonds wasn't there."

"Oh Jesus, Annie, why didn't you tell me this last week?"

"Honestly, when it came up, I couldn't believe it. It was such an unusual situation. I've never lost anything in my life. Just my keys, you know . . ." She waited for a laugh but didn't get one.

"And then you sounded so angry at me when your father wanted it back. It was just crazy. After what Matthew did to Ben, I just . . . I don't know. I didn't want to lose you as a friend. I'm sorry."

"A quarter of a million dollars. How long were you going to hold out on me, Annie?"

"I wasn't holding out," Annie said. "I was digesting. I'm really sorry."

"Oh God. Jesus. Would you have kept this secret if my dad hadn't said anything?"

"No," Annie said quickly. "No, no. It would have been taken care of. You'll be reimbursed." She wanted to spill her suspicion that Carol's father had the bonds, that he was trying to double his money. But how could she do that the day her mother was buried?

"Does your manager know all this?"

"Of course. He knows everything. He's the one who assured me insurance would take care of it. After the investigation, of course." Now she was talking reimbursement; what happened to her principles?

"Are you having an affair with him?" Carol said suddenly.

Oh God, why was she back on men? "Of course not," she said quickly.

Carol let her breath out in a whistle. "Well, that's one good thing."

"Why?" Annie was practically drowning in all her lies.

"I like him," Carol said. "Maybe he'll call me so we can talk about all this."

"Ah, yeah. I'll tell him," Annie promised.

"And tell Mag I'm thinking about taking her to Florida. Call it a belated graduation present."

"Really?" Annie was stunned. Where did that come from?

thirty-seven

AS SOON AS ANNIE WAS OUT OF THE APARTMENT, Brian called her on her cell phone. He thought it was important to tell her again he'd had a good time, that he respected her as a broker and a woman, and that everything was going to be all right. Unfortunately her cell phone was off, so he couldn't tell her. Furthermore, he didn't think it would be right to leave that kind of message. He shrugged to himself and put the phone aside only to pick it up and try again five minutes later. The cell was still off.

He poured himself another drink, then sat on the sofa naked, fondling his penis as he thought about all the things he liked about Annie. It was a very pleasant occupation for a few minutes. But soon his drink was all gone, and only the melting ice was left. Then he started worrying about her having to go home to a husband she hated. No one should have to do that. He headed for the shower, thinking that he was going to rescue her from a terrible fate. As he soaped himself down, he congratulated himself on his plan for getting Annie for himself. Of all the women he knew, she was the one he liked the most. Ever since they'd met, she'd been his unattainable ideal, the good wife who'd both worked *and* stayed home. Everything about her was exactly right. She never went to the free lunches the big corporations threw for their IPOs. She wasn't a parasite on the firm, or her clients. She didn't buy and sell just to generate income for herself as some brokers did. Most of the complaints he had to deal with were frivolous cases of people trying to get back money they'd lost in the course of doing business and taking risks. But some cases were well founded. Brokers did a lot of things they shouldn't do, buying and selling when they felt like it, just for the commissions. Most of the time they didn't get caught. Sometimes they did, and the firm had to pay reparations. And sometimes brokers became ensnared in messy situations not of their own making. Ben came to mind.

Brian knew that Annie really did think of the needs of her clients first. It hadn't been smart to help her friend Carol, but getting caught up in the mess had humbled

her. And frankly he liked her better humbled. Gone was
the know-it-all Annie. This Annie wasn't in such a hurry
to go home to her washed-up husband. She wasn't so
snippy and contemptuous of him. And surprise, she was
a tiger in bed. But there was more to Brian's attraction
than this short list. He admired her for having no enemies. Everybody liked her. Everybody. Nobody had a
mean thing to say about Annie Custer. Her girls were
beautiful. He wouldn't mind being a stepdad to them.
One of them was out of the house, graduated from high
school and gone. The other one could live with her
father. He didn't know anything about children, but
these children were already grown. He didn't think they
would be a problem to the relationship.

Brian was already planning the rest of his life when he
got out of the shower and dialed her number. The phone
rang while he toweled himself dry. Annoyed that the cell
phone was still off, he checked his watch. Even if Annie
had walked home, she should be there by now. He considered dialing her home number. After all, he was the
branch manager. He could call any employee anytime he
wanted to. He hesitated, not really wanting to talk with
either Ben or the two pretty girls. He decided that the
thoughtful thing would be to wait a little while in case
she was having dinner. And that led him to food.

Meals in general made Brian anxious, so Annie's having dinner somewhere else, and without him, was doubly upsetting. He did not like to eat alone. Every lunch
and every dinner was an issue. He had to come up with
some date, some male friend, someone to eat with him
every day. Managing a stream of people with whom to
eat was more time-consuming than managing the office.
Tonight he was disappointed that his new love interest
had gone home, and he knew that he could avoid the

dinner issue by going to the gym. But after the martilas and the lovemaking, he didn't feel like getting all sweaty on a stupid treadmill.

Since he couldn't think of anyone to call this late and didn't feel like ordering in, he finally pulled on a pair of jeans, a black Polo shirt, and a leather jacket. Still a little buzzed from the alcohol and the prospect of a new life, he walked slowly over to Third Avenue. As he walked, he dialed Annie's cell a few more times just in case she'd turned it on again. She hadn't, but that didn't daunt him. He was just so elated.

Annie on his sofa had been an excellent event, better than Mary Beth, who was actually quite a dullard in bed. She'd moved in a wooden kind of way and hadn't been able to learn how to touch him right. Annie, however, had the touch. She didn't need instruction. And she had the look. *And* everybody liked her. That meant a lot to him. He went over his list and it didn't change. Annie seemed very right.

Outside, night had settled in, but Third Avenue was crowded with people on their way home or their way out, people looking for food and maybe an instant friend. Brian mingled for a while without talking with anyone. As he did every night, he was thinking that it was time for him to settle down, but tonight he really had someone in mind. He was cranked up enough to enter the raucous Café Daum and seek out a solo table, so pleased with himself that he didn't even mind ordering a skirt steak and frites, then eating them all by himself. He'd sorted everything out in his mind. He was done searching for love.

thirty-eight

AFTER DINNER WAS OVER AND DINA WAS GONE, Annie took a quick bath, put on a pair of Bebe's cast-off jeans and a tank top, and went to see her older daughter. Maggie was lying on her bed, depressed and watching a rerun of *Top Model*. When Annie opened the door of the room, the first thing she saw was the hole in the ceiling around the chandelier where moldering plaster used to be.

"Oh God, when did that happen?" she asked, certain that this morning the ceiling had been intact.

"Today. It was a huge mess." Mag seemed unconcerned about it.

"Who cleaned it up?"

"Dina."

"On her last day?" Annie shook her head. "Margaret, you've seen that show a dozen times. Could you look at me for one minute?"

Mag took her eyes off the screen. "Surprise. Gift Boxes doesn't have any openings," she announced.

Annie's heart sank. She'd forgotten all about that. "Oh, that's too bad," she murmured.

"It was a stupid fiasco," Mag said bitterly. "I felt like a total idiot. Thanks for the help, Mom."

Annie searched for some comforting words. "Oh well, something else will come up."

"Yeah, right." She paused. "Are you and Dad getting divorced?"

"What?" Annie was taken aback.

"It's a simple question. Yes or no?"

Annie didn't know what to say. "Did you and Carol talk about that?"

"No. Have you told Dad what you're up to?" Maggie sat up and made room for her mother on the bed. Finally Mag wanted to talk, but Annie wasn't in the mood.

Annie sat down and wished she could give her daughter a hug and a pep talk. She knew that a hug would be taken the wrong way, and she was ambivalent about the pep. Life was complicated. Planes crashed into buildings. Countries made war. People disappointed each other in so many ways. Marriages imploded. And people cheated when they shouldn't. Even mothers were human. For the first time in her life Annie couldn't talk about any of that. She didn't think mothers should be human. She herself had wanted to be better than human. Now that she'd lost the moral high ground, she had to change the subject.

"Carol's mother was buried today, did you know?"

Maggie nodded. "Of course, but she doesn't care. They weren't close." The way she blew it off offended Annie.

"Oh, she cares. Mothers are important even when they're not good ones." Well, she could say *that*.

Mag gave her a look. *Please.*

"It's true. I still miss my mother. I think about her all the time. What did you and Carol talk about?"

"She's sorry she didn't have kids, like you're sorry you did."

"Hey, I'm not sorry I had kids," Annie protested. "I love my kids."

"Oh please." This time Mag said it out loud. "Even

my room is rejecting me. Maybe I should go and be Carol's daughter. She has a great guest room and no problems with her ceilings."

"No." *Only her father, mother, and husband,* Annie thought.

Mag laughed softly, and the cold damp wind that chilled Annie so often settled over her again. Even though she knew that daughters were born to hurt and she shouldn't let it get to her, she was mortally wounded. Then Mag did something that truly amazed her.

"God, give me strength," she said dramatically, putting the back of her hand against her forehead and gazing up as if for help from above. Mag thought she was parodying her mother, but sounded instead exactly like the grandmother she'd never met.

Annie was shocked. Brenda had used this exact gesture and tone of voice whenever her children annoyed her, but Annie was sure she'd never made that gesture herself in her whole life. "I love you, Maggie. You and Barbara are all I have," she said softly.

Mag gave her a skeptical look. "If you break up with Dad, I'll go live with Carol. Then you won't have to worry about me anymore."

Annie punched a pillow. She was getting into deep water here. She didn't want her daughter knowing her thoughts before she did. "I'm not worried about you. I know you're all right." Instead of going on about all the good that might come of a divorce, she knew enough to shut up.

"Not with this brain tumor, I'm not," Mag said.

"You don't have a freaking brain tumor. You had a brain scan, remember? Your brain is perfect," Annie reminded her. It cost more than a thousand dollars. *She* wasn't going to forget it.

"That was two months ago. The tumor was too small to see then. Now I'm much worse," Mag said.

"Well, if you're so sick that you can't go to college and you can't make a real effort to look for work, how come you're doing so well at those expensive *golf lessons*?" Annie instantly hated herself for being a mean-spirited accountant who had to add up what everything cost. Why did she do that?

"What does golf have to do with anything?" Now both of them were hurt, and Mag turned back to the TV. Annie was forced to return to her room with some seriously lost ground.

As she headed down the hall, she reviewed the situation. Why couldn't Carol find her own man and children? Better yet, why couldn't Ben go and Dina come back? At least Dina was useful. When Annie opened the door, she was surprised to find the husband she intended to leave sitting there waiting for her.

"Hi." She hesitated in the doorway.

"Did you see Mag's ceiling?" he asked.

She nodded, still hanging back.

"I had a long talk with the super. He wants to open up the whole ceiling and take a look. I said I thought it was a good idea. It'll be a mess, but I'll be here to oversee the project. Maybe we'll get it right this time." He sat in the armchair by his side of the bed. He was wearing long pants for a change. He'd even shaved and gotten a haircut that day.

Annie didn't say anything. For once he'd said the right thing and taken the wind out of her sails.

"You look really pretty. Did you do something different?" he asked.

With this she froze. "Different?" Numbly, she shook her head. How did they know these things?

"Well, you look just great. Did anybody ever tell you how great you look in a tank top?"

"I don't know. Maybe a long time ago," she said slowly.

"Maybe too long ago. How was your day?" He had a pleasant expression on his face and vaguely resembled someone she used to know but hadn't seen in quite a while. Considering the situation, it was a disturbing sight.

Why was he asking about her day? She answered slowly, "There are problems with Carol. Her father's making a complaint."

He looked concerned. "How much is at stake?"

Annie lifted a shoulder. "Two hundred and sixty thousand."

He whistled. "Why is he suing?"

She thought she'd told him this. "He set me up. A little bait and switch. I put the bonds in the bag. He took them out. It looks as if I stole them."

"Jesus, Annie. This sounds familiar."

She nodded.

"Are you just going to stand there, or are you coming in?"

She had the sinking feeling that she was caught cheating, probably tattled on by her own daughter. "I can see how people just disappear and never come back," she murmured.

"It's not that bad, is it?"

Yes, it was. She took a few steps into the room and tried not to look at the bed. The marriage was over. She did not want to get in bed with him. Then he surprised her again.

"I've been really tough on you," he said after a moment. "I'm sorry."

He was sorry. It was the last thing she expected to hear.

"I can be difficult. I understand why you want to run away. I've been a slug."

Silence.

"Annie, I really meant to get going a lot sooner. But the days kept going by, and I couldn't count them. I don't know how to explain it. But as soon as you're out of the game, it doesn't seem so important anymore." He sat with his head bent and his hands between his knees. "I know I've let you down."

Annie's eyes filled with tears. She realized that this was what she'd been waiting for. Her husband was confessing. And he seemed so genuinely contrite that for a second she had to fight the impulse to save him from any further pain by telling him it was all right.

"Must be something in the water," she said. "We have three divorced guys in the office alone right now, and not because they want to be. Carol's divorcing Matthew."

Ben sucked in his breath. "Really?"

Annie shook her head. "It's not like the old days when you guys dumped us for younger women just because you could. It's different now. We're the ones walking out. And frankly a lot of us don't care if we never get another man for the rest of our lives."

"What's this *we*? Are you leaving me, Annie?" Ben asked.

"Think of the advantages. No one will tell you what to do anymore. No one will complain. You won't have to hear my opinions. You can live exactly the way you want to. Never wash up. No responsibilities . . ." She lifted her hands.

He grimaced. "Is that how you see me?"

"I just want you to be happy, Ben. And that's not something I can do for you." God knows, she'd tried.

"But what do you want for yourself?" If he was angry, he didn't show it. He just asked the question as if he really wanted to know.

The phone rang before she could answer. She hurried across the room to pick up. She had a feeling it was Brian, but she said, "Hello, Carol?"

"No, it's Brian. I'm dying here. Have you told him about us yet?" he asked.

thirty-nine

CAROL DIALED BRIAN REDFIELD'S HOME NUMBER WITH some trepidation. She'd found it in the Manhattan phone book and studied it for an hour before daring to call. She thought she'd go out of her mind if she didn't talk to somebody, and frankly she didn't know who else to call. Her crazy father had told her that her best friend was a thief. Her best friend had just admitted that a whole bunch of money was missing from her father's stash and that Annie hadn't been about to tell her.

At first she'd really believed what Annie told her. She thought their friendship was more important than money. But an hour later she wasn't so certain. Two hundred and sixty thousand dollars was a lot of money, and she knew that Annie needed it. It occurred to her that Matthew's case had involved the same amount of money and that Annie might have taken her father's bonds to get back at them for the Ben debacle. What if, after all they'd been through as friends, money was more important to Annie than she was? She knew that Matthew would behave this way, but Annie? Carol wanted to tear her hair out when she thought Annie was capable of such a thing. After a long debate with herself, she finally called Brian. She figured he'd know.

He picked up after about six rings. "Hello?" His voice was fuzzy.

"Hi, were you sleeping?" Carol's voice was tentative. Annie had told her he had a girl a week. Maybe he was with one of them now.

"Who is this?" he asked.

"It's Carol, Carol Mack. I wanted to thank you for the flowers. They were beautiful." She almost swooned at the sound of his voice. He sounded so nice, just the opposite of her mean-spirited husband.

"Oh, Carol. Sorry, I just walked in the door from dinner. Just give me a second to go to the other phone . . ."

"I'm sorry to bother you so late. Is this a bad time?"

"No, no. Of course not. I told you to call me anytime. What can I do for you?"

"I got some disturbing news," Carol said slowly.

"Oh?"

"How well do you know Annie Custer?"

"Pretty well. What's the problem?"

Carol hesitated. "I'm really sorry to call you at home. I have no one else to ask. My father is unreliable."

"It's not a problem. This is what I'm here for. Fire away."

"My father called and told me some bonds were missing."

"Uh-huh."

"And I didn't believe him."

"Uh-huh," Brian said again.

"Then I spoke to Annie a little while ago."

Silence.

"She told me my dad was right. A lot of money is missing. What's the story?"

She could hear Brian inhale. "You know, I'm not really sure. Nothing like this has ever happened before."

"Did Annie take the bonds?" Carol said slowly.

"Oh no, no, no. We don't think that's a possibility."

Carol realized that she'd been holding her breath. "How do you know?"

"Oh, I'd stand by Annie in a tornado. She's as straight as they come. There has to be some simple explanation. Do you have any ideas yourself?"

Carol thought of the mess in her father's house. She knew he could lie. She could think of a lot of simple explanations. "Maybe I should ask my father again. We could search the house. Who knows, maybe . . ."

He jumped on it. "That would be a good idea. Would you do that? I wouldn't like to have to send an investigator out to bother him at a time like this."

"Oh God. My father told me he's going to sue. What will happen?"

"Don't worry, we'll take care of you," he said.

"You will? No matter what?" Carol was doubtful.

"Yes. It's not going to be a problem." Brian's voice was confident.

Carol wondered what would happen to Annie if she'd done something wrong. She wondered what Brian really meant about taking care of her. She liked him and could almost feel the heat of his body right through the phone.

"Great," she murmured. "I feel a lot better now."

forty

ANNIE WAS IN BRIAN'S OFFICE BY NINE A.M. RIGHT
away she was distressed by the clumps of brown powder
on his desk from spilled cocoa mix. Why couldn't he just
drink coffee like everybody else? Instead of feeling transformed by their romp on the sofa and the knowledge
that he was a good lover, she was flooded by her feelings
from the past: that Brian was just a little boy playing at
being a man.

"Brian, I'd appreciate it if you didn't call me at home
again," she said in a starchy tone.

"Good morning, Annie," he replied serenely. "And
how are you today?"

"I'm a little edgy." That was an understatement.
She'd slept with a colleague. She'd succumbed to the
biggest no-no in the book. It had been a terrible night,
and she was late coming in.

"Want some cocoa?" He offered her a packet from his
drawer.

"No thanks," she said coldly.

"Calm down, Annie. Everything's going to be fine,"
he promised.

She shook her head. "No, I can't calm down. I want
to talk about your calling me at home last night. You
can't do that, okay. Let's get our boundaries straight."

"You told Ben about us, right?" Brian was impecca-

bly dressed in a heather tweed suit. His tie was blue, and
he smelled delicious even from all the way across the
room. But Annie happened to know that his bed was
merely two mattresses on the floor, and that he slept in a
tangle of sheets and damp towels after working out and
downing way too many vodka martinis.

"No, Brian, I didn't tell Ben anything," she said.

"But you know how I feel about you," he said with
the whine she knew so well.

She closed the door to his office and sat in her usual
place. "I wouldn't have told Ben for anything in the
world. It would have been stupid and cruel." Annie put
her lips together firmly. On the most practical level,
telling him would only make a divorce settlement much
more expensive. But that wasn't the real reason. The
night before, Ben had been rational, even distinctly sweet,
for the first time in years.

"Ben, let's just admit it's over and get a divorce,"
she'd said, and he'd just nodded.

"If that's what you want, Annie. I won't stand in your
way." His shoulders weren't hunched in any sort of
brokenhearted way. He was as straight as the clubs in
his golf bag. "Don't worry about me, honey. I can manage. I'll be fine," he'd said bravely.

With men, particularly spoiled men, this sort of thing
just didn't happen. "What?" It was the last thing Annie
expected to hear, and she had been completely taken
aback.

"It's not a problem. I can move out, or you can move
out. It's fine. We'll manage." Then, in an amazingly generous gesture, he'd held out his arms. "Come here, baby.
Give me a hug." And they'd hugged all night.

This morning Annie had some second thoughts about
Brian and wanted to take a few steps back. In fact, she

wanted to take the entire drunken experience back. How could she manage the situation?

"Look, we have to be careful and think about this, Brian," she said slowly.

"Well, I don't have to think about it. I had a great time. I like you." He smiled as if his liking her covered it all.

"Ah, but there's more to life than a great time." She happened to be very sober now. "There are issues that have to be resolved before we can think about ourselves," she went on.

"Well, I guess you're just not the afterglow kind of girl," he summed up irritably.

"Brian, one quick fling on a sofa doesn't change everything overnight—"

"It wasn't *that* quick," he protested.

"You know what I mean," she murmured.

"Well, you could move in with me. That would change things overnight."

She held up her hand. The idea of paying for her own apartment and all of her family's living expenses so she could sleep on the floor with Brian was not what she had in mind.

Brian opened another envelope of Swiss Miss. More brown powder spilled out on his desk. "Okay, I can see where you're going with this."

"Be sensible. You know there can't be any appearance of a personal relationship. We got ahead of ourselves. Now we have to step back."

"You're right, of course. Until this Teath case is resolved, we'll have to go away for the weekends. What?"

"Brian, I have a family. I can't go away for weekends."

"Fine, fine. Then I'll have to get a settlement. That's all there is to it."

"A settlement of what?" Annie needed to get out of there. She was having trouble breathing.

"I'm telling you. This isn't going to be a problem. I'll get insurance to cover those bonds, or most of them. Well, at least half." He shrugged.

"Why can't we have an investigation?"

"Oh, we don't need an investigation. I've got it covered. Now tell me about Carol Mack," he said.

Annie was alarmed. She was distracted. Had she missed something? "What about her?" she asked cautiously.

"Well, she called me last night at home."

"Oh no." Annie groaned.

"Uh-huh. She wants my advice about her situation with her father, allocation of assets, all kinds of things. And she wanted to know if you had taken her bonds. She sounded so upset I felt sorry for her."

"Jesus, Brian, you have to be so careful here. If she thinks you and I have a relationship, it would be really dangerous."

"Why?" He looked innocent.

"Brian, listen to me. Carol is off-limits for now, okay?"

"Why?" Brian stirred his cocoa.

"If she thought you and I were—" Annie wiggled her fingers. "She'd kill me."

"Why?" he asked again.

"Women are competitive, okay." Annie wanted to leave it at that.

"What does that mean?" Brian shook his head as if he didn't get it.

"It's hard to explain. You'll just have to trust me on this."

"Can't I give her investment advice?"

"No, Brian, you can't. As long as it's my account, I

have to manage it my way. You have to tell her I'm great and leave it at that."

"Okay, fine . . . Annie are you going to be available for a Yankee game on Friday?"

"What?" Annie didn't know how they'd gotten to the Yankees. They'd been talking about discretion, her need to manage her own clients. She couldn't let him mess up her life in the name of liking her. The man was needy. Needy men were loose cannons. She stared at him with dismay.

"I have tickets for the game. I'm going to take clients and I want you to be there with me."

"Ah." Annie didn't know why air was having so much trouble getting down into her lungs. She'd just told him she wasn't going away for weekends. She'd told him she couldn't gallivant around town with him, either, and he hadn't heard a thing. The man was a management problem. No wonder all his girlfriends left him. Someone knocked on the door.

"Come," Brian said.

Annie grimaced at the word as Petra stuck her head in.

"I need you, Annie," she said.

"Great, I'm coming." Annie tried to unclench her jaw as she hurried out into the hall.

"Vartan Vole is here," Petra said excitedly.

"No kidding." Annie hurried around the curve of the building to her office and stopped at her door. The mystery man who had them all running around like headless chickens was sitting in her office with a leather briefcase on his lap, and he looked like a thug. Thick-necked and bushy-haired, he had a belligerent face and a cheap suit that smelled of sweat even across the room.

"How do you do, Annie Custard? Isn't that a famous battle?" He did not stand to greet her.

"Ah, not really," she murmured.

From his sitting position, he stuck out his hand, expecting her to move forward and take it. She hesitated just a second, then slowly crossed the space between them and offered two fingers.

"How nice to finally meet you. Please sit down," he said as if it were his office and not hers.

She frowned.

"It's okay. I have some business for you. I know you'll be pleased." He flushed as he said it. He certainly was pleased.

She moved to the swivel chair behind her desk and sat down without a word. He immediately opened his briefcase and took out a wad of stock certificates.

"A personal delivery. Now you'll be happy," he said with a big grin.

"What's this?" Annie asked, excited in spite of herself.

"Ten million dollars' worth of IBM. I want them deposited in my account pronto." He smiled some more.

Numbly, Annie reached for one and studied it. The date was September 23, 1989. What was IBM in '89? The name on the certificate was Andre Albertise. She sighed.

"Ah, Vartan, I can't deposit this. It's not registered in your name," she told him.

"It's okay. He's deceased," Vartan said happily.

Annie frowned. "That doesn't make any difference, Vartan. It's not in your name."

"So what, I bought it at auction. Worth ten million. I bought it for five. That's a good deal, huh? I want you to deposit them. I'll leave four million in the account and we transfer six out to my account in Canada."

Well, there was no question Annie wanted Vartan's account. She'd wanted it since the first time he'd called with one of his crazy promises. It would be so nice to get a second major account in only days. But she was suspicious. It didn't ring true. "I didn't know you could buy stocks at auction," she said slowly.

"Oh, Annie Custard, you can buy anything at auction. Motorcycles, boats. Coins, antiquities. Anything."

"But how would stock certificates get to an auction house?" She'd never heard of such a thing.

"Andre lived in Europe. He died. His relatives didn't know how to negotiate the American system, but I'm a savvy businessman. I know a good deal when I see one. Of course I bid on them, and I got them. It's very good to give you business, Annie Custard." He dumped the pile on her desk. "Please deposit them right away. I need that transfer immediately for good works."

Annie punched a button on her phone. "Petra, would you ask Brian to come into my office?" She'd just gotten away from Brian. It was just her luck that Vartan was bringing him back.

forty-one

BRIAN HURRIED INTO ANNIE'S OFFICE, SMILING AS IF she'd summoned him for a tryst. He stopped short when he saw a stranger sitting in his usual chair. His face made an almost comical change.

"This is Vartan Vole. Our branch manager, Brian Redfield." Annie introduced them quickly.

Vartan stuck out his paw, and Brian shook it somberly.

"Pleased to meet you," Vartan said in a hearty voice with a trace of an accent.

Brian eyed him coolly and nodded, making a point of not staring at the pile of stock certificates on Annie's desk. "Pleased to meet you, too." He glanced at Annie for clarification, but she wouldn't help him out.

Vartan's chest puffed. "I have ten million dollars in IBM that I want deposited in my account, and I don't have all day to talk about it. My limo is waiting for me downstairs. I'm flying to Zurich at noon."

"Really," Brian said. Then he did the same thing Annie had done. He picked up a certificate and studied it.

Vartan bristled. "I've never seen people like you. I bring you a ten-million-dollar account and you turn up your nose."

"Nobody's turning up a nose," Brian replied genially. "But this is highly unusual." He held up the certificate and leafed through to the middle of the stack where he chose another three at random.

"I told Miss Custard here that I need six million wired out to my Canadian account before four P.M.," Vartan said impatiently.

"These aren't in your name." Brian glanced up from the two certificates he held in each hand.

Vartan pointed a thick finger at him. "I get it. You're not the manager," he said. "Where's the real manager?"

Brian flushed a deep red. "Oh, I'm the real manager. Where did you get these?"

Vartan's fleshy face said *None of your business*, but his lips moved with another set of words. "I bought the lot at auction for five million dollars. I want this nice lady to have my account. I pledge that I'll leave four million here, okay? I like her. She can invest it for me. I need the rest for my good works." He said this in a magnanimous tone.

Brian shook his head as if puzzled.

"What's your problem?" Vartan demanded.

"They're not in your name."

"They're perfectly legit," Vartan sputtered.

"That may be. But we'll have to do some checking."
Brian didn't want to chase the account away, but he had
to be honest. "It will take a few days."

"A few *days*? Why?" Vartan showed outrage.

Brian gave him his wolfish little smile. "It's just routine."

Annie nodded. *Thank you, Brian.*

He turned to grin at her. See, it was easy taking care of
a woman. There was a high five in his smile. He could
keep Annie happy, no problem. Maybe the account
would pan out.

Vartan glowered. "Check it out for what; don't you
trust me? Billions of dollars flow through my accounts
every day. I'm strictly legitimate, ask anybody."

Well, they had asked around, but no one seemed to
know anything about Vartan Vole. Brian pushed the pile
of certificates back across the desk.

"Look, if you need money in a hurry, you can try to
take these somewhere else. If they're legitimate, they will
get deposited in due course. But," he added, "I'm certain
that no one will let you margin anything on this today."

"It's not margining to draw on an account with ten
million in it."

"We can't let you take millions out before the millions
go in," Brian said seriously. If they allowed a transfer of
money from an account with stolen or fake certificates
in it, the money would be gone and Hall Stale would be
the loser. They were hungry, but they weren't stupid.

"Oh well. I understand." Vartan made a move to
leave. Then he stopped. "How about transferring the

bare bones for me? Say two million? I have a school program for Head Start kids that's going into deficit."

Brian shook his head. "I'll be happy to do it as soon as our compliance people give us the go-ahead."

"Okay, of course. Check it out." Vartan conceded defeat and paced all the way to the door. There he paused to give Annie a hard look. "I'll call you from the airport, Mrs. Custard," he said. "I hope you'll have it sorted out by then."

Ten minutes later Frisk, Darian, Annie, and Brian were gathered around the table in the conference room with Vartan's pile of stock certificates in front of them.

Frisk flipped through them and whistled. "I can't believe two certificate cases in one month. I've never seen anything like it. Who is this Albertise anyway?"

"Vartan said he's deceased," Annie said.

"Oh, another deceased person, of course." Frisk frowned. "Is this a relative of a client, too?"

"No," Brian said quickly. "This is nothing like the Teath case." Instantly he was sorry he said it, because they all looked at him expectantly.

Darian was the one to mention the elephant in the room. "What are you doing about that?" she asked.

"We're probably going to settle." Brian didn't look at Annie.

Frisk jumped on it. "So fast? What's the hurry?"

"We don't need any more negative press. Dr. Teath is a litigious guy. If there was a clean way to save the firm the money and the loss of face, I'd go for it in a heartbeat. But let's face it. Better to settle up and keep the account." Brian shrugged.

Everybody looked shocked, so he added quickly, "I'm opting for the human solution."

Annie shook her head.

He glared at her. "What?"

Darian quickly changed the subject to the Vartan Vole certificates. "So where did *this* little stash come from?"

"Some ridiculous story. He says he purchased them at auction," Annie said.

"What auction?" Darian sniffed.

"I gather we don't have any provenance on this," Frisk said.

"Doesn't mean they aren't genuine," Brian said equitably.

"Okay, fine. I'll take one and send it out for verification." He held the certificate up to the light and shrugged. "Who knows, maybe it's genuine."

"Good," Brian said. It wouldn't be hard to find out. Every stock certificate was registered. If the name and numbers didn't pop up, then they'd know in a few days.

"What about the serial numbers on those bonds?" Annie asked. "Now that they're officially missing, can we do something about it?"

Frisk glanced at Brian. "I'm glad you asked about that. I took the liberty of sending out a memo on it. All of our offices and several hundred banks have the serial numbers on their lookout list. They're pretty careful about checking those numbers before paying out. If someone tries to redeem them, we may get lucky."

Brian nodded absently. He was doing the human thing and feeling good about it. He planned to give Carol a call, maybe ask her to lunch so he could explore how much she'd be willing to accept in settlement. He was annoyed with Annie because of all the cruel things she'd said that morning. And he remembered that he'd always thought that she had a cold and withholding streak in her personality.

forty-two

CAROL'S WORK HAD BEEN INTERRUPTED BY HER mother's sudden death. She'd been collecting small summer pleasures in a tropical theme for the summer span. Not Caribbean or Hawaiian this year but more in the style of Florida. Everything with shells, with fish, with palm fronds and coconuts. She was thinking neon flamingos. She was thinking Florida, where her father planned to go. As her mother had hung on in her private limbo, Carol had been stuck in the quicksand of Easter. She hadn't had a moment to breathe before summer was sucking her into its two-part program of planning items that would both sell in the flagship stores that dotted the major cities and tempt readers of the catalogs that were mailed to tens of thousands of homes nationwide. Her assistant, a fussy man she called Herm the Germ, was trying to usurp her. Whenever she was out of the office, he undercut her by lying about where she was and what she was doing. So now she didn't dare leave.

A death in the family, like sex, had no place in her busy schedule. She and the rest of her department had already been planning for the following autumn long before they ever attacked spring. The problem was the seasons came on them at a punishing pace, always pushing them forward into a future they themselves never had time to enjoy. They worked on their concepts more than a year ahead, praying that the economy would support their projections, and war wouldn't shut down their factories abroad. For her it was an endless cycle of buy, buy, buy. No matter what the state of the world or the economy was, the company needed new merchandise to spread across the nation in every season.

When Matthew hadn't taken a few extra hours off to commiserate with her after her mother's funeral, and then hadn't come home to take her out to dinner as he'd promised, she'd finally known that her marriage was as irreparable as Humpty Dumpty after his fall. But she had work to do. She couldn't take time for anything else or else Herm would cause mischief. She didn't have time to get a killer lawyer to defend her against her husband, or brood about her mother's sad life, her own loss, her confusing situation with Annie, or even her father and his missing bonds. She had a theory, but she didn't have the time to pursue it.

On Thursday, however, she got a break. Herm the Germ, who was a fanatic about his health, had a toothache and left early to go to visit his dentist. Carol left soon after to have a heart-to-heart talk with her dad and to search the house before he had a chance to dismantle it. She took off at three to travel out to Staten Island for the third time in a week, and didn't even think of buying fancy food at Zabar's. She was done with that. She didn't go by limousine, either. It was Matthew's firm's car service, not hers. She was done with that, too.

She had a lot of grievances about Matthew, and this was another one. Matthew had never been nice about dropping her off at work. He liked to take the West Side Highway down to Wall Street and swing around the tip of Manhattan to get to his office at One New York Plaza. He went there by car service every day. On the rare occasions when they left the apartment at the same time, he had not been good-natured about taking a detour into crowded Midtown to give her a lift. It seemed appropriate that she take the subway today, then the Staten Island ferry as she used to do so often when she was a young woman. Back then it had always seemed like such a long way, and today was no different. The train was hot and crowded, and the ride to Wall Street evoked a thousand memories that receded like the tide all the way back to her most tender childhood years.

When Carol emerged into the brilliant afternoon sunshine at Battery Park, she felt sweaty and raw, almost as if she had shed her grown-up's skin and was a hopeful little girl again. The leaves on the trees were beginning to yellow, and a fall wind nipped at the open neck of her blouse. She hesitated on the tip of Manhattan where the immensity of the city spread in three directions, remembering how hard she had studied to figure out the geography of the area.

From where she stood in Battery Park, she could envision the boroughs like pieces in a puzzle she'd learned. Manhattan and the Bronx were to the north. Queens was tucked in the curve of the East River up in the northwestern section of Long Island. Brooklyn was adjacent to Queens in the southwestern section of Long Island. Brooklyn was a peninsula bordered by the East River, Upper New York Bay, the Narrows, Gravesend Bay, Lower New York Harbor, the Atlantic Ocean, Rockaway Inlet, and Jamaica Bay. All those bodies of water circled Brooklyn, which was the fourth largest city in the United States. Not many people knew that. Only Brooklynites were impressed by it.

Staten Island was also huge, probably twice the landmass of Manhattan. More than half of its long coastline curved around Bayonne, Elizabeth, Linden, Carteret, and Perth Amboy, New Jersey, and was less than a mile away from the mainland in many places. The vast beaches on the ocean side of Staten Island faced the wide-open Raritan Bay and Atlantic Ocean. Five miles of water in Upper New York Bay separated the tip of Staten Island from the tip of Manhattan.

When she was little, Carol had thought Manhattan was as far away as Europe. When she was in high school, her head turned toward it like a flower toward the sun. Just the view of the Wall Street area from the ferry slip had filled her with awe. Everything that symbolized the power and the lure of New York was right there: quirky old Wall Street with the Stock Exchange and Trinity Church, the Fulton Fish Market, South Street Seaport, and tall ships. Matthew's building hadn't been there twenty-five years ago, but Carol could see it now. The old Wall Street and the new were both right in front of her, and she was filled with the same excitement.

Everything that had lured her to Manhattan—the sophistication of the restaurants, the style of the clothes people wore, the jazzed feeling of being at the center of the world—was unchanged. Manhattan's command to be a somebody, not a nobody, was unchanged. She still felt the tug of ambition now. Even without the stature of the World Trade Center, New York's power and challenge to stand out and succeed at something had not been wiped away. It pulsed away in her heart. She'd picked a husband for his ambition and she'd paid for it in neglect, but she herself was the same. She now felt that she'd badly neglected her own parents, especially her mother. It wasn't an easy lesson to learn.

Carol boarded the ferry with the tourists and commuters and stayed outside on the open part of the deck to watch the city slide away from her. With the wind picking up her hair and the tangy salt in her nose, she felt a surprising nostalgia for the young woman who'd crossed the water to get away, no different from any girl fleeing small-town life.

She watched the other side approach. Staten Island was big but it was small. It had been important as a port and refuge for loyalists in the Revolutionary War, but had never been developed as intensively as its neighbors. By the middle of the nineteenth century, Staten Island had already acquired a reputation as a sleepy outpost where not much ever happened. Its old ports and pleasant homes in quiet suburban settings gave it plenty of charm. But all the charm in the world could not lift it out of the shadow of its more populous neighbors.

Carol reached for her cell phone as the ferry nudged the dock. "Come and get me, Dad, I'm here," she said when he answered.

"Here, where?" he said as if he didn't know what she was talking about.

"I'm at the ferry," she said.

"This is not very much warning," he complained.

"I called an hour ago from the office. Don't you remember?" She didn't want to sound panicked, but this was the kind of thing that worried her about him. He didn't remember anything. How could he be left on his own? How could he manage, and what should she do about it?

"You didn't call," came the querulous reply.

"Yes, Dad, I did. But if it's too much trouble, I can take a taxi . . ."

"No, no. I'll be there," he assured her. "But I wish you'd told me earlier."

Fifteen minutes later he pulled up in the battered Toyota. The car was a mess, but her father looked like a different person from the broken-down old man he'd been at his wife's funeral. Carol's mouth fell open in surprise. Since Monday he'd cut his shaggy hair. He was wearing brand-new glasses and attractive new clothes. In fact, the yellow shirt and blue jacket he was wearing seemed very familiar to her. As she looked closer, Carol could almost swear she'd bought them several years back from Bergdorf Goodman. She frowned at the possibility that her father had lied to her about returning her gifts.

"Hop in, did you bring me my bonds?" he demanded, as if they hadn't gone over this a number of times.

She ignored the question. "Dad, you look great," she murmured as she buckled her seat belt.

He shrugged, pleased with the compliment. "How about taking your old dad to dinner?"

"In a little while. I want to go home first."

"What for?" He put the car in gear and pulled out too fast. She lurched forward into her seat belt. The car approaching from the other direction honked wildly as it swerved to avoid him.

"Jesus. Slow down." Carol's blood pressure didn't abate until he'd gotten safely on the road. Then she glanced suspiciously at his trousers. She was certain the outfit had come from Bergdorf's. She recognized the braided belt and was horrified. He'd kept her gifts and never worn them.

"Dad, I need to go home and look around. I want to go through Mom's things," she told him.

"Junk," he said. "I got rid of it all."

"What?" she squealed. "You got rid of Mom's *stuff* without asking me?"

"Oh God. You have everything you ever wanted, Carol. What do you care?" He lifted a hand off the wheel. He was wearing her grandfather's watch and a ring with a deep blue star sapphire in it that she'd never seen before. The watch was hers. The ring was probably hers, too. Her heart stopped, then started beating again. Why did he do that? Why did he have to lie about everything? She could argue and complain, but there was nothing she could do about it.

"Jesus," she whimpered, shaking her head as he turned onto Forest Avenue. She knew he was heading toward his favorite restaurant in the Plaza Shopping Center and protested again.

"Dad, I can't eat yet. It's not even five o'clock."

"Well, I'm glad you came. Where are the bonds? I want this to be over," he said jovially.

"What?" She was confused. What did he want to be over?

"I've waited a long time. Now I need to get on with my life," he said.

Waited a long time? The words burned. "Dad, you told me the bonds were stolen. If they were stolen, how could I bring them back?"

He waved his hand again. "You know what I mean."

"No, I don't know what you mean."

"I need my money." His mood sharpened and he glanced at her angrily. "You got what you wanted. Now I need my own back."

She was overcome with the helpless feeling that trying to deal with him always produced. Much of the time she didn't know what he was talking about. He'd always seemed as harmless as a sparrow, a man dug deep in a trench of his own making. But now she wasn't sure what he was. A liar, certainly. But what about her mother? A deep fear gathered in her gut. "Look, I need to go home for a few minutes."

"I told you, nothing's there anymore." He kept going in the wrong direction.

Carol wanted to grab the wheel from him and turn the car around herself. It was just like him not to change course no matter what she said. He was just like Matthew, and she was appalled once again to think that she'd married a younger version of her own father. She'd never been in control of her own life.

"I want to see the house," she said stubbornly.

"Okay, it's up to you." Annoyed, he made a dangerous U-turn. The car careened back and forth across two lanes until he got it firmly set in the other direction.

"Thanks," she murmured sarcastically.

Neither spoke as they passed the familiar landmarks all the way home. When he drove up to the house fifteen minutes later, Carol was shocked by the enormous change that had taken place there. The Christmas sled was off the roof, and the icicles were gone from the gutters. The shrubbery had been pruned, and several pots of rust and gold chrysanthemums had been artfully placed around the front door. Then she saw other changes. The house had been pressure-washed. The peeling paint was gone from the bricks. The windows and screen doors were clean, too.

The house was still a very small bungalow, but now it looked quaint instead of pathetically shabby. Something had happened. Dean Teath, who'd been famously unable to take action on anything, annoying family and neighbors alike, for decades, had sprung to life as soon as his wife was gone. It was a miracle. Carol stepped inside the place the Teath family had called home, and was stunned to find it nearly empty.

"Planned Parenthood took the furniture," her father announced proudly. "Your mother would have liked that. Goodwill took the clothes. And of course, the funeral people gave me the name of a cleaning service. Your mother wasn't much of a housekeeper, you know."

He looked around at the empty space he had created. "It cost a bundle, let me tell you, but it was worth it to get rid of that old junk."

Carol stood there in shock. She hadn't cared much

about the house or the furniture. Her history had been an embarrassment to her. She'd left it behind years ago, planning to create a better one for the future. But now she missed it. Her life with Matthew was over, and now her birthright was gone, too, wiped away by its own guardian. Speechless, she checked the pantry where her mother had kept so many useless things. Gone were the pickle crocks where her jewelry and small amounts of cash used to reside. Ditto everything in the closet in Carol's old room. Her record collection and school yearbooks had disappeared. Upstairs, the tiny attic had never been so clean. Gone were the alligator purses, the dress-up hats and shoes, her old baby carriage and tricycle. Gone were the dust and mold and photographs of herself on roller skates and her wearing her prom dress. She wanted to cry.

"Where are the photo albums?" she asked.

"Don't you have them?" her father replied innocently.

She shook her head. "You threw my pictures away. How could you do that?"

"No, no, I didn't do it."

"Dad, you threw my stuff away!" She was furious. How spiteful was that? "How do I know you didn't throw away the bonds, too?" she demanded. How did she even know they were his bonds? Like the watch and the ring he was wearing, they could be hers.

"The bonds? Why would I do that?" He sounded surprised by the very idea.

"Something's not right here." Carol looked around at the empty home. She had a bad feeling about this, a bad feeling about her mother's sudden demise and her father's metamorphosis. She missed her mother—well, not really her mother; she missed what her mother could have been. It was a weird feeling, and not at all what she'd expected. She was overwhelmed by grief . . . and suspicion.

"I'm hungry," her father muttered, scratching his ear as if he couldn't remember where he'd left his dinner.

"Something's not right, Dad."

"I know, honey, but Matthew will help us get the money back."

Carol shook her head. "No, he won't help. We're separated."

"Why? I thought you liked him."

"I already told you. We're getting a divorce. He packed up while I was at work yesterday. I didn't even know he was moving out until he called to tell me he was gone. Sound familiar?" She glared at him. The two men were the same, and she'd never seen the resemblance.

"He's still a lawyer, isn't he?" The old man refused any comparison. "Isn't that his job?"

"Well, we can't sue, Dad. Matthew already did that to Hall Stale. We can't go there again." If Carol had returned home hoping for a little sympathy for her failed marriage, she didn't find it. Her father was outraged by the thought that Matthew wasn't going to help them.

"What are you talking about?" he thundered.

"Look, Dad, he already sued Hall Stale on a bogus case. We can't try that again."

"Bogus. I don't know what you're talking about. They stole my bonds."

Carol shook her head. "I really doubt it. I've known Annie Custer for fifteen years. She's my best friend. She would not steal your bonds. Maybe you threw them out by accident."

"I didn't throw them out," he insisted.

"Then maybe your accountant took them."

"Brad retired to Sarasota. Can we have dinner now?"

She tried one more time. "Dad, I think you have the bonds somewhere."

He shook his head. "Look around. If you find them, fine."

She accepted his offer and searched carefully, but the closets were empty. His things were gone.

"What are you doing with this house?" Carol asked after she'd satisfied herself that nothing of any value remained there.

"That real estate lady who came out from the funeral home, she put it on the market for me."

"Is she the one who had it cleaned up?"

"Yep, she took care of everything."

"You didn't waste any time." Carol was deeply angry that she'd been left out of another major decision.

"No need to wait. I'm moving on," he said with satisfaction.

That was exactly what Matthew had said last night. Amazing. She'd mentioned the D word Monday, and by Wednesday he was out the door. Maybe he felt he'd waited long enough, too. Right at that moment, Carol didn't have a high opinion of men. The only good thing about it was, if her father moved on, she wouldn't have to take responsibility for him. He'd get what he wanted, to be out of sight and on his own.

She went outside and got back in the car. He followed her, eager for food. This time she took the wheel and drove to the Italian dump he liked. He had a big appetite for his lasagne but did not have anything more to add about where his stuff had gone. Even though she pressed him for more information, he didn't seem to remember much. It could be an act; she just couldn't evaluate the situation. She had no idea what the truth was. Before she got back on the ferry, she took the name of the real estate lady who'd helped him clean the house. The last thing she did was take a good look in the trunk of his car. Nothing much in there but some old tools. She thought about it all the way home.

forty-three

JUST BEFORE NOON ON FRIDAY, FRISK CAME INTO Annie's office with the news she'd been dreading all week.

"I just got word about those certificates your friend brought in," he said.

Annie sat up with a jolt. *Please, please let them be genuine.* She knew as she prayed it was a lost cause. Frisk was jingling the coins in his pocket, a sure sign of a problem. She waited. He kept her in suspense.

"So?" she asked after what seemed like a very long pause.

"I thought you'd want to be the first to know." He kept her waiting a little while longer.

"I do want to know. What?"

"They're phony."

Annie gasped. "All of them?"

"I would suspect so." Frisk jingled away.

"Oh God! That prick put us through hell. He's called me six times a day for a month. I can't believe this. What an asshole!" Annie hit the desk with her fist.

"You or him?" Frisk quipped.

"Oh shit!" Annie fumed. She'd so wanted something good to happen. What a futile wish.

Frisk stood there jingling.

"What?" Annie asked. "Don't tell me there are legal issues."

"Nope, not for us. For him, probably."

"I've always had a bad feeling about that guy." Annie couldn't get over it. What if they'd deposited phony certificates? She hated to think about it.

Frisk stopped jingling. A second later he started rocking back and forth on his toes. He was a man who always had some body part moving. "Well, let the fish go," he concluded.

Annie's phone rang, and he was out the door. She picked up. "Annie Custer."

"Annie, what's your final word on that Yankee game?" It was Brian, still hopeful about her accompanying him tonight.

"I already gave you my final word," she said, more irritably than she meant to.

"I know, but that was yesterday. What's your final word today?" he demanded.

"I can't go to the Yankee game tonight," she said, doodling on her calendar.

"Annie, I need someone to go places with me," he complained.

Well, that was his problem. She couldn't drop everything even if she wanted to. "The certificates are phonies," she told him.

"What certificates?"

"The ten million in IBM stock that Vole brought in."

"Aw jeez," Brian lamented. "We didn't need that."

There were many things in life they got that they didn't need, Annie thought. He was one of the things she didn't need.

"Where do you want to go to lunch?" His voice was eager. He was a man who didn't give up easily.

"Ah, I can't. I've got an errand to run," she hedged.

"Really?" He sounded as if he didn't believe that.

"Really."

"Fine, I'll see you later." Now he sounded angry, and would sulk all afternoon.

Why did men always have to be like that? She wasn't his slave. Disgusted with the male sex, she hung up and hurried out of the office. She was desperate for a little freedom, or at least a breath of fresh air. But as soon as she was down on Third Avenue she felt the rush of the city around her . . . and a powerful sense that something else was about to happen to her. Something worse than stolen bearer bonds and stock fraud combined. She suppressed the panic and tried to think of something she actually needed to do. The only errand she could think of was to retrieve the roll of film Dina had taken of her last dinner. Annie had left it at the one-hour photo shop early in the week. Okay, she'd do that. She headed for the hole-in-the-wall around the corner, always so empty she didn't know how it stayed in business, presented her receipt to the clerk at the counter, and paid for the prints. Then, lingering outside in the brisk early-October morning for just a while longer, she opened the envelope.

She had some vague hope that the new family photos might inspire the same sense of nostalgia the old ones always did. There was no question that the Custers always seemed to look happy in their photos. They didn't stare off in different directions like family members in so many Christmas cards. Bebe and Mag were always smiling. They had their arms around each other, laughing at some private joke. Annie and Ben were inevitably squashed together to fit in the frame. The marriage had been rocky for a long time, but the frozen moments of happiness preserved on film presented a different reality.

There were twenty-four exposures on this roll of film. Quickly Annie flipped through them. There were the expected group shots around the table, the dog, the cake, Dina. The obligatory images of the girls making faces at each other. Annie smiled and moved on. Then, in the place she least expected the second shoe to drop, it dropped.

It was a picture of Bebe in her bathroom. She was wearing a shower cap. She was wrapped in a towel. Her eyes were closed. She was holding something that Annie knew from the movies was a bong. A cloud of smoke obscured one side of her face. Shocked, Annie flipped to the next picture. Bebe's mouth was glued to the bong, and Annie realized that someone had actually taken a picture of her daughter smoking what she guessed was marijuana. Why Bebe was wearing a shower cap was instantly clear. Bebe had covered her hair so no one would smell smoke in it.

"Jesus." Bebe had been caught in the act without appearing to know it. And also caught in a very big lie. She claimed that she didn't smoke dope.

Dina must have known about this for a while, and waited until she was far away to reveal the secret to Annie. Seething, Annie flipped to the next picture. This one was a wide-angle shot of Mag poking at the hole in her ceiling with one of her new golf irons. Around her on the floor were chunks of plaster. "Oh my God!" Dina had caught Mag, too, knocking down the plaster ceiling of her own room. Horrified, she moved on to the next one. Worse and worse, in this one Mag was sitting on the floor of Annie's closet. The bottom drawer of Annie's dresser was open, and on the floor were the new bras and panties she'd bought at Victoria's Secret. Mag's face was turned toward the door, where Ben was standing with his hand raised to his forehead.

Her heart lurched at the pain on his face. Slowly she walked back up the block and into the Lipstick Building. Slowly she presented her identity card and pressed the elevator button. Fourteen. Slowly, with the pictures still clutched in her hand, she waded through the halls to her office. The jig was up. Bebe smoked dope. Mag was a snitch. And she was no prize herself. She sat down at the desk and dialed her home phone. Eventually Ben answered.

"Hi, Annie," he said in a pleasant voice. "What's up?"

Annie was silent. Now that her husband was on the phone, she didn't know where to begin. She stared out her window at the bank of windows in the building across the street. People were still going about their business over there, just as they had been half an hour ago. They were talking on the phone, working on their computers, moving paper around. The same things she did, as if it all mattered. Another line rang. Outside in her cubicle, Petra said her name. And still Annie couldn't find the right salutation.

"Hello, hello. Annie, I know it's you. What's up?" Ben's voice took on that slight tinge of impatience that always drove her nuts.

What's up? was too big a question. A whole lot was up, but she needed a little question to get her mouth moving.

"Are you all right?" he asked.

"No," she said in a tiny voice. "I'm not really all right at all."

"Do you want me to come over?" he said immediately.

Yes. Yes, she did want him to come over. But she

didn't want him to run into the loose cannon, Brian, who unwisely thought she was his new girlfriend.

"Maybe you could meet me for lunch," she said slowly. She checked her watch. It was eleven thirty. She'd taken all the office she could take. She wanted to go home and circle the wagons.

"Sure, lunch would be great. You choose," Ben said.

"You'll have to choose. I can't choose anymore," she told him.

"Fine. Walk up to Colonial. I'll see you there at noon." His voice sounded strong. It gave her some hope.

forty-four

BEN ORDERED THE SPICY STEAK SALAD, CHICKEN salad with peanut sauce, and a whole crispy snapper. He handed the menu back to the waiter and studied his wife as if he hadn't seen her for a long time. He was dressed in his navy blazer and cavalry twill trousers, and Annie's first thought when she saw him was that clothes did make the man.

"You look good," she said.

"You, too, what's going on?" He eyed her suspiciously, as if the revolution was about to take his head.

She handed him the photographs.

"What's this?"

"Just look," she said, then ordered an iced tea.

He opened the envelope curiously and went through

the mundane photos quickly. "So . . . ?" Then he got to Bebe smoking the dope. "What the hell?"

"What *is* that?" Annie asked.

"Well, it's not a cigarette," he said slowly. "But let's not get nuts."

"She's smoking dope, and she's doing it in our home," Annie exploded.

"Well, it's better than her doing it in someone else's home." Ben studied it.

"No, we can't take that position," she said angrily. "I mean it. We have to take a stand."

"Who took that picture?" he mused. "Margaret?"

"Dina took the picture."

"How do you know?"

"She's always got that damn camera in her hand, and she's quiet. Go on."

He turned to the next picture. "What the hell!" he said again. It was his face looking at Mag holding up the sexy underwear. "I followed her into the closet," he said. "She was late for her interview, and I was just bugging her to get going. I didn't like the fact that she was going through your stuff . . . but I didn't see Dina take that. I had no idea she was there," he said, musing about how it had been possible.

Annie was relieved that he didn't say anything about the underwear, not a word. He just moved on to the next photo, and squinted at the picture of Maggie with her ceiling at her feet.

"Gee, I didn't know she took down the ceiling herself. I had no idea. She's over the top." He looked at the pictures again, one after another. "Wow."

"Everybody's over the top. I'm quitting my job," Annie told him abruptly.

"What?"

"The girls need me. So do you."

"What?" he said again as if she couldn't possibly have said what she said.

"I told you things were out of control."

"So what, you used to smoke dope. What's the big deal?"

She knew what he was doing: attempting a smoke screen to cover his ignorance about his daughter's activities. It didn't work. "I was in college. I tried it a few times. It wasn't my thing. Bebe's fifteen and very shaky in school. Nodding off in the bathroom is not the key to her salvation," Annie retorted.

"They all have problems at this age." Frowning, Ben took up the photo of his daughter smoking the bong. "Let's not overreact."

"I'm not overreacting. Our kids are floundering. Mag can't get out of bed except to play golf. You can't keep pretending everything's peachy."

Ben was quiet for a long time. "All right, I'll admit things have been better," he said finally.

"A lot better." Annie dipped her chin. She didn't want to say what she was thinking. He'd dropped the ball. But clearly he knew it anyway.

"You think this is my fault, don't you?"

She didn't answer.

"Well, look, I told you the other day if you want a divorce, you can have it. I won't fight you. Go ahead," he said almost recklessly. "The ball's in your court."

Annie shook her head. That would be too easy for him. He could just slide away and leave her to pick up the pieces. Uh-uh. She wasn't going to let him do that. And it wasn't what she wanted anyway. She wanted them to pick up the pieces together, make some important decisions about how they intended to spend the rest of their lives. Still, for a moment she pretended to think about it.

"Dina retired. You retired. I just told you I want to retire like the two of you. That's what I want." The salads came, and Annie was surprised to find herself hungry. She dug in.

"Huh?" He looked at her blankly. "You've always worked."

She chewed and swallowed. "Maybe I'll do something, but I don't want to be a stock jockey anymore. I don't want to manage money for people who think I'm a crook. I don't want to see if I can cut a deal that I know is illegal just to get an account."

"What deal?" he demanded.

"It doesn't matter what deal." The whole business was plain wrong. She couldn't do it. She was furious with Brian. She knew he was trying to take advantage of her just because he needed a new girlfriend, and she was disappointed in herself that she'd fallen for it.

"Yes, it matters what deal. Come on, baby, you can tell me." Now Ben was interested.

Annie ate some more salad. "A ridiculous thing. A really sleazy thing. I was taking it seriously because I thought we needed money. But, honey, you're right. We don't need to make money."

He looked startled. "When did I ever say we don't need to make money?"

"Ben, I want to be a stay-at-home mom. I don't want out of the marriage. I want back into it."

He'd picked up his fork. Now he put it down again. "Is that what the underwear was all about?" Here was the core of his concern, and his sudden change of attitude.

"Yes, sweetheart," she said solemnly.

"All week I thought . . ." He nodded at the photo. "When I saw that stuff, I thought . . ." He swallowed.

"No, no, it was for you," she said quickly. She used to be an honest woman. Now she was lying left and right. But what did it matter, as long as he bought it?

"So how are we going to work this out?" he said slowly.

forty-five

FRIDAY WAS DRESS-DOWN DAY AT CAROL'S OFFICE. Most people came in jeans and T-shirts. When Brian Redfield called at eleven thirty and asked her if she was free for lunch, he suggested they meet at Fives, the up-scale restaurant in the Peninsula Hotel. She happened to be free but didn't want to show up there in her worst work clothes.

She hesitated. "It's dress-down day. Are you dressed down?"

"No, but you're the client, so it doesn't matter what you wear," he said smoothly.

"I'm wearing jeans."

He laughed. "I like women in jeans."

Oh ho ho, she thought, *he's flirting*. She told him she'd be happy to meet him there.

When she marched up the set of carpeted steps at twelve thirty on the dot, he was waiting for her. He was wearing a formal blue suit, a light blue shirt with white French cuffs, and a yellow tie. She thought he was absolutely darling.

"Thank you for joining me on such short notice. So many people aren't flexible that way." He made a face, squeezed her hand, then led the way up the second set of stairs to the dining room.

"It was nice of you to ask," she replied demurely, glancing around the beautiful room overlooking Fifth Avenue.

The tables were placed far apart and covered with arctic white cloths. It was a nice change from the crowded bistros that had popped up everywhere, taking the place of the pasta restaurants that had taken the place of the Japanese sushi restaurants that had taken the place of the Chinese restaurants that used to dot every Manhattan corner. She appreciated his good taste and almost didn't mind the fact that she was wearing tight black jeans that showed off her ass, a white peasant shirt, and the silver necklaces and bracelets that gave her an entirely misleading bohemian air.

Brian helped her with her chair. Their pencil-thin waitperson shook out her napkin and placed it carefully in her lap as if she were helpless to do it herself. Carol beamed at the attention. "Thank you."

The server disappeared and Brian murmured, "Tough week, huh?"

At those words, Carol's carefully made-up eyes opened wide in an unexpected moment of déjà vu. She'd only just met him, but the way he said *tough week* made her feel as if she'd known him all her life. The concerned expression on his handsome face resonated deeply. He was so different from Matthew, who'd been the only one in their household allowed to have tough weeks.

"You know, then?" she said.

"Your mother passed on." Brian touched her hand. "That's always very sad."

"No. Well, yes. But my husband and I split up." Carol

said it with no emotion, as if Matthew were someone in the news who'd passed on.

Brian's eyebrows shot up. "Really?"

"You didn't know?" She was surprised. She'd guessed the reason for the lunch was that he'd heard about the divorce. She could always tell when a man liked her. He'd returned her call the very next day, proof enough of interest. It made her think that she'd been way off track in her original theory that something was going on between him and Annie.

"How would I know?" he protested.

"I thought Annie might have told you. You're pretty close, aren't you?"

"She's a great girl, but very discreet. No, she didn't tell me anything about your private life." He touched the napkin to his lips, and she wondered if he was telling the truth.

"Can I get you something to drink?" Their server was a young woman with a blond bun stuck on the back of her head that looked as small and hard as the dinner rolls on their plates. "A cocktail or a glass of wine?" She looked hopefully from one to the other.

"Oh, it's Friday, I'll have something," Carol said. "Chardonnay."

"The same for me," Brian said. The server went away. "This changes the picture," he announced.

"In what way?" she asked.

"I thought Matthew would be representing you. He's not well liked at Hall Stale." He smiled at the understatement.

Carol looked away. She didn't want to talk about Matthew. She wanted to talk about Brian.

"That case was rough for all of us. I was in the middle of my divorce. The only good thing about the outcome was the damage it did to my bonus." He gazed out at Fifth Avenue.

"What do you mean?" That interested her.

"Oh, the way the system works is the branch pays for settlements of complaints out of its earnings. A portion comes out of the manager's bonus." He laughed. "I'd been there only a few months and certainly hadn't been the supervisor at the time in question, but I had to pay anyway."

He shrugged off the loss. "I didn't really care. All it meant to me was that Sally didn't get it."

"So Ben didn't pay?"

"Oh no. The firm paid, but it was not a good thing for anybody." He gazed at her without discomfort. "Didn't you know that?"

"Uh-uh. I couldn't talk to Annie about it. We kind of fell apart after that. I mean, I kept my account there, and I talked to her about business, but it wasn't the same. And Matthew was really mean about it. He wanted a complete break, of course, but I couldn't do that to Annie. I don't have that many friends," she admitted.

"Well, he took us for a costly ride," Brian said.

She looked out the window at Fifth Avenue. It was all so uncomfortable. Matthew's scam, now missing bonds. She wasn't sure what she should do. "What about my case?" she asked faintly.

"Oh, don't worry about it. We'll do the right thing," Brian assured her.

What exactly was that? she wondered.

He waved his hand. "That's a cute outfit."

"Thanks." She flushed.

"I can't believe you're getting a divorce," he said. "It's just so amazing."

"I think you just changed the subject." She laughed.

"Sorry. It just came into my head. I'm really surprised.

I wasn't prepared for your divorcing old Matthew. He's quite the powerhouse, isn't he?"

"Yes, a real sweetheart. Tell me about *your* divorce."

"It was my wife's idea."

"What was her beef?" Carol asked.

"Oh, she'd been so straight in college. She wanted to break out and party all the time. I was too square for her. I go to the gym, take vitamins, drink hot chocolate . . ."

"You do?" She laughed.

"It's better for you than coffee," he said defensively. "And I like to hang out at home after work. Things got away from Sally . . ." He didn't go any further.

"Silly girl." Carol studied him. His eyes didn't stray everywhere, looking at everything but her, the way Matthew's always did. And Annie had told her he was nearly forty, but he seemed younger. His good looks had quite an effect on her. And the attraction seemed mutual.

"Of course, Annie's getting divorced, too. Do you two do everything together?" he asked.

"No, no. Only one of us is getting divorced. Annie will never leave Ben." Carol wanted to nip that idea in the bud.

"Really?" He actually recoiled as if she'd punched him.

She shook her dark hair emphatically. "Never. She adores him. That's the difference."

"She adores him? But she says he's a total slug." Brian seemed confused.

"Oh well. You can't always believe what people say. Trust me on this one. She adores him. It's possible to adore a slug. I used to." She glanced down at her menu. "Um, everything looks so good. What should I have?"

"Oh, have the foie gras. It's great here." Looking

rather stricken, Brian ordered two more glasses of Chardonnay.

As she finished her first one, Carol watched him try to recover from the news about Annie. Once again it seemed clear that he had a crush on Annie, and didn't know that much about her. Maybe he'd just invited *her* to lunch because of the bonds, after all. That possibility upset her. She really liked him.

"You started to tell me about doing the right thing? What would that be?" she asked abruptly.

"Well, we don't just write a check for large amounts of money without a very good reason. We try to work things out first." He smiled. "Did you talk to your father again?"

"I went to see him yesterday." Carol picked up her wineglass. She was still troubled. Many more things were missing than bonds.

"And?"

"Oh, he's convinced the bonds went out the door with Annie. Where does that leave us?"

"I'll try to get you a settlement."

"What do you mean, *a settlement*?" she said slowly.

"Well, we know the bonds were in your father's house when Annie recorded the serial numbers there. We don't know for sure they left your father's house. Do you see what I mean?"

"No," she said flatly.

"Annie spent some time with your mother." He didn't go on.

"You think my mother took them?" Carol was horrified.

"No, no, no. Of course not. It's just that it can't be proven either way whether they were in the bag with Annie, or whether someone else took them out of the bag before she left."

"The accountant?"

Brian nodded. "Exactly. Four people were there."

Carol was silent. One of those four people was dead now. "I hate money," she said suddenly.

Brian laughed. "It's funny that you say that. Every rich client we have tells me the happiest time in his life was when he didn't have any."

"Well, that's because they don't remember what it's like," Carol countered. "My parents were ridiculous. They didn't spend on anything. I grew up thinking we were paupers."

"Believe it or not, a lot of people are like that," Brian said.

"Matthew cheated his best friend. I guess he thought it was okay because the firm would pay. I'm sure he'll do the same to me in the divorce." She felt like putting her head on the table and weeping.

"Maybe not," Brian murmured.

"Oh yes. I'm sure he'll punish me for being loyal to Annie."

"But, Carol, you have your own money now. It doesn't matter what he does."

"No, of course not. It's the principle of the thing. Cheating isn't nice," she said primly.

He smiled. "You two girls are something. I think I'm in trouble."

Carol studied the menu again. "You know, I will have the foie gras," she said.

He shook his head, smiling. "You aren't by any chance free to go to a Yankee game tonight, are you?"

"What?" She knew the rules of dating from the dark ages, before she'd married Matthew: You weren't supposed to go out with someone for lunch and then a sporting event that same evening. It made a girl too available and not worthy of respect. Also, you ran the risk of running out of things to say too early in the relationship. If a girl was interested, she was supposed to let time go by before accepting a second invitation, preferably a week or two later . . . but maybe things were different now.

"I mean, if you don't have anything to do. We have a great box, but if you're busy, don't worry about it." Brian wiggled his finger to summon the server with the tight bun.

Busy, Carol thought wildly. *She was the opposite of busy.* But it was too good to be true to have a date with a doll only two days after separating from her jerk of a husband. Still, she had to think for a minute before giving her positive answer. She wrinkled her nose trying to remember. Were Yankees baseball, or football?

forty-six

THE APARTMENT WAS QUIET WHEN ANNIE AND BEN got home, hours before the market was due to close. The silence gave her an eerie feeling. She wasn't used to being home on a weekday without Dina and Spanish TV, or at least one kid, to annoy her. Privacy had been a nearly lost concept only dimly remembered from her prebreeding age. She stopped short in the foyer as Curly trotted over and stuck his muzzle into her hand. Without the chatter, the music, the commercials of a single TV, he seemed puzzled, too.

"Hey, baby, where is everybody?" she asked. He wagged a hopeful answer. *You're here.* Right behind her Ben touched the small of her back in a signal she also vaguely remembered from long ago. *Want to fool around?*

She was startled. Only yesterday the prospect of fooling around was pretty much a thing of the past.

"Maggie," he called to their daughter.

No answer. His fingers caressed Annie's waist as he waited for a reply. He definitely wanted to, and she was definitely tempted, but she was distracted by the possibility of a returning adolescent barging into the room without knocking. Ben read her mind.

"I'll go see if she's here," he said, and took off down the hall.

The very second he was out of sight a chill entered the foyer. A shadow unfurled in the corner, and Curly's tail dropped like the starting flag at a race. He tensed and growled. Annie turned her back and hurried into the kitchen. "Come on, baby. Come in here," she called to the dog.

The poodle hesitated, then hastily followed her just before she shut the door. The draft moved right through it, however, and Curly broke into a frustrated howl.

"Shh, it's okay, Curl." Annie gave him a freeze-dried liver treat to calm him down, then addressed the cold spot near the door. "Mom, you've got to stop this. You're making him crazy. You're making us all crazy," she amended. "What do you want?"

No answer.

"I know you're here. You have to stop it. Go away, I can take my life from here."

She thought she heard a knock somewhere, like her mother's knocking wood for luck in her childhood. Curly heard the sound, too, and ran to the back door barking his head off. She didn't bother to look in the back hall; she knew no one was out there. She sighed and glanced around the kitchen where she'd spent so much money upgrading and so little time enjoying. The country table, where the family had wolfed down so many uncomfortable dinners together, was littered with the morning papers and nothing else. She bent to look under the table and didn't see any smoke or shadow of her mother lurking there.

Come out, come out wherever you are. Her eyes moved to the sink. A few dishes and cups were stacked in there from breakfast, but surprisingly the kitchen hadn't become the disastrous mess she'd anticipated in Dina's absence. "The least you could do is wash up," she grumbled to the ghost.

Silence. All seemed quiet, but Annie knew better. She took her usual place at the kitchen counter by the phone and checked her messages. There were a few. Despite the fact that she was never at home on a Friday afternoon, Petra had phoned there to say that Vartan Vole was on the rampage, wanting his millions transferred. Three clients needed to reach her before the end of the day. Brian demanded to know if she was coming back. And Carol had left an urgent message, too.

"I told them I didn't know your schedule. Are you coming back?" Petra asked in her message. "I tried your cell, but it's off," she added as an explanation for the call to her home.

How did people know everything about her? Annie wondered. Irritated that she could be located so easily, Annie called Petra back to tell her she was out of the office with a client all afternoon. Then she looked around her kitchen one more time. Except for the freezing cold, nothing was out of whack. The clocks all told the correct time. No ceiling or undercabinet lights were flashing messages in code. The appliances were still. Only the refrigerator hummed, but refrigerators were supposed to hum. Maybe. Maybe . . .

Ben opened the door and came in without his jacket. "No one's home. Want to fool around?" he asked with a hopeful smile.

He didn't seem to notice the temperature as he approached the stool where she was shivering. He kissed her forehead, then gently teased the nape of her neck with his fingertips. The stroking was a gesture that had always been certain to soothe her in the past. His forearm brushed her breasts with a touch of the old electricity. She shivered some more.

"It's going to be okay," he whispered. "We've got this under control."

Annie nodded, uncertain which way to swing. The lunch had been a serious exploration of their options, but she was skeptical about the possibility of enormous changes at the very last minute. She knew well enough that when asked for a divorce, some men shot their wives dead with assault weapons for wanting to leave them. Some begged for forgiveness and promised to change, then remained exactly the same. And still others had been waiting for a chance to escape all along and said "Fine." Matthew turned out to be a husband in the third category. Annie had always thought Ben was the second type. He might say the right things, but he'd never leave the sofa.

She wondered what had prompted this sudden passion: the floundering children or the underwear lie? But what difference did it make? She was caught in an answered prayer and shouldn't start playing the accountant. Still, it was embarrassing. She'd bought some underwear dreaming of sex with someone new. A guy with a hard body and a history of poor choices in women. And why not? Ben had abdicated in the sex-and-everything-else departments, while Brian talked sex all day long. Whether he'd done it to let off steam or to encourage her to wonder what she was missing, Annie had certainly wondered. Maybe she wasn't supposed to think about other men, but she'd brooded about Brian and it had gotten her in trouble. Now with Ben's arms circling her waist, Annie was sorry about the lapse.

"I really missed you," Ben murmured into her neck.

Murmuring was very nice, but she remained suspicious. Did he hope she'd change her mind about quitting her job, about selling the apartment and using the cash to start a new life far from New York City? At lunch they'd calculated its value. It was worth at least a couple of million by now. They could take Bebe out of the costly private school she loathed and relocate in a brand-new house in a golf community somewhere warm. "Why not?" If he could learn the game, so could she. And he'd perked up at the G word.

After a long pause in which she didn't speak, he said, "Your turn."

"I missed you, too," she replied dutifully. But she couldn't help remembering how many times she'd said that to him after he'd taken to his bed and abandoned her. Once again he read her mind.

"I'm back," he whispered. "You called, I came. Don't hold out on me now."

And still she hesitated. Then other words flew in on a stiff wind. *Give up the accounting.* Annie shivered.

"What is it?" He checked his watch, fearful that their children would be home soon.

"Didn't you hear that?" Annie asked.

"Uh-uh." He played with a lock of her hair.

"It's freezing in here. Aren't you cold?"

"Uh-uh."

Then she saw it curling out of the corner. The ghost of her mother had become like the spam in her e-mail that appeared unbidden every day with tantalizing promises of a thinner body and a bigger dick.

"Okay, let's get out of here." She wiggled off the stool and fled the kitchen, holding Ben's hand as she led him down the hall. Her excitement tingled in the small of her back, awakening a thousand memories of better days. Nice. Just the feeling of his body so close to her and so obviously eager to love again was stunning in its familiarity and ability to arouse the old passions. More than nice.

In seconds they were in their warm bedroom shedding their clothes. Neither hesitated now. Their hands and lips and tongues sought out the special, well-loved places, and rekindled intense pleasures that had been on hold for a long time. No housekeeper or child was around to chastise or tease or inhibit them. All alone they remembered what their home had been like before their children had come, before a housekeeper had been necessary, when it had been just them. They revisited the known territory of each other's bodies, panting like the young people they still wanted to be. They were too preoccupied to hear the front door, or Mag calling them.

She was at the bedroom door before they had a chance to cover up. She came in without knocking. "What's going on? Oh shit." The door slammed behind her.

forty-seven

CAROL HAD NEVER BEEN TO A BASEBALL GAME IN her entire life. The idea of actually going to a massive stadium for no work-related reason was completely foreign, even terrifying. Anything could happen in a place with tens of thousands of people all jammed together and only a few exits. The possibilities for pandemonium were practically limitless. Starting with a riot ensuing from the home team losing and moving right up the list to suicide bomber, poison gas, sniper, and total blackout of the entire tristate area—well, death by stadium could come from anywhere. She got the willies just thinking about all the risks a baseball game presented. She was 99.5 percent sure it was baseball. She must have been dead drunk when she'd agreed to go.

As she walked back to her office after lunch with the totally dreamy Brian Redfield, however, she still had a pretty nice buzz. She weighed her options. She could make herself unavailable by workload and hope for another opportunity. Or she could try to persuade him to do something else she'd enjoy more—not a good plan if he was a serious sports fan. Or she could bite the bullet and go to Queens, or was it the Bronx? She wasn't sure, but she thought it was the Bronx. Carol, like all New Yorkers, was a borough snob. For every resident of New York, Manhattan lived at the top of the borough list.

Queens, Brooklyn, the Bronx, and Staten Island were ranked in descending order, depending on where you came from. For Carol going to the Bronx for the evening was about the equivalent of traveling to the second circle of hell.

Still, she hadn't had a date with a single, adorable, straight man in—give or take a few minutes—eighteen long years. Or indeed any man at all. Given that fact, she thought it might seem ungrateful to cancel almost immediately after being asked for the very first time. For all she knew she might have to wait eighteen years for another chance. Add to that Brian's promise to get the lost bond money back without hurting Annie in any way. *Well,* she asked herself, *what choice did she really have?* She didn't think Annie had stolen her money.

Despite the unpleasant prospect of going to the Bronx and running the risk of never returning, she was in a great mood when she got back to the office. Her desk was still cluttered and unmanageable, but in one corner some space had been made for a vase of really stunning Casablanca lilies tied with a white ribbon. The intoxicating aroma of the huge pure white flowers filled the small space, and she was almost staggered by the lovely gesture. That was really fast, she thought. *Really* fast. How could Brian have managed such speed? He must have dropped into a florist on the way back to his office and had the delivery person run all the way to her office to get there before she did.

Anticipating a smile at his thoughtfulness, she reached for the card in the envelope, and instantly she was crushed. It was a sympathy card from Arnold Angelico. She frowned as she read it: "I was so sorry to hear of your loss. Call Audrey to reschedule the Monday meeting."

Carol was hugely annoyed. She didn't want to reschedule the Monday meeting. She'd been planning and working on it for weeks. Doubly disappointed, she sat down at her desk to call Audrey, Arnold's assistant.

"Hi, it's Carol. Is Arnold there? I want to thank him for the beautiful flowers. It was very thoughtful of him. Or you," she added in case Audrey had sent them.

"Oh, it was him, and he's gone for the weekend. He told me to tell you not to worry about taking Monday off. He lost his mother last Christmas, so he knows how sad it is."

"What? I'm not taking Monday off," Carol protested. "Monday's my fall presentation. I wouldn't miss it for anything."

"I know. And we had a breakfast scheduled, but Herman told me you're not ready."

"He told you that?" Carol looked for her assistant, but didn't see the Germ at his desk. When she found him, she was going to kill him.

"He said you'd missed a few days, including yesterday, and wouldn't be here to present Monday. It's not a big deal. Except that Arnold will be traveling for the next ten days. We can plan it for when he gets back. How's that?" she said.

Carol's voice was steady as she replied, "No, it's fine. We don't need to delay. I'll be here Monday. I'm ready for it. I don't know where Herm got that idea— I didn't tell him to call you. In fact, I would have called myself if I had to reschedule. Is Arnold mad?"

"Nooo. Well, a little," Audrey admitted.

"Jesus, Audrey. You canceled everybody without speaking to me directly?"

"We thought you must really be upset. It didn't sound like you at all," she admitted.

"Well, it wasn't me. What can we do about this? Is there any way we can get back on line for Monday?"

Carol held her breath. She didn't want to wait ten days for her meeting. She didn't want to be late for the fall span. Every year after she presented, the department heads always argued and changed their minds a bunch of times. It would put her way behind. She started hyperventilating. She knew she had a reputation for erupting and didn't want to start screaming at Audrey, who'd only tell everyone. Herm must have been counting on her temper to sink her. Her throat constricted as she tried to control her rage. Why hadn't she gotten rid of him six months ago when he'd first started this nonsense?

"Oh, I don't know at this point. I suppose I could check around."

"That would be really nice, Audrey. I need that meeting to move forward." Carol sat back in her chair. Her heart was pounding. It was just like yesterday, when she'd found out that her father had stripped the house of all her souvenirs and memories. It was like the day before that, when Matthew moved out and quit their marriage while she was at work. It was like Annie's not telling her that a quarter of a million dollars was missing. She wanted to pound the table and scream. Hello, this was her life, and she wasn't in control of it. What was wrong with people? she wanted to know. What were they thinking? Her assistant was the one person she was supposed to be able to trust, and he'd made her look like an irresponsible flake.

"Well, I could make some calls, but you know how people are. They might think you're troublesome, Carol. And I know Arnold has already filled the time slot. It would have to be Tuesday. After that, he's away."

"Okay, Tuesday would be fine. I appreciate it." Carol was out of her chair the minute she hung up with Audrey. She knew she couldn't use the phone because Herman would only appear from nowhere, skulk outside her office, and listen in. And she couldn't e-mail the head of Human Resources, because even though she changed her password every few days, Herm still knew how to get into her mail. She knew this because he made references to things he couldn't know about any other way. It was unacceptable. She'd relied on him, and this was her thanks. A cumulative effect of many disloyalties fired her into an indignant frenzy. HR would not be able to talk her out of it this time. There was no other reasonable response to this kind of interference. Herman had underestimated her one time too many. He was history.

forty-eight

AS SOON AS THE MARKET CLOSED, BRIAN RAN home to shower and change for the game. After the long week full of work dramas and Annie's ridiculous excuses for not going out, he was delighted to have someone to take to the game—and a really stunning woman at that. Never mind that she was old. He could overlook the fact that, like Annie, Carol was probably as old as he was. It didn't matter, he told himself (his dating mantra); it just didn't matter. On a Friday night, it was humiliating going out with Bill and Carl. Those old guys with their paunches and thinning hair prowled the bars and went to singles parties arranged by desperate women for the over-fifty set. Sometimes they even went on the baseball websites to get blind dates for the games. They did everything they could to meet women. They carried Viagra with them and slept with anybody once, then bemoaned their fate of never finding the right girl, and kept on trolling. The whole scenario was depressing. Just being with them made Brian feel like a loser. And since he knew he looked just like Brad Pitt, he couldn't be a loser, right?

There was another reason he was so delighted Carol was going out with him. He could tell she liked him, and he hoped this would prove to be an advantage in both keeping her account and getting a good settlement out of her. If she liked him enough, she might accept half. Yeah, he was looking to settle at half. He didn't plan to come on to her. She was a client, and that would be a big no-no. He wouldn't do it anyway. All he wanted was company at the game and a leg up on the settlement. So he dressed accordingly.

He called a car service and picked Carol up at her apartment at five forty-five. The doorman in green livery looked him over and told him to go up.

"Twelve C, elevator on the left, sir."

"Thanks." Brian glanced at his watch, hoping this wouldn't take too long. He didn't like to be late.

"Hi, you're early." Carol opened the door for him and led him into the living room.

He didn't think he was early. He thought he was right on time. Then he sucked in his breath, dazzled by the splendor of the place. "Wow!"

He hadn't expected an oversized living room with a large stone fireplace at each end and the most amazing modern furniture he'd ever seen scattered about. "This is something!"

"Oh well, we bought it cheap, before the real estate boom," Carol said modestly.

"It's beautiful. Did you do it yourself?"

"Yes, of course. We knocked down the wall between the living room and dining room for drama. But I decorated with Matthew's taste in mind. I don't really like modern. Too cold," she said disparagingly.

"Oh I agree. Absolutely," Brian threw in quickly. "But you did a magnificent job."

She tossed her head to show her contempt for it. "Now that Matthew's out of the picture, I'm going to do it over."

"I'm sure that will be spectacular, too." Brian's eyes boggled at the view of Central Park. He wasn't exactly a hick, but this was fantastic.

"Well, thank you." She smiled at all the compliments.

Then he noticed *her* and was blown away. Carol Mack had dressed for a club date. She was wearing a butterscotch-colored leather jacket with a white halter top, tight white pants, and white go-go boots. "Is it all right?" she asked anxiously about her outfit.

"Wow," he said again. With her silky dark hair, deep red lipstick, and flawless complexion, she looked like a movie star. She really did. He liked the turquoise jewelry and matching watch. "You look amazing."

"Is it all right?"

He nodded, still a little stunned. He was wearing a long-sleeved practice jersey, jeans, and black-and-white two-tone retro Adidas.

"Are you sure?" She seemed a little puzzled by the shirt and sneakers.

"Absolutely. You look very stylish. You definitely outshine me." Somehow he doubted that she'd ever been to a game of any kind.

"Well, thanks. Would you care for a drink, or shall we go?" she asked.

"I like to be there for the opening pitch. Do you

mind?" In fact, he liked to be there for batting practice, but it was too late for that.

"Not at all," she said gamely. "I could bring a pitcher of cocktails for the ride."

He raised his eyebrows, triply impressed by this extraordinary woman. "That would be terrific."

They decided on a fashionable exotic drink and built it together from her well-stocked bar. Ten minutes later they were in the car sipping apple martinis from a leather travel martini set.

"This is very cool," Brian said of the drink transport. The leather case had compartments for small bottles of liquor and mixers, and of course oversized martini glasses. He was particularly impressed by the way the ice cubes were separated from the vodka in the shaker, so they could keep the cocktail cold without diluting it. The whole thing was for serious drinkers, and very clever. It seemed as though they had martinis in common. He sneaked a glance at Carol. She'd even thought of bringing along extra green apple slices and bright red cherries for color. She was a woman who thought of everything—very detail-oriented.

"I thought so, too. It was in our summer necessities collection two years ago." She laughed, and it was a very pleasant sound. "Of course, I had to have one. We had a cute picnic basket that year as well," she reflected. "I got them both, but I've never had a chance to use them." Her expression clouded over.

"Why not? This is great."

"Oh God." She rolled her eyes. "Matthew and I never went anywhere. Isn't this fun?"

It was indeed. They thoroughly enjoyed themselves on the trip north through Central Park and all the way up First Avenue. By the time they hit the bridge traffic that fed into the Bronx and points north, Brian was telling the story of his life and pouring seconds. It was an altogether unique experience for him. For one thing, no one he knew took limos to ball games; they took the subway. He'd guessed that the subway would not be a good move with Carol. For another thing, if they did use limos, they certainly didn't drink martinis in them. It took just under an hour to get to Yankee Stadium. Brian was a little plastered by the time they made their way to the right gate, handed over the tickets, and were examined for contraband, then released to their seats. Everyone looked at Carol, and Brian imagined they all thought she was a movie star.

"Wow, we're close," she said, looking back at the stadium that rose up in tiers behind her.

"Yes," Brian said proudly. They were in a box right behind home plate with a dugout visible on either side.

"We're right on the field! We can see everything," Carol said with wonder. "This is so great. Which side are we for?"

Brian guffawed. She was a funny girl. "The guys with the stripes on their pants."

"Oh yeah. Blue hats. I knew that."

"Right, the guys with the blue hats. We call them Yankees."

"Go Yankees!" Carol screamed into the dugout.

Everybody all around them turned to look at her again, and Brian grinned like a fool. He hadn't been this smitten since Tuesday, and that was a lifetime ago. Bill and Carl hadn't shown up, and he didn't know a single soul in the box. Every seat had been given away. It was an unusual thing. They were alone among strangers, and right on time.

"All rise for the national anthem," said the announcer.

They rose, everybody sang off key, and they all sat

down. Da da da dum da dum. Out went the first pitch, and the game was on. After three players went up to bat—the first one struck out, the next two walked—Carol started commenting on their physiques and their proficiency at the game.

"That one has a great ass," Carol said, pointing at Derek Jeter. "Not a very good batter, though."

Brian laughed. "Are you hungry?"

"Starved. What do we get, hot dogs?"

"No, no. This is first class all the way. You can have a lot of things. How about a sandwich?"

"Beer?"

"Of course, lots of beer." He was delighted. She liked beer.

"They could have better costumes, though. That gray color on the Yankees isn't very inspiring. Why are they so fat?"

"They're not fat, and I think it's white," Brian protested.

Crack.

"Look at that! He hit the ball," she yelped.

"We call that a home run."

"Go Yankees!" she cried. "This is so fun." Then she struck a serious note. "These fans won't riot and stampede the field if they lose, will they?"

Brian cracked up. She was the funniest person he'd ever met. "That's soccer. They don't have that kind of trouble here." Then he looked around for a waiter to order food, and saw something so small-world he couldn't believe it. Matthew Mack was also in a field box, but he was three rows behind them, sitting with a bunch of guys who hadn't changed out of their business suits. Unlike everyone else, who looked at Carol for a moment, then moved on to checking for other celebrities, Matthew was boring a hole in them with his eyes. Brian turned quickly around.

"Husband alert," he said without thinking.

"What?"

"Your husband is here."

"Nooo, you're mistaken. Matthew doesn't go to ball games." Carol laughed. "Must be someone else."

"Behind you, ten o'clock."

Carol turned around and saw him right away. "Oh my God, you're right. Unbelievable. Oh my God! What's he doing here?"

She turned back to Brian. "Doesn't he look terrible?"

"I'm sorry. Maybe I shouldn't have said anything."

"No, I'm glad you did. He looks *awful*. Did you see his suit? Looks like he slept in it."

"Are you going to get back together?" Brian was overwhelmed by that thought. If they got back together, he wouldn't be able to go out with her again. He needed a drink quickly, and looked around frantically for a waiter.

Carol caught him with a dazzling smile that almost knocked him from his chair. "Why would I do that?"

"Uh, lots of people make up," Brian said. "Long marriages and all that. And frankly being single is no picnic. I mean, except for now. You know what I mean."

"Yes, I do. I'm having a ball. And, I won't make up with Matthew. I couldn't. I'm very nice and easygoing until I figure things out. Then if someone's hurt me, he'd better get out of the way." She turned to glare at ten o'clock, but only for a second. Then she was back, smiling at him again.

Brian was thinking that Matthew Mack was a jerk. Nothing new there.

"He never took me to a baseball game," she said slowly.

"I'll bet there are a lot of things he didn't do, but maybe I shouldn't say that." Brian smiled.

Carol smiled back. "Oh look. Peanuts in the shell. I'd love some peanuts."

"I'll get you some." He searched for that elusive waiter, then forgot his task and turned back to Carol. She really didn't seem upset that her husband was sitting right behind her. She didn't really seem to be thinking about him at all. What a woman! "I was wondering," he said slowly. "If you're not too busy, maybe we could do something tomorrow."

forty-nine

"MAGGIE, I NEED TO RENT A KID." CAROL WAS ON the phone early Monday morning, using the ploy that had worked for years whenever she needed to take Mag and Bebe to animated movies and all the kitschy events that no adult with any self-respect could attend alone.

"Ha, ha, Carol. You can have two. Mom hates us." Mag was awake and lying in her bed in a deeper funk than ever before. She felt as if her life were ending for the very last time. Beside her on her bedside table was a list of chores five miles long that she had to do before the stock market closed and her evil mother came home. Bebe was grounded for life, and Mag was the new housekeeper.

"Oh, I'm sure that isn't true," Carol burbled. "I know your mother loves you very much."

"Oh, believe me, it's true."

Mag thought her parents were sooo messed up she didn't know what to do. Since about three A.M. she'd been practically dead with a fatal aneurysm thinking about what she'd caught them doing. Disgusting! Perverted beyond belief! Ugh, they were naked, and they were doing it in plain sight. Gross. She thought sex at their age should be banned, but she also thought sex at any age was absolutely revolting. She couldn't imagine why anybody did it. Horrible. It was like having the plague in her own home. She wished they would die like Carol's mother and leave her a pot of money so she could have a real life far, far from them. But instead of dying, they'd gotten up as if nothing had happened, put on their clothes, and gone to war against *her*. It was so unfair. Before, they'd been annoying. Now they suddenly had scruples, and she was being punished. Her life had become such a nightmare that all morning she'd thought about jumping out her window.

"What's going on?" Carol asked, suddenly concerned. "Is everything all right?"

"No. Mom freaked out." Mag clicked her tongue.

"Freaked out, why?"

Mag rolled over on her side and stared at the wall. "It's a long story, Carol. Dina left, and Curly pooped in Bebe's room. The place is a total mess. And Bebe's a drug addict. Mom wants to send her to rehab. Then when Mom started ranting, Bebe busted me and told her I started her on the freaking weed in the first place. Now she wants to send both of us to rehab, and I don't even like the shit. I really don't."

"Really," Carol said.

"No, I don't like it. It makes me paranoid," Mag insisted. "I'm the good one."

"Oh, Mag, of course you're a good one," Carol cooed. "Of course you are."

"I am. But she blames me for everything. Like I had a choice about anything. She scheduled every single moment of my life since I was *two*. Camp and summer school, and spring break school, and SAT tutors and art lessons and piano lessons and tennis lessons. It was horrible. I wanted to rip my face off." Mag couldn't even describe how ridiculously demanding her mother had been her whole life. Even in prison they got time off for good behavior. But not her.

"Oh, Mag, honey. I can't believe this. You were always so good at everything. I thought you loved all that." Carol sounded very concerned.

"I hated all that, but at least I tried. Bebe's such a fuckup she won't even try. All she does is go shopping and smoke weed. She could be the stupidest person on earth. And she's made my life a living hell."

"Oh, for heaven's sake, Maggie, some people's lives are a living hell, but your life is *not*. And don't say that about your sister. She's hardly a fuckup. She's a lovely girl."

"I'm sorry." Mag gulped and felt guilty for complaining. Carol was always so nice to her. And her mother just died. It was just too bad that the wrong mother died. "Are you okay?" she asked in a small voice.

"Well, I need your help, Maggie."

"You need my help? What for?" Suddenly Mag was suspicious. She didn't think it was a good idea to trust any grown-up.

"Well, Matthew and I are getting divorced. And I'm just overwhelmed at work," Carol said slowly.

"Mom told me about the breakup. I'm sorry. So many things are going wrong for you. I shouldn't complain."

"No, no. Don't be guilty. I'm fine. The marriage was not a good one, I just didn't want to admit it. You know what? Matt didn't want to have children. That pretty much says it all, don't you think?" Carol's voice was smoother than Mag had heard it in, like, forever. *She* wasn't freaking out because her life wasn't going well. Mag felt a surge of love for her.

"Wow, I didn't know that," she said. They'd all assumed Carol didn't have children because something was wrong with her. Or Matthew didn't have enough sperm. Ewww, he was a monster. What kind of person didn't want children? *Poor Carol,* she thought.

"Well, there are a lot of things you didn't know, Miss Margaret. And your father didn't do anything wrong. Matthew is just a prick."

Mag didn't say anything. The conversation was getting a little too deep for her. Her father was a total jerk. Everybody knew that. But he'd bought her beautiful golf clubs and arranged for the one set of lessons she really liked. She loved him for the golf, so she wasn't going there.

"And I fired my assistant," Carol went on. "I'm cleaning up my whole life."

"Huh?" Mag rolled over and looked at her sick ceiling, which hadn't been repaired yet.

"So, I need somebody to be on top of things in the office, someone to follow through. Make my travel plans. Maybe sometimes even travel with me. I go to a lot of neat places."

What was Carol talking about? Mag had no idea where this was going, but she felt sorry that Carol's life was so out of control.

"I know you know that you're a computer whiz," Carol was saying. "And you got great grades at a tough school. If you went into marketing, maybe you could use your work experience here for credit toward a degree. Pay it forward, know what I mean?"

"My work experience?" Mag had no work experience. She'd been in school all her life. She had no idea what Carol was talking about.

"Mag, I work at a great company. I don't have to tell you that."

"I love the company," Mag said quickly. "I-I study the catalog. You have really cool stuff." And then she stopped. "I don't know what you're talking about, Carol."

"I'm talking about a job, Maggie. How would you like to be my assistant for a year?"

Mag was speechless. Carol's assistant was about thirty-two. He was very anal and organized. She, on the other hand, couldn't be counted on even to pick up her clothes, or walk the dog. All she ever wanted to do was jump out a window. She was a poor choice for anything, the only kid in her class not to go to college. She couldn't begin to imagine what Carol was thinking.

"It would be like working for your aunt," Carol warned. "I'll be tough on you, but you'll learn a lot. And we'll have fun. Wouldn't it be nice to have fun for a change?"

Mag found her tongue. "But how could I get a job like that? Aren't there human resource people to go through and hundreds of college graduates looking for jobs? How could I compete with that?"

"Thousands of people looking for work. But . . . you'll be part of this program I'm starting. You'll be an intern. You'd have to promise me you'd stay through next summer. And if you want to quit then and go on to college next fall, great. But that's up to you."

Mag was now sitting up on the edge of her bed. Her spine had stiffened without her being aware of it. It was totally unbelievable. She was sure Carol had gone crazy. Everybody knew she wasn't qualified; they'd told her so at the temp agency. Not even qualified to answer the phone.

"You'd do that for me?" she asked in a small voice. She didn't think such a thing was possible. Nobody hired their best friend's kids, even when they weren't dropouts. All she'd expected from Carol was a lunch and a lecture.

"Mag, you're a total darling. I've known you since you learned your ABCs. I know you can do this."

"But *why*?" Mag started panicking. Why would Carol take this kind of risk? She'd be terrible, and everyone would think Carol was nuts for hiring her.

"Let's just say I need the right kind of help, honey. And you're it." Carol sounded confident.

"I can't be *it*," Mag cried. She almost sounded sullen. She almost whined in her very worst tone. Almost.

"Well, you can. You need me, and I need you. It's a perfect match of needs. We can do this together, Mag." Carol sounded like a whole new person. No whine from her side for a change.

"Are you sure?" Mag said in a teeny-tiny voice.

"I'm sure. Just don't tell your mom yet. I want to tell her myself."

"Okay." Mag forgot to ask if she was getting paid for her internship. She forgot to ask what she had to do, who she had to talk to. All she could think of was how much she hated her mother for trying to make her clean the house. And she didn't have the heart to say no to Carol.

fifty

VARTAN VOLE WAS WAITING FOR ANNIE WHEN SHE
came in to work on Monday morning. Petra caught her
just as she rounded the bend in the building.

"Annie, I'm so glad you're here. I found Mr. Vole in
your office when I got back from a bathroom break. He
refused to wait in reception! I'm so sorry. Should I call
someone?" she asked anxiously.

"Oh no." Annie took a step backward as if to flee. Re-
flexively she glanced at her watch. Eight thirty was a little early for an unscheduled meeting. What was the man
doing there?

As soon as she asked herself the question, a number of
frightening thoughts popped into her head. Where were
the code-yellow buffers that Homeland Security advised
for all public places? What was wrong with the security
man in the lobby of the building? He'd let an outsider
walk right in, then only minutes later hassled *her,* a legitimate employee he'd known for years. What was wrong
with everybody? The receptionist at Hall Stale let him
walk right in, and Petra hadn't been at her station to
stop him. Too many holes in the fire-wall. She trembled
thinking about how easy it was to breach security. So
now the man was in her office. For all she knew, he was
an evil genius who could use her own computer to transfer anybody's money to himself—even hers. Or he had a

gun in his pocket and planned to shoot her dead if she denied him the millions he was so desperately trying to acquire. What to do? What to do? Fight or flight? She hesitated, considering her options.

"Is Brian here?" she asked.

"Not yet," Petra said.

"Frisk?"

"Frisk and Darian are here," Petra replied.

Darian could probably fight off a tiger, but Frisk was burly. He was the one Annie wanted. Security on the fourteenth floor? That was a laugh. She had no idea who that might be. "Alert Frisk, will you? We need him to return Vole's certificates," she said.

"What about you?" Petra said. "You want me to come with you?"

"Go get Frisk," Annie said, "and anybody big you can round up."

Annie was wearing a black suit with a black T-shirt to suit her no-nonsense mood. She was ready for war on all fronts. From the door, she could see a three-quarters view of Vartan Vole, who still didn't look the part of a world-class financial player. He was a hairy, heavyset man in a cheap and wrinkled suit with a bulging brief-case hugged tightly to his barrel chest. Luckily he wasn't anywhere near her computer. He was hovering by the glass-topped coffee table in front of her sofa, appearing to study a photo of her family taken at camp some years ago. Inside their gold frame, the Custers were all wearing shorts and polo shirts with the camp's logo on the pocket, and they were grinning like happy fools in the sunshine of that long-past summer.

"Mr. Vole, what a surprise. I didn't have you on my schedule this morning," Annie said coldly.

Vartan turned to face her like an eager suitor at a dance.

"Heelllo, Annie Custard," he said heartily. "I came on the red-eye just to see you."

She didn't ask him where from, only wished him to return there as quickly as possible. She could see through his large black eyeglass frames that his eyes were indeed puffy and red. He could well have had a sleepless night. The condition of his suit also indicated exceptional usage without benefit of a good dry cleaner. But he was a liar about everything else, so why believe this?

Vartan started talking before she was even halfway in the room. "I am about to show you more money in one place than you have ever seen in your life," he said excitedly. "You won't believe this."

"Funny you should say that. I don't believe it already," Annie remarked.

"Oh no. Oh yes. This is amazing indeed. A chance of a lifetime. Come in and sit down, yes? Hold out your hand, you will feel the riches of kings rush through your blood. Believe me, Annie Custard, this is the deal of a lifetime."

Annie sat down at her desk. She no longer had any hope for deals of a lifetime from Vole. "Mr. Vole, the IBM certificates you gave me last week are phony," she told him bluntly.

"What!" He acted like an innocent bystander in a war zone, shot in a crossfire by a sniper's bullet. One hand smacked the briefcase over his heart. His eyeballs rolled around in his head. He actually staggered a step and had to steady himself on the back of one of Annie's plaid wing chairs. "Don't do this to me," he cried.

"I can't do anything for or against you. Your certificates are phony. End of story. You'll have to leave."

"They aren't," he protested. "There's been a mistake."

She shrugged. "It doesn't matter. There's nothing we can do for you."

"But wait. I know they're good as gold. Anybody would take them," he argued.

"Fine, you can try them somewhere else."

"But I bought them at auction. Southebee's," he protested.

"You mean Sotheby's," she corrected. He didn't even know the name of the auction house.

"That's right, Southebee's. Do you think they would handle phony certificates? No, they wouldn't."

She shrugged again. It wasn't her problem.

"But I want you to see this," he said wildly.

Out of nowhere came his passport. He flapped it across the desk at her. "U.S. passport, the real thing. I'm a citizen. Would a U.S. citizen fool you? Would I spend five million dollars on phony certificates? Never."

Frisk strode into the room without his suit jacket and without knocking. He was a well-muscled young man, with broad shoulders and powerful arms. Board-stiff from Chinese laundry starch, his white dress shirt displayed an impressive expanse of chest. Annie exhaled in relief. He looked every inch a Wall Street warrior. Darian followed close on Frisk's heel, with Anderson, a young broker who played on the firm's baseball team. No one wanted to miss a show. Today Darian's hair was curly and soft, and she was wearing another pink suit. Annie saw a bulge in her jacket pocket and guessed it was the can of pepper spray she normally kept in her purse.

"Hellooo, everybody," Vartan said without missing a beat.

Before Frisk had a chance to wrestle him to the floor or Darian could spray him with the pepper, Vartan had his briefcase open. A pile of coins clattered down on the coffee table. One flipped over onto the rug, and he sank down to his knees to locate it.

"Gold!" he exclaimed, retrieving it with relief. "Solid gold, thousands of years old. You will never see so much wealth again."

Gold? For a second they all froze in their places. Then Vartan climbed to his feet. "Are you happy now? I have something really big for you!" he said triumphantly.

"I have an appointment, Mr. Vole. Mr. Frisk here will return your certificates. I need you to leave quietly," Annie said firmly. "Hall Stale does not deal in coins."

"What are you talking about? You don't want to see a hundred million dollars' worth of lost treasure?" Vartan looked amazed.

"No," Annie said. "I don't want to see it."

"Where's it from?" Darian piped up, peeking at a coin without picking it up.

"I acquired it from an Arab gentleman—"

Oh God, Iraqi plunder, Annie thought, and cut him off before he could say another thing. "Mr. Vole, Mr. Frisk will escort you to the elevator."

"No, no. You don't understand. If you deposit this in my account, we'll all be rich," Vartan said frantically.

"We understand, but we can't deposit coins," Frisk told him.

"But take a look at this king's ransom that's never been available before." He shook the last one out of a leather pouch. It was thick and dull and not perfectly formed, clearly produced by hand and not in some modern machine. It clinked on the glass, but failed to impress them the way the IBM certificates had. The dull gleam gave a suggestion of gold, but no one made a move to take a closer look at the pile. Annie actually shuddered. She had trouble enough without adding foreign plunder to her list of transgressions.

"Whatever it is, we can't take it." Frisk echoed her thoughts. "Why don't you come with me?"

Vartan ignored him. "Believe me. It's completely on the up-and-up. Put it in my account. A little trade, that's all. Treasure for cash." Up went his bushy eyebrows. He had his own belief system. It didn't include defeat.

"Mr. Vole. We're a brokerage firm. We deal in stocks and bonds, not coins. That's it. And we all have work to do." Frisk jerked his head toward the door.

"Well, I gave you stock. You wouldn't take my stocks, either," Vartan said in a hurt tone.

"No, they're fake," Frisk told him.

"But I can sell *these* anywhere." Vartan wasn't finished.

"Goodbye, Mr. Vole," Annie said.

"But I came all the way from Turkey for this," he protested.

Annie didn't say anything more. Frisk moved in, and Vartan stuck his hand out.

"You told me you were a full-service broker. Where do you expect me to go now?" His hurt eyes made a circuit of the room.

"Try Charles Stack," Darian said quickly. "They deal in coins."

"Do you think they'll take the stock, too?" he asked earnestly. "I only have today."

fifty-one

AFTER VARTAN WAS GONE, ANNIE'S HEART POUNDED. Coins. Coins! The nut wanted cash for coins. It was the craziest thing she'd ever heard. Thank God for Frisk. The lights flickered, and she jumped out of her chair. Oh God, please no more blackouts! No more. Hurriedly she looked down at the street. Oh God. She couldn't take a power failure now. Down on Third Avenue the traffic lights were green. All the lights were on in the building across the street. False alarm. She must have imagined it. She sat down again, trying to calm herself. She needed to talk to Brian. She couldn't babysit him anymore. She couldn't be his girlfriend, or even his lunch friend. She and Ben had spent the weekend reconciling their differences. They were going to save their girls by selling their apartment and starting over in another office outside New York. Brian had bad luck with women, so she dreaded having the conversation. But it had to be done, so she waited nervously for him to come in.

Her phone rang, and Petra answered. "Ann Custer's office."

Her intercom sounded. "Yes, Petra."

"It's Carol."

"Thanks." Annie picked up. "Hi, Carol. How are you doing?"

"I'm ready to see you now," Carol announced.

"Great. Are you coming over?"

"No, let's have lunch. We haven't had lunch in ages."

"Fine. What do you feel like?"

Carol heaved a great sigh. "Oh, a lobster salad. How about the Brasserie in the Seagram Building?"

"Too noisy. It gives me a headache," Annie said quickly.

"I'm the client, Annie."

"Fine, the Brasserie it is," she conceded immediately.

"See you at twelve."

Annie waited and waited, but Brian didn't show up all morning. She didn't know where he was, and had no chance to talk with him. At twelve on the dot, she walked into the aggressively modern Brasserie and cringed at its new look, which hadn't been new for a number of years. She hated to come here, hated it. She'd been back a few times since the renovation and found it too changed to please her taste for the old burnished bronze Brasserie, and yet too familiar a room to prevent the memories from flooding back. Of all the restaurants in New York, this was the place where she most missed her mother.

In the old days when Annie was a little girl, and later a young woman, she and Brenda used to come here often. They'd always ordered the same thing: *fromage* burgers. Back then, no other restaurant in the city put cheese inside the sirloin patty instead of on top of it. Annie had thought the gooey melted Swiss inside the pink ground beef was a miracle. The place had even smelled different then. In the past it had smelled of baguettes and ratatouille. She still remembered the crunchy bread and the garlic that stayed with her all after-noon every time she'd eaten it. She remembered the rich, yeasty kugelhopf with lots of powdered sugar and raisins. Most of all she remembered her mother's lecturing her to death. Brenda had preached endlessly on every subject, the do-not-no-matter-whats. Do not tweeze any dark hairs on her upper lip. Do not wear clothes so tight they showed her jiggling fanny. Do not let boys get fresh. Do not take off her panty hose (keep them on at all times to ensure the above). Do not eat too much chocolate or touch herself (pimples). Do not eat too much bread or dessert. *Fat.* Do not date anybody too seriously before the age of twenty-five.

After Annie had graduated from college and gotten her job, then started dating Ben, her mother never had anything good to say about him, either. At her job she'd worked too hard, strived for success too hard, never had any time for her mother. Ben–The Boyfriend—liked the girls. He wouldn't be a faithful husband. Brenda nagged Annie about birth control, about being oh-so-careful about every single thing.

"You don't want to get pregnant on your honeymoon, do you?" she'd scolded.

Annie hadn't wanted to get pregnant immediately, but it had happened. Practically. She'd gotten pregnant at twenty-two, only a few months after she and Ben tied the knot at the Plaza Hotel. Brenda had had a lot to say about pretty much everything. She'd wanted Annie married, but not so very fast, and not to Ben. She'd wanted grandchildren, but not too soon. A thousand cigarettes went with every single one of her salvos, and in the end Brenda Flood finished herself off before Annie could prove her competence in any area. Her father followed along not many years later. They'd both died young.

Inside the Brasserie, Annie took a deep breath, remembering those two relationships that never had a chance to evolve, to change and mellow and grow up.

Eighteen years later she was still mourning the losses. She didn't know why she couldn't get over her mother's death. She was forty years old, too old to be an orphan, and yet she still felt like one. Ever since her mother passed on, she'd hated seeing those mother–daughter duos walking arm in arm on the street, endlessly talking. She hated watching them have lunch together in the coffee shops, shopping at Saks and Bergdorf Goodman, sipping coffee at the museum restaurants. All those mothers giving their daughters advice on every subject— whether they wanted or needed it or not—kept renewing the longing Annie had for all that she'd lost. The longing had kept her anxious over the years. She still worried about the negatives. The girls not thriving. Ben's not turning out the way she wanted him. Her not being a perfect wife and mother and provider. The challenge for women in her day had been to prove they could do it all well, and she hadn't been able to.

Now she was kept waiting on the top of the stairs, just the way she'd always had to wait for the ever-late Brenda. Even though the place was almost empty at this early hour, the girl with the reservation book wouldn't seat her until her party was complete. Carol touched her arm as she hung on to the banister.

"Hi, have you been here long?"

"All my life," Annie murmured.

Carol gave her a hug. "Sorry, my boss called just as I was leaving. We had to sort a few things out. Herm fucked me over as usual."

"You should get rid of him," Annie murmured, grateful for her fabulous Petra. *Petra* happened to be the Greek word for "stone," or "rock," which Petra was.

"Um-hmmm." Carol turned to follow the girl with the menus down the stairs to the dining room. She was wearing a black-and-white tweed pantsuit, black boots, and a stunning red Hermès scarf—one of the big ones—and she virtually bounced down the stairs like a happy ball. Annie was startled by the change in her old friend. Only a few weeks ago Carol had been a nervous and jerky girl who bit her nails until they bled, and had frown lines so deep that not even Botox could soften them. And of course, her voice alone could shatter glass. Now she looked and sounded . . . well, completely different.

She studied her, wondering how Carol's eyes could be so unclouded and bright. What made her look so good? Only last week she'd buried both her mother and her marriage. *Look at those shoulders*, Annie marveled. *Not a hunch or a bunch or a sign of tension or misery anywhere.* She was standing tall. They took their places in a booth. Carol spread the napkin in her lap and actually grinned!

Something was definitely up. Annie inhaled and exhaled a few times, readying herself for an important revelation. Or a blow. Carol had summoned her. It had to be something big. She guessed it was that Matthew was back in the picture.

"How are you doing?" Annie asked as soon as they'd learned their server's name, pretended to listen to his list of specials, then both ordered iced tea.

"Well," Carol replied quickly. "Very well."

Her father probably killed her mother. How could she be doing well? "How's your dad?" she asked cautiously.

"Oh, he's moving to Sarasota." Carol's fingers flew to her temple as if the very thought gave her a headache.

"What?" Annie was flabbergasted.

"I know, isn't it something? All these years he wouldn't even come into the city and now he's relocating to the

Vail of the South." Carol shook her head. "I really can't get over it. People, right?"

Annie was stunned. *"Sarasota?"*

"It's on the west coast of Florida."

"I know where it is," Annie said. "Archie Cooper is the branch manager of the Hall Stale office down there. He's been trying to recruit us for years." The office was on the second floor, and no planes flew into buildings there. She and Ben had both spoken to him over the weekend and were going to visit before the end of the week.

The iced teas came, and they both grabbed pink packets of sweetener.

"No kidding. Small world, right?" Carol sipped her tea.

Even smaller than Carol thought, but after she'd sustained so many losses, Annie didn't want to tell her that they, too, were considering leaving her. Annie didn't think they had any choice. When she thought of all the wholesome things a simpler life in a smaller town offered—lots of water and golf courses for Ben, an art school for Bebe, a house with a swimming pool for her, and grass for Curly—it wasn't so hard a decision.

"How did your father choose that particular place?" She cut off her musing on the subject.

"I don't know. He's a complete mystery to me," Carol told her, "but that's where he's going, and thank *God*, I don't have to go there with him."

Annie smiled.

"What?"

"Nothing." But she had a new idea about the bonds. In Florida, she could track Dean Teath. It wasn't an incentive to move to the same city where he was going, but it would be a benefit, a definite benefit. She wanted to know. So, apparently, did Carol.

"Those missing bonds are really bothering me," Carol said. "I went home last Thursday to look for them—"

"Did you find them?" Annie asked eagerly.

"Nope, I found the house cleaned up and empty of everything. My books, my yearbooks. The photographs. He'd wiped us out, erased us. It was horrible."

"I'm sorry," Annie murmured.

"And he's selling the house, of course." Carol's hand flew to her head again. Then she brightened. "He'll do all right with it. The lot is worth more than the bonds anyway. It's only a block from the beach."

"I still miss my mother," Annie said suddenly. She figured it was her turn to say something. "And I miss Dina, too."

Carol nodded. "Well, I know you do. It's hard not having a family. I've always wanted aunts and uncles and old people who could tell stories about my history. Last week my dad told me my grandfather was a pirate. It's not true, of course. Last week he told Brian he was a bootlegger . . . go figure."

Brian? Her Brian? How did Brian enter the picture? Annie was puzzled, and more than a little alarmed.

"So we don't have family, Annie. But we have each other. You've been my rock all these years." Carol favored her with more wattage.

Annie stared at her. What was that about Brian? She pressed her lips together, suddenly suspicious about her friend's brilliant smile despite her mother's possible murder and her marriage so precipitately ended. If Carol was poaching on Brian, she'd have a cow. But she didn't want to go there just yet.

"Has your mother visited you?" she asked warily.

"Visited me? No, she never visited me. She stayed on Staten Island all her life. She wouldn't leave for anything. Well, my graduation. My wedding . . ." Carol counted the times.

"No, I mean her spirit." Annie lowered her voice.

"Her spirit?" Carol made a face for a word she wasn't used to saying. "What are you talking about?"

"Her—" Annie leaned closer. "—ghost."

Carol burst into laughter. "Oh, my mother isn't sophisticated enough to have a ghost, Annie. She was a retard. Retards go to simple heaven, and don't venture out for anything."

"Where did you get that word, *retard*?" Annie was shocked at the cruelty and familiarity of the awful term.

"Oh, Mag uses it," Carol said, offhand.

"She certainly does, to describe her sister. I don't like her talking like that." And since when was Maggie talking to Carol about her retard sister? Annie bit her tongue. There was a lot under the surface here.

Carol gave her a penetrating look. "What's the matter, Annie?"

"I feel bad about so many things."

Carol shrugged. "Oh, don't worry about the bonds, Annie. Brian's cutting a check for me. It's not the whole amount, but so what?" And there was that thousand-watt smile again. "Some things are more important than money. Friendship is more important."

"Brian is cutting a check?" Annie said slowly. What about investigating the accountant? Brian had promised to do that. And she knew he hadn't done it because she'd called Brad herself, and he'd told her no one had contacted him. This was fraud pure and simple, and Brian was becoming an accessory. Or something.

"He's a doll, Annie," Carol cooed.

Brian? "Go on." Annie tapped her fingers on the tablecloth, and the server appeared.

"Have you decided?" he asked. He was tall and thin and looked like a movie star.

"Not yet." Carol beamed at him. "We need a little more time."

The place was filling up. This time Carol was the one to lean across the table confidingly. "He's completely turned my life around," she announced.

Annie's heart almost stopped. She seriously doubted that a mere check for the bonds—and not even the full amount—could do that for the Carol she knew. She licked her lips. She'd known Brian for three years. She'd lunched with him literally hundreds of times. He'd always had eyes for her. She'd known it, and he'd known it. Last Tuesday he'd told her he loved her and wanted to spend the rest of his life with her. He'd told her that Wednesday, Thursday, and Friday. Now it was Monday, and Carol was telling her he'd turned her miserable little life around. She waited for the blow.

"He took me to a baseball game, can you believe it?" Carol said.

Annie shook her head in total disbelief.

"Well, he did. And I loved it. And he loves my apartment. We have so much in common. And, you know, one thing led to another." She lifted her eyebrows. "The man is hung like a moose. God, it was incredible."

Annie shook her head again. That remark didn't say much for Matthew. She didn't think Brian's was *that* great. Not incredible. Now, Ben was incredible . . .

"What?" Carol demanded.

"Nothing. I just warned you he's a little boy. He has a woman a week." Annie was so disheartened by the defection of her first lover in half a lifetime that she considered telling Carol she herself had been Brian's woman of last week.

"No, no. He's not like that. We spent the night together. It was so fun. Like, all night, Annie! Then he went home to change and called me right away. There was no backing off at all. We spent Saturday together. Then Sunday. He's so *there*, you know what I mean, so present." Carol sounded ecstatic.

"We call that needy, Carol."

"He wants me to decorate his apartment. Have you seen it? It's going to be so cute when I'm finished. I'm telling you, the whole thing is absolutely fabulous. A completely blank slate. He's so perfect, I can't believe it."

"I can't, either," Annie said, wondering if steam was rising out of her ears. "I gather you're going through with your divorce."

"Oh my God. You won't believe this, either. Matthew was at the game. He saw us together, and he's been calling every hour. I mean it, every *hour*. The bastard wants me back." Carol pumped her arm, like an athlete. *Yeah*.

"Well, did he say anything about me?" Annie asked in a tiny voice.

"Who? Oh, Brian? Honey, he thinks you're fabulous, of course. He calls you his best friend. Isn't it great that his best friend and my best friend are the same person?"

Annie sucked in her breath and looked down at the menu. Three years she'd been loyal to the fucker who might, for all she knew, have sold her husband down the river, and he wouldn't even come into the office to tell her he'd spent the *weekend* with her best friend. Obviously he hadn't told Carol about their little adventure last week. He'd just flipped them, the way people flipped real estate.

"Annie?"

Annie had wanted to think her relationship meant something to Brian. But she herself had known from the start that it didn't mean that much to her. Why shouldn't he move on—the louse! She gazed at her delirious friend. *I can tell you, or I can let it go. Just like the murder of your mom—a horrible crime that can't be proven one way or another.* She thought about it for a few seconds. What was the right thing here? It was true that Carol needed someone to hold on to her really tight, and Annie hated being in a viselike grip. She shrugged. So maybe it would work out between her and Brian. She decided to be generous and flip her lover to her best friend without telling the truth about that, either.

"I'm so happy for you," she said finally. "You deserve it."

"He wants to have children," Carol cooed.

Annie went numb on the idea of Carol and Brian having children. Now, that was a scary thought.

"And there's something else, too." Carol's grin widened even further.

"Oh yeah?" Annie didn't dare ask.

"Something else really great has happened. I finally fired Herm. Maggie's coming to work for me. Isn't that terrific?"

Annie stared.

"You wanted her out of bed. I got her out of bed. I gave her a job. I love your daughter, Annie, and a little push is all she needs. Isn't that what friends are for?" Carol pressed Annie's frigid fingers. "Aren't you glad?"

"Thank you, Carol. I'm thrilled." But Annie had as much trouble processing this information as she had the previous news. It seemed that everything she'd feared had come to pass. New York had been attacked. Her husband had collapsed with the Trade Center. Her children had lost their way. She'd made some big mistakes at work, and now her best friend had stolen both her lover and her child. Humiliated, she stuck her face into her iced tea glass to recover.

When she returned to the moment, the items on the menu were so blurry she couldn't read them. Okay, she understood the lesson. Bad things happened in life, but life itself went on in one form or another. The key was learning to accept the changes. That thought came to her and she started feeling a little better. Then she found some negatives to cling to. Mag was no more capable of holding a job than she was of flying to the moon. And Brian, well, Brian had alienated his wife and every girl-friend he'd ever had. All that cocoa, please. It couldn't work out with Carol, could it? As she was chalking up negatives, she heard a familiar voice and froze.

"Don't be jealous, Annie. It's time to learn how to let go."

What? Annie knew who'd spoken before she investi-gated. Then she slowly turned her head to look. And there at the next table she saw her mother, wearing an old black-and-white tweed Chanel suit that was just like Carol's.

This vision was an unusually clear one. Brenda looked exactly as she had before she'd been diagnosed with can-cer. Only her expression wasn't clear as she sat alone in the restaurant she'd loved so much. And despite the regulations against smoking in public places, she was puffing on one of her ever-present Marlboros. For a sec-ond Annie was filled with an overwhelming sensation of pure joy. Then she looked down at the menu again and saw *fromage* burger and ratatouille just where they'd al-ways been. *Plus ça change, plus c'est la même chose.* The French saying jumped unbidden into her head. The more things change, the more they stay the same. Annie couldn't resist. She ordered them.

fifty-two

"LET IT GO. IT JUST DOESN'T MATTER." BRIAN WAS
annoyed with Annie because she wouldn't stop demanding an investigation of Dean Teath.

"It may not matter to you," Annie told him. After all,
her little indiscretion had brought him a wealthy girlfriend more than eager to lavish all her attention on him.
Carol was his dream come true. What did he have to
worry about? "But it matters to me." It had become an
ongoing battle between them.

"Oh come on, you have to be philosophical about
these things. Think of it as water under the bridge."

In pretty much the blink of an eye he'd returned to
being her manager, and he never mentioned their little
tryst again. That might have been gallant of him, but she
wasn't letting Dean Teath off the hook. She didn't care
that he was an old man. She believed he had murdered
his wife because she wouldn't sign over her stock to him.
The Staten Island police might have let it go. Hall Stale
certainly wanted to let it go, but Annie wasn't letting it
go. She had many unanswered questions about the case.
One thing, however, was transparent. Even though the
Teaths had hidden their wealth from their daughter and
neighbors, they hadn't hidden it from the IRS. Annie
talked to Brad Rosen, their accountant, several times,
and he told her they'd always paid taxes.

No one else seemed to care what happened. Annie was the only one who was preoccupied by Dean Teath, and she started following the money. It wasn't very hard. All she had to do was put the situation to Brad Rosen in a persuasive way.

"Brad, I left you in the kitchen with a quarter of a million dollars in bearer bonds that Dr. Teath claims I stole from him," Annie told him. "Do you understand my predicament?"

"I understand," he said nervously, "but I didn't take them. The old man was with me every second."

"That may be true, but somebody is going to have to repay that quarter of a million. Could be you, could be us . . ." She hung up to let him think about it. A few days later she called him back and said the same thing.

"You're scaring me," he replied.

"Well, so far, my firm is not naming you as a codefendant in this case, but I could change that in a heartbeat. I don't want this on my record. It's a lot of money to lose."

Silence. "What do you want?" he asked after a moment.

"How much do you make a year, Brad?" Annie felt like a detective. This was how they did it.

"Thirty-two-five," he said slowly.

"You make thirty-two thousand, five hundred dollars? Do you own your own home?"

"Not yet. My wife and I made an offer on a place last week. We're still negotiating." His voice quavered.

"Last week. Really," Annie murmured.

"We need a bigger place, we're having a baby," he explained.

"Well, congratulations." She paused. "I guess you need a lot of money to buy a house and raise a child these days." She could hear him breathing.

"I didn't do anything wrong," he said after a moment.

"That's what Martha Stewart said; I'm sure *you* didn't," she added quickly. "But I didn't do anything wrong, either, and maybe our lawyers won't be as trusting about you as I am. Trust can be a dangerous thing. I trusted you in that room with him, and something happened there that got me in trouble. I'm not letting it go."

"What do you want?" Brad asked again.

"I want to see your records. The tax returns, the account statements."

"There's a privacy issue. I'll have to ask my boss," he replied slowly.

"This is important to all of us. I'd be happy to ask your boss for you," Annie offered.

"What are you looking for?" he asked timidly.

"Maybe I can find a way to get us both out of hot water."

"How far back do you want to go? We keep everything that's more than two years old in a warehouse. When Brad retired, a lot of it was thrown away."

"When do you start throwing things out? Six years?"

"I don't know. I'd have to check."

"That's great, Brad. And I'll need Brad Meltzer's address. I want to talk to him."

"No problem. She lives in Sarasota."

"*She* lives in Sarasota!" Annie was stunned.

"Yeah, her name is Bradley, but everyone calls her Brad."

Annie was exhilarated, but she did not run to Brian with that interesting piece of information. The Teaths had had a woman accountant, who'd moved to Sarasota, where Dean just happened to have relocated as well. She wanted to put the whole story together before she said goodbye. She was taking all her clients with her

when she left the Third Avenue office. A big chunk of
Brian's business was going out the door.

A few days later Brad sent her copies of the Teaths'
tax returns and their work product for preparing them.
Three file boxes full of stuff. She and Ben spent time
studying them at night. Then she asked Frisk and Darian to help her. In the file boxes, she'd found Teath's
bank statements from several banks on Staten Island;
the accounts had been closed. She asked Frisk to memo
all the banks in Sarasota again about the missing bearer
bonds. Frisk was able to locate the bank where Teath
had deposited the money from the sale of his house. The
bank that had issued the mortgage to the new owners
provided the name of the bank that received the funds.
It was on the canceled check returned to them. The bank
was Colonial. That was their target.

Frisk got in touch with the president of Colonial
Bank, and they waited. The day after Hall Stale received
a signed release of liability from Teath and issued him a
check for $160,000, Annie flew to Sarasota. She planned
her visit to coincide with his receipt of the check. She
took the seven-forty-five flight from Newark and arrived
at ten forty.

By noon, after much driving around a huge subdivision in Palmer Ranch, she located the home of Brad
Meltzer and rang the bell. Brad, an attractive blonde of
indeterminate age, was waiting for her.

"So nice to meet any friend of Dean's. Come in," she
said.

"Thank you for agreeing to talk to me about real estate in Sarasota," Annie said, entering a house where
everything was peach—the sofas, the floor, the paintings
on the wall, the lamps on the table.

"Oh, it's a pleasure. I love the company." Brad was

plump and cute. Her hair was carefully coiffed and she wore quite a bit of makeup. She led the way to a huge kitchen–family room. "Houses here all have the open plan. You're going to find that quite a change from up north. How do you know Dean?"

"His daughter is one of my clients," Annie said.

"Carol, yes . . . well, it's sad to lose someone. I lost my husband recently, so I know how hard that is." She shook her head, and her hair didn't move.

"Are you and Dean close?" Annie asked.

"Oh well, he's a delightful man. I'm helping him find a home." She laughed. "It's not easy, he's very tight—but that's not uncommon in men of his generation. Would you like some iced tea?" She bustled around her large kitchen, gathering up plates and glasses and turkey wraps that she must have purchased at the deli counter of her grocery store.

"That would be great. Did you know his wife?" Annie sat in a white chair at the kitchen table. Brad poured tea, and she sipped it gratefully.

"No, I always worked with Dean. I was their accountant. Some people find that surprising, but my husband and I always worked together. We had a wonderful life."

Annie smiled. "What did you know about the Teaths?"

"Well . . ." Brad joined her at the table and leaned in confidingly. "His wife had all the money. She kept him on a tight rein, I'll tell you, and he wasn't very happy. I guess you know that Carol got all the money. Poor man, he hasn't had an easy life. But we all carry some baggage, don't we?"

Not as much as he does, Annie thought. She sat with Brad for an hour and a half, learned a few things and guessed others. On his wife's instructions, Dean had reinvested some of the dividend income in her name. But he'd skimmed part of it off over the years to purchase the bearer bonds for himself. Furthermore, when Brad's husband died and she retired to Sarasota, Dean told her he was moving there soon himself.

"People always say that, and sometimes they do," she said brightly. "What brings you here, dear?"

"The weather. I know Carol will be happy to know her father has a friend here. Are you two dating?"

"Oh my, no. My Bernie was a wonderful man. I'll never marry again, but it's nice to have a friend."

Brad passed the wraps with a smile, and Annie wondered if Dean had received the check yet. She knew he would not try to cash the bonds until he'd been paid for them. Of course, he could hold on to them for months, or even years, but she didn't think he would. After all, he'd started divesting as soon as his wife was gone.

At two o'clock she said goodbye to Brad. She was nearing her new office building downtown when Frisk called on her cell. "Bingo," he said. "Teath tried to cash in the bonds at Colonial Bank an hour ago. We got him."

epilogue

EVERYTHING WAS DIFFERENT IN FLORIDA. MORNINGS came more slowly and with no rumblings of the subway underground, no trucks on Second or Third Avenue, no screaming sirens or city noises of any kind. Just before dawn the birds began to stir. Gray doves, green parrots, red-headed woodpeckers. White and blue herons, ducks and geese and swans appeared from their night habitats, walking, swimming, and flying in to herald the new day. The sun came up nearly an hour later in the South, so Annie was always awake to see its arrival. Just as the soft swish of sprinklers on the green at the ninth hole of the Gulfside Golf Course went off, the coffee machine came on in the kitchen. The alluring aroma drew her out of bed to the changing light.

As the sprinklers on the golf course went off, the fountain in the middle of the water hazard nearest to them came on, spouting a dozen tandem spikes of water high into the blue sky. To Annie, mornings alone were proof of the existence of God. Each new morning helped restore some long-forgotten pleasure. The quiet cup of coffee. The activities of birds. Sailboats in the Gulf. Fruit ripening on the trees. There were a lot of things to study in Florida, and fewer things to fear.

To fear: Bebe and eighty-year-old people behind the steering wheels of fast cars. In two months she would have her learner's permit. That, and art classes and sunshine and the promise of a car if she stayed straight, made the challenge of a new high school worthy of effort. Anyway, Bebe looked good in her bikinis. That was something for Bebe to live for and Annie to fear.

Other things to fear: sudden lethal bolts of lightning appearing from nowhere on the golf courses and the beaches. The five-foot alligator in the pond less than twenty-five yards from their pool cage. When Annie complained to the overseers of the grounds about the creature, the subdivision elders told her it was a harmless pet. When she pressed harder, they further said that alligators weren't removed from golf course and subdivision ponds until they grew to eight feet, or started chasing golf carts. But not to worry, they didn't attack people very often. They lay submerged to the eyes in the water waiting for something small to come along, like birds and dogs. The alligator was certainly something for Curly to fear.

Each day as Bebe and Ben slowly moved from sleep to action, Annie watched the gray lighten to rose. By the time both of them hit the kitchen, the white brilliance of day had illuminated the blue of the pond between their pool cage and the sharp, grassy bank that sloped up to the green of the invisible ninth hole above them. Over coffee, Ben and Annie marveled at a view they'd never expected to enjoy in their lifetime. Nestled inside the picket fence that bordered their yard and kept Curly safe were an orange tree and an avocado tree. In January both were heavy with ripe fruit. Not far away, a large mango tree was not yet in bloom for its summer harvest. Those three specimen trees, along with the row of palm trees on higher ground in the distance, looked like a picture postcard of paradise. A paradise with an alligator wrinkle. Sometimes its flat head could be seen as it moved across the pond. And sometimes it disappeared altogether. From time to time, the alligator came out on land and walked to the next water hazard between the tee and the fairway of the tenth hole. And it stayed there for a while.

The alligator on the golf course was Annie's new metaphor for life, a symbol of hidden dangers and treachery even in the safest of places. The golfers ignored the predator the way investors ignored the perils of a stock market that could both sustain and destroy, depending on the season. And the brokerage business, which had repelled Ben three years ago in New York and her only six months ago, drew them both back into the game again in Florida. Ben had a new reason to prevail.

As they said in New York, go figure. A change of venue had restored Ben's interest in the business. His incentive included two recovering children and a happy wife. Industry and recreation were, after all, the American way of life. They purchased a large Mediterranean-style house with an open plan, a swimming pool, and a spa. A membership in a golf course. Two cars for the three-car garage. Ben and Annie moved to the Hall Stale office in the Colonial Bank building with its mirrored windows and prime view of Golden Gate Point and the Gulf of Mexico. In his exuberance, he bought Annie an expensive set of golf clubs and oversaw her lessons with the pro. While she wasn't very good at it yet, she had to admit she liked the outfits. The satisfaction in recovery, however, went much deeper.

Mag, too, was a new girl, working for Carol in the buying business and living in the guest room of her apartment. She talked with her mother and sister every day and planned to try college in the fall. Brian's apartment was in renovation. Carol had gutted it to give it character. She was also redecorating her own apartment and fighting for an equitable divorce settlement. Six months later, despite Carol's moving her account to the Florida office with Annie, she and Brian were still a devoted couple. Brad Meltzer, however, met someone else and quickly lost interest in Dean Teath. He didn't get to keep the Hall Stale check.

One last unexpected thing happened. After Annie moved to Florida and was happy with her life, she realized that the visitations from her mother had stopped. The day she had lunch with Carol at the Brasserie turned out to be the last time she saw her.